A Garland Series
Foundations of the Novel

Representative Early

Eighteenth-Century Fiction

A collection of 100 rare titles
reprinted in photo-facsimile in 71 volumes

Foundations of the Novel

compiled and edited by
Michael F. Shugrue
Secretary for English for the M.L.A.

with New Introductions for each volume by

Michael Shugrue, *City College of C.U.N.Y.*
Malcolm J. Bosse, *City College of C.U.N.Y.*
William Graves, *N.Y. Institute of Technology*

A Tale of a Tub

and

An Account of a Battel between the Ancient and Modern Books in St. James's Library

and

A Discourse Concerning the Mechanical Operation of the Spirit

by

Jonathan Swift

with a new introduction
for the Garland Edition by
Malcolm J. Bosse

Garland Publishing, Inc., New York & London

1972

The new introduction for the

Garland *Foundations of the Novel* Edition

is Copyright © 1972, by

Garland Publishing, Inc., New York & London

All Rights Reserved

Bibliographical note:
This facsimile has been made from a copy in the
Houghton Library of Harvard University
(EC7 SW55 704t A)

Library of Congress Cataloging in Publication Data

Swift, Jonathan, 1667-1745.
  A tale of a tub.

  (Foundations of the novel)
  Reprint of the 1704 ed.
    I. Swift, Jonathan, 1667-1745. An account of a
battel between the ancient and modern books in St.
James's Library. 1972. II. Swift, Jonathan, 1667-1745.
A discourse concerning the mechanical operation of the
spirit. 1972. III. Title. IV. Series.
PZ3.S9765Tal11 [PR3724]   823'.5   71-170512
ISBN 0-8240-0520-1

Printed in the United States of America

Introduction

In the 1704 volume of A Tale of a Tub, *Swift offered three satires, the longest being the title work, which consisted of sixteen parts, including five elaborate introductory sections in which a variety of narrative voices appear. The "tale" proper is a satire on religion and alternates with digressions that constitute a satire on learning. Uniting these two themes is Swift's vision of a world gone mad in which the modern man substitutes newness for originality, words for meaning, and form for substance.*

Swift makes perfectly clear the allegorical content of the tale: Peter, Jack, and Martin stand respectively for Catholicism, Protestant Dissent, and the Church of England. The story of three young men who come to town to make their fortune is also the history of the break with Rome, the ensuing conflicts brought on by the Reformation, and the corruption of the spirit of primitive Christianity. Peter's artful manipulation of the meaning of their father's will (Scripture) and Jack's retaliatory shifts in doctrinal thought are ultimately balanced by Martin's sensible resolve to follow a via media, *the only hope for institutional religion. Woven into the story is a satiric commentary on mankind's love of fashion. The three young men fall under the spell of sartorism, a theology based on clothes. Its chief tenet is*

INTRODUCTION

that the outer covering of man, which changes with the times, is of more spiritual importance than the inner being. In a search for new beliefs Jack turns to Aeolism, a religion of enthusiasm in which spirituality is so pervasive that the gullible, ecstatic followers of the cult finally worship the wind because it has no substance.

A counterpart to corruption of religious spirit is corruption of intellectual activity, exemplified, in the digressions, by pompous critics, Grub Street hacks, the wits of Will's Coffee House, and the virtuosi of Gresham College where the Royal Society met. In this Tubbian world, common sense and experience are swept aside in the pursuit of novelty. The unnamed writer, so modern that he has no past and therefore no memory, endlessly analyzes minutiae and gravely contemplates scientific projects which have no basis in reality. The final apocalyptic vision of "universal darkness" later to be found in Pope's Dunciad *is given a wryly humorous cast in Section IX of the* Tale, *where the chaos of the preceding digressions is at last focused upon a major theme: the attainment of happiness comes through an assiduous pursuit of madness. The writer argues that what actually separates the inmates of Bedlam from other men is the clothes they wear. In the Tubbian world, he explains, fancy dominates the mind because only through delusion can pain be removed and in its absence be found happiness.*

In the final two parts the writer practices what he preaches; he implements his praise of folly by showing increasing loss of control over his narrative structure.

INTRODUCTION

The story of the three young men and the digressions on learning all merge, involved sentences proliferate, subjects appear suddenly and just as suddenly disappear, until at its most chaotic, when lacunae take the place of words, the work ends on the dying fall of complete and hopeless madness.

The second satire in the 1704 volume was An Account of a Battel between the Ancient and Modern Books in St. James's Library, *occasioned by the "Phalaris controversy," which had pitted the Oxford wits, led by Sir William Temple and Charles Boyle, against William Wotton and the great philologist Richard Bentley. The issue around which the intellectual battle had raged had been the validity of the letters of Phalaris, a tyrant of Sicily. Temple and his adherents had claimed that they were authentic, but Bentley claimed that these epistles were in fact spurious. In defending Temple, his former patron, and following his own preference for the classics, Swift begins the work as a historical explanation of the quarrel between advocates of modern and ancient writing, a quarrel which had engaged French and English intellectuals since the mid-seventeenth century. Having joined the opposing sides in battle, Swift shifts to a mock-heroic treatment and ends this epic fragment by skewering Wotton and Bentley like "a Brace of Woodcocks" (p. 277). Though Swift's is a skillful performance, especially so in his conjuring of the* Iliad, *time has proved that Dr. Bentley had justifiably dismissed the Phalaris manuscript. However misplaced his literary loyalty, in this work Swift has put one of his*

INTRODUCTION

most famous allegories, the tale of the Spider and Bee. The modern writer, like the spider, spins out of his own self and mistakes the usefulness of mathematical design for beauty; the writer who respects tradition takes sustenance, like the bee, from a variety of rich sources. In this inspired metaphor Swift gives visual form to his intellectual judgment that excellence is neither old nor new but perennial, its essence being sweetness and light.

The third satire in the 1704 volume was entitled A Discourse concerning the Mechanical Operation of the Spirit, *cast in the form of a letter to a friend. The letter writer is another of Swift's "moderns," thoroughly materialistic in his philosophy, who reasons inaccurately from the wrong premises and reaches the right conclusion. This is a fast-paced satire of men who seek universal faith while professing simultaneously that the soul is wholly mechanical in its operations. The writer develops the thesis that religious enthusiasm is simply an outcome of physical action and describes in funny, if sometimes offensive Swiftian detail, the arts of ogling, humming, canting, and snuffling among religious fanatics.*

A Tale of a Tub *won notoriety for Swift, once his authorship had been established. In the 1710 edition, the fifth, Swift included an "Apology" in which he clearly stated his intentions. He never intended to attack Christianity but the corruption of it; moreover, his employment of humor had a serious motive, which was to point out the folly of the world. It is in this spirit that Swift wrote in the Preface to the* Battel: *"Satyr is a*

INTRODUCTION

sort of Glass, wherein Beholders do generally discover every body's Face but their own."

Malcolm J. Bosse

Treatises writ by the same Author, most of them mentioned in the following Discourses; which will be speedily published.

A *Character of the present Set of* Wits *in this Island.*

A Panegyrical Essay upon the Number THREE.

A Dissertation upon the principal Productions of Grub-street.

Lectures upon a Dissection of Human Nature.

A Panegyrick upon the World.

An Analytical Discourse upon Zeal, Histori-theo-physi-logically *considered.*

A general History of Ears.

A modest Defence of the Proceedings of the Rabble *in all Ages.*

A Description of the Kingdom of Absurdities.

A Voyage into England, *by a Person of Quality in* Terra Australis incognita, *translated from the Original.*

A Critical Essay upon the Art of Canting, *Philosophically, Physically, and Musically considered.*

A TALE OF A TUB.

Written for the Universal Improvement of Mankind.

Diu multumque desideratum.

To which is added,

An ACCOUNT of a BATTEL BETWEEN THE Antient and Modern BOOKS in St. James's Library.

Basima eacabasa eanaa irraurista, diarba da caeotaba fobor camelanthi. *Iren. Lib.* 1. C. 18.

———— *Juvatque novos decerpere flores,*
Insignemque meo capiti petere inde coronam,
Unde prius nulli velarunt tempora Musæ. Lucret.

LONDON:
Printed for *John Nutt,* near *Stationers-Hall.*
MDCCIV.

TO
The Right Honourable,
JOHN
Lord SOMMERS.

My LORD,

THO' the Author has written a large Dedication, yet That being addrefs'd to a Prince, whom I am never likely to have the Honor of being known to; A Perfon, befides, as far as I can obferve, not at all regarded, or thought on by any of our prefent Writers; And, I being wholly free from that Slavery, which Bookfellers ufually lye under, to the Caprices of Authors; I think it a wife Piece of Prefumption, to infcribe thefe Papers to your Lordfhip, and to implore your Lordfhip's Protection of them. God and your Lordfhip know their Faults, and their Merits; for as to my own Particular, I am altogether a Stranger to the Matter; And, though every Body elfe fhould be equally ignorant, I do not fear the Sale of the Book, at all the worfe, upon that Score. Your Lord-

DEDICATION.

ſhip's Name on the Front, in Capital Letters, will at any time get off one Edition: Neither would I defire any other Help, to grow an Alderman, than a Patent for the fole Priviledge of Dedicating to your Lordſhip.

I ſhould now, in right of a Dedicator, give your Lordſhip a Liſt of your own Virtues, and at the ſame time, be very unwilling to offend your Modeſty; But, chiefly, I ſhould celebrate your Liberality towards Men of great Parts and ſmall Fortunes, and give you broad Hints, that I mean my ſelf. And, I was juſt going on in the uſual Method, to peruſe a hundred or two of Dedications, and tranſcribe an Abſtract, to be applied to your Lordſhip; But, I was diverted by a certain Accident. For, upon the Covers of theſe Papers, I caſually obſerved written in large Letters, the two following Words, *DETUR DIGNISSIMO*; which, for ought I knew, might contain ſome important Meaning. But, it unluckily fell out, that none of the Authors I employ, underſtood *Latin* (tho', I have them often in pay, to tranſlate out of that Language) I was therefore compelled to have recourſe to the Curate of our Pariſh, who Engliſhed it thus, *Let it be given to the Worthieſt*; And his Comment was, that the Author meant,

his

DEDICATION.

his Work should be dedicated to the sublimest Genius of the Age, for Wit, Learning, Judgment, Eloquence and Wisdom. I call'd at a Poet's Chamber (who works for my Shop) in an Alley hard by, shewed him the Translation, and desired his Opinion, who it was that the Author could mean; He told me, after some Consideration, that Vanity was a Thing he abhorr'd; but by the Description, he thought Himself to be the Person aimed at; And, at the same time, he very kindly offer'd his own Assistance *gratis*, towards penning a Dedication to Himself. I desired him, however, to give a second Guess; Why then, said he, It must be I, or my Lord *Sommers*. From thence I went to several other Wits of my Acquaintance, with no small Hazard and Weariness to my Person, from a prodigious Number of dark, winding Stairs; But found them all in the same Story, both of your Lordship and themselves. Now, your Lordship is to understand, that this Proceeding was not of my own Invention; For, I have somewhere heard, it is a Maxim, that those, to whom every Body allows the second Place, have an undoubted Title to the First.

THIS, infallibly, convinced me, that your Lordship was the Person intended by the Author. But, being very unacquainted

DEDICATION.

in the Style and Form of Dedications, I employ'd thofe Wits aforefaid, to furnifh me with Hints and Materials, towards a Panegyrick upon your Lordfhip's Virtues.

IN two Days, they brought me ten Sheets of Paper, fill'd up on every Side. They fwore to me, that they had ranfack'd whatever could be found in the Characters of *Socrates, Ariftides, Epaminondas, Cato, Tully, Atticus,* and other hard Names, which I cannot now recollect. However, I have Reafon to believe, they impofed upon my Ignorance, becaufe, when I came to read over their Collections, there was not a Syllable there, but, what I and every body elfe, knew as well as themfelves: Therefore, I grievoufly fufpect a Cheat; and, that thefe Authors of mine, ftole and tranfcribed every Word, from the univerfal Report of Mankind. So that I look upon my felf, as fifty Shillings out of Pocket, to no manner of Purpofe.

IF, by altering the Title, I could make the fame Materials ferve for another Dedication (as my Betters have done) it would help to make up my Lofs: But, I have made feveral Perfons, dip here and there in thofe Papers, and before they read three Lines, they have all affured me, plainly, that they cannot poffibly be applied to any Perfon, befides your Lordfhip.

DEDICATION.

I expected, indeed, to have heard of your Lordship's Bravery, at the Head of an Army; Of your undaunted Courage, in mounting a Breach, or scaling a Wall; Or, to have had your Pedigree trac'd in a Lineal Descent from the House of *Austria*; Or, of your wonderful Talent at Dress and Dancing; Or, your Profound Knowledge in *Algebra*, *Metaphysicks*, and the Oriental Tongues: But to ply the World with an old beaten Story of your Wit, and Eloquence, and Learning, and Wisdom, and Justice, and Politeness, and Candor, and Evenness of Temper in all Scenes of Life; Of that great Discernment in Discovering, and Readiness in Favouring deserving Men; with forty other common Topicks: I confess, I have neither Conscience, nor Countenance to do it. Because, there is no Virtue, either of a Publick or Private Life, which some Circumstances of your own, have not often produced upon the Stage of the World; And those few, which for want of Occasions to exert them, might otherwise have pass'd unseen or unobserved by your *Friends*, your *Enemies* have at length brought to Light.

'Tis true, I should be very loth, the Bright Example of your Lordship's Virtues should be lost to after Ages, both for their sake and your own; but chiefly, because they

DEDICATION.

they will be so very necessary to adorn the History of a *late Reign*; And That is another Reason, why I would forbear to make a Recital of them here; Because, I have been told by Wise Men, that as Dedications have run for some Years past, a good Historian will not be apt to have Recouse thither, in search of Characters.

THERE is one Point, wherein I think we Dedicators would do well to change our Measures; I mean, instead of running on so far, upon the Praise of our Patron's *Liberality*, to spend a Word or two, in admiring their *Patience*. I can put no greater Compliment on your Lordship's, than by giving you so ample an Occasion to exercise it at present. Tho', perhaps, I shall not be apt to reckon much Merit to your Lordship upon that Score, who having been formerly used to tedious Harangues, and sometimes, to as little Purpose, will be the readier to pardon this, especially, when it is offered by one, who is with all Respect and Veneration,

  My LORD,

   Your Lordship's most Obedient,

    and most Faithful Servant,

      The Bookseller.

       THE

THE BOOKSELLER TO THE READER.

IT is now Six Years, since these Papers came first to my Hands, which seems to have been about a Twelvemonth after they were writ: For, the Author tells us in his Preface to the first Treatise, that he hath calculated it for the Year 1697, and in several Passages of that Discourse, as well as the second, it appears, they were written about that Time.

As to the Author, I can give no manner of Satisfaction; However, I am credibly informed, that this Publication is without his Knowledge; for he concludes the Copy is lost, having lent it to a Person, since dead, and being never in Possession of it after: So that, whether the Work received his last Hand, or, whether he intended to fill up the defective Places, is like to remain a Secret.

The Bookseller to the Reader.

If I should go about to tell the Reader, by what Accident, I became Master of these Papers, it would, in this unbelieving Age, pass for little more than the Cant, or Jargon of the Trade. I, therefore, gladly spare both him and my self so unnecessary a Trouble. There yet remains a difficult Question, why I publish'd them no sooner. I forbore upon two Accounts: First, because I thought I had better Work upon my Hands; and Secondly, because, I was not without some Hope of hearing from the Author, and receiving his Directions. But, I have been lately alarm'd with Intelligence of a surreptitious Copy, which a certain great Wit had new polish'd and refin'd, or, as our present Writers express themselves, fitted to the Humor of the Age; as they have already done, with great Felicity, to Don Quixot, Boccalini, la Bruyere, and other Authors. However, I thought it fairer Dealing, to offer the whole Work in its Naturals. If any Gentleman will please to furnish me with a Key, in order to explain the more difficult Parts, I shall very gratefully acknowledge the Favour, and print it by it self.

THE
Epistle Dedicatory,
TO
His Royal Highness
PRINCE POSTERITY.

SIR,

I HERE present *Your Highness* with the Fruits of a very few leisure Hours, stollen from the short Intervals of a World of Business, and of an Employment quite alien from such Amusements as this: The poor Production of that Refuse of Time which has lain heavy upon my Hands, during a long Prorogation of Parliament, a great Dearth of Forein News, and a tedious Fit of rainy Weather: For which, and other Reasons, it cannot chuse extreamly to deserve such a Patronage as that of *Your Highness*, whose

B numberless

number'efs Virtues in fo few Years, make the World look upon You as the future Example to all Princes: For altho' *Your Highnefs* is hardly got clear of Infancy, yet has the univerfal learned World already refolved upon appealing to Your future Dictates with the lowest and moft refign-ned Submiffion; Fate having decreed You fole Arbiter of the Productions of human Wit, in this polite and moft accomplifh'd Age. Methinks, the Number of Appellants were enough to fhock and ftartle any Judge of a Genius lefs unlimited than Yours: But in order to prevent fuch glorious Tryals, the *Perfon* (it feems) to whofe Care the Education of *Your Highnefs* is committed, has refolved (as I am told) to keep You in almoft an univerfal Ignorance of our Studies, which it is Your inherent Birth-right to infpect.

It is amazing to me, that this *Perfon* fhould have Affurance in the face of the Sun, to go about perfuading *Your Highnefs*, that our Age is almoft wholly illiterate, and has hardly produced one Writer upon any Subject. I know very well, that when *Your Highnefs* fhall come to riper Years, and have gone thro' the Learning

PRINCE POSTERITY.

ing of Antiquity, You will be too curious to neglect inquiring into the Authors of the very Age before You; And to think that this *Infolent*, in the Account he is preparing for Your View, designs to reduce them to a Number so insignificant as I am ashamed to mention; it moves my Zeal and my Spleen for the Honor and Interest of our vast flourishing Body, as well as of my self, for whom I know by long Experience, he has profess'd, and Still continues a peculiar Malice.

'Tis not unlikely, that when *Your Highness* will one Day peruse what I am now writing, You may be ready to expostulate with Your *Governour* upon the Credit of what I here affirm, and command Him to shew You some of our Productions. To which he will answer, (for I am well informed of his Designs) by asking *Your Highness*, where they are? and what is become of them? and pretend it a Demonstration that there never were any, because they are not then to be found: Not to be found! Who has mislaid them? Are they sunk in the Abyss of Things? 'Tis certain, that in their own Nature they were *light* enough to swim upon the Surface

Surface for all Eternity: Therefore the Fault is in Him, who tied Weights so heavy to their Heels, as to depress them to the Center. Is their very Essence destroyed? Who has annihilated them? Were they drowned by *Purges* or martyred by *Pipes*? Who administred them to the Posteriors of —— But that it may no longer be a Doubt with *Your Highness*, who is to be the Author of this universal Ruin; I beseech You to observe that large and terrible *Scythe* which Your *Governour* affects to bear continually about him. Be pleased to remark the Length and Strength, the Sharpness and Hardness of his *Nails* and *Teeth*; Consider his baneful abominable *Breath*, Enemy to Life and Matter, infectious and corrupting: And then reflect whether it be possible for any mortal Ink and Paper of this Generation to make a suitable Resistance. Oh, that *Your Highness* would one day resolve to disarm this Usurping *Maitre de Palais*, of his furious Engins, and bring Your Empire *hors du Page*.

It were endless to recount the several Methods of Tyranny and Destruction, which Your *Governour* is pleased to practice

ctice upon this Occasion. His inveterate Malice is such to the Writings of our Age, that of several Thousands produced yearly from this renowned City, before the next Revolution of the Sun, there is not one to be heard of: Unhappy Infants, many of them barbarously destroyed, before they have so much as learnt their *Mother-Tongue* to beg for Pity. Some he stifles in their Cradles, others he frights into Convulsions, whereof they suddenly die; Some he flays alive, others he tears Limb from Limb: Great Numbers are offered to *Moloch*, and the rest tainted by his Breath, die of a languishing Consumption.

But the Concern I have most at Heart, is for our Corporation of *Poets*, from whom I am preparing a Petition to *Your Highness*, to be subscribed with the Names of one hundred thirty six of the first Rate, but whose immortal Productions are never likely to reach your Eyes, tho' each of them is now an humble and an earnest Appellant for the Laurel, and has large comely Volumes ready to shew for a Support to his Pretensions. The *never-dying* Works of these illustrious Persons, Your

Governour, Sir, has devoted to unavoidable Death, and *Your Highness* is to be made believe, that our Age has never arrived at the Honor to produce one single Poet.

WE confess *Immortality* to be a great and powerful Goddess, but in vain we offer up to her our Devotions and our Sacrifices, if *Your Highness's Governour*, who has usurped the *Priesthood*, must by an unparallell'd Ambition and Avarice, wholly intercept and devour them.

To affirm that our Age is altogether Unlearned, and devoid of Writers in any kind, seems to be an Assertion so bold and so false, that I have been sometime thinking, the contrary may almost be proved by uncontroulable Demonstration. 'Tis true indeed, that altho' their Numbers be vast, and their Productions numerous in proportion, yet are they hurryed so hastily off the Scene, that they escape our Memory, and delude our Sight. When I first thought of this Address, I had prepared a copious List of *Titles* to present *Your Highness* as an undisputed Argument for what I affirm. The Originals were posted

posted fresh upon all Gates and Corners of Streets; but returning in a very few Hours to take a Review, they were all torn down, and fresh ones in their Places: I enquired after them among Readers and Bookfellers, but I enquired in vain, the *Memorial of them was loſt among Men, their Place was no more to be found*; and I was laughed to scorn, for a *Clown* and a *Pedant*, devoid of all Taste and Refinement, little versed in the Course of *preſent* Affairs, and that knew nothing of what had pass'd in the best Companies of Court and Town. So that I can only avow in general to *Your Highneſs*, that we *do* abound in Learning and Wit; but to fix upon Particulars, is a Task too slippery for my slender Abilities. If I should venture in a windy Day, to affirm to *Your Highneſs*, that there is a huge Cloud near the *Horizon* in the Form of a *Bear*, another in the *Zenith* with the Head of an *Aſs*, a third to the Westward with Claws like a *Dragon*; and *Your Highneſs* should in a few Minutes think fit to examine the Truth; 'tis certain, they would be all changed in Figure and Position, new ones would arise, and all we could agree upon would be, that Clouds there were,

were, but that I was grosly mistaken in the *Zoography* and *Topography* of them.

But Your *Governour*, perhaps, may still insist, and put the Question; What is then become of those immense Bales of Paper, which must needs have been employ'd in such Numbers of Books? Can these also be wholly annihilate, and so of a sudden as I pretend? What shall I say in return of so invidious an Objection? It ill befits the Distance between *Your Highness* and Me, to send You for ocular Conviction to a *Jakes* or an *Oven*; to the Windows of a *Bawdy-House*, or to a sordid *Lanthorn*. Books like Men their Authors have no more than one Way of coming into the World, but there are ten Thousand to go out of it, and return no more.

I profess to *Your Highness* in the Integrity of my Heart, that what I am going to say is literally true this Minute I am writing: What Revolutions may happen before it shall be ready for Your Perusal, I can by no means warrant; However, I beg You to accept it as a Specimen of our Learning, our Politeness and
our

PRINCE POSTERITY.

our Wit. I do therefore affirm upon the Word of a sincere Man, that there is now actually in being, a certain Poet called *John Dryden*, whose Translation of *Virgil* was lately printed in a large Folio, well bound, and if diligent search were made, for ought I know, is yet to be seen. There is another call'd *Nahum Tate*, who is ready to make Oath that he has caused many Rheams of Verse to be published, whereof both himself and his Bookseller (if lawfully required) can still produce authentick Copies, and therefore wonders why the World is pleased to make such a Secret of it. There is a Third, known by the Name of *Tom Durfey*, a Poet of a vast Comprehension, an universal Genius, and most profound Learning. There are also one Mr. *Rymer*, and one Mr. *Dennis*, most profound Criticks There is a Person styled Dr. *B-tl-y*, who has wrote near a thousand Pages of immense Erudition, *giving a full and true Account* of a certain *Squable* of wonderful importance between himself and a Bookseller: He is a Writer of infinite Wit and Humour; no Man raillyes with a better Grace, and in more sprightly Turns. Further, I avow to *Your Highness*, that with these Eyes I have be-
held

Dedication to

held the Perfon of *William W-tt-n*, B. D. who has written a good fizeable Volume againſt a *Friend* of *Your Governour* (from whom, alas! he muſt therefore look for little Favour) in a moſt gentlemanly Stile, adorned with utmoſt Politeneſs and Civility; replete with Diſcoveries equally valuable for their Novelty and Uſe; and embelifh'd with *Traits* of Wit fo poignant and fo appoſite, that he is a worthy Yoke-mate to his fore-mention'd *Friend.*

W H Y ſhould I go upon further Particulars, which might fill a Volume with the juſt Elogies of my cotemporary Brethren? I ſhall bequeath this Piece of Juſtice to a larger Work; wherein I intend to write a Character of the preſent Set of *Wits* in our Nation: Their Perſons I ſhall deſcribe particularly, and at Length, their Genius and Underſtandings in *Miniature.*

I N the mean time, I do here make bold to preſent *Your Highneſs* with a faithful Abſtract drawn from the Univerſal Body of all Arts and Sciences, intended wholly for Your Service and Inſtruction: Nor do I doubt in the leaſt, but *Your Highneſs* will
peruſe

perufe it as carefully, and make as confiderable Improvements, as *other* young *Princes* have already done by the many Volumes of late Years written for a Help to their Studies.

THAT *Your Highnefs* may advance in Wifdom and Virtue, as well as Years, and at laft out-fhine all Your Royal Anceftors, fhall be the daily Prayer of,

S I R,

Decemb.
1697.

Your Highnefs's

Moft devoted, &c.

THE

THE PREFACE.

THE Wits of the prefent Age being fo very numerous and penetrating, it feems, the Grandees of *Church* and *State* begin to fall under horrible Apprehenfions, left thefe Gentlemen during the Intervals of a long Peace, fhould find leifure to pick Holes in the weak fides of Religion and Government. To prevent which, there has been much Thought employ'd of late upon certain Projects for taking off the Force and Edge of thofe formidable Enquirers, from canvafing and reafoning upon fuch delicate Points. They have at length fixed upon one, which will require fome Time as well as Coft, to perfect. Mean while, the Danger hourly increafing, by new Levies of Wits all appointed (as there is Reafon to fear) with Pen, Ink, and Paper, which may at an hour's Warning be drawn out into Pamphlets, and other Offenfive Weapons, ready for immediate Execution:

The PREFACE.

It was judged of absolute necessity, that some present Expedient be thought on, till the main Design can be brought to Maturity. To this End, at a Grand Committee, some Days ago, this important Discovery was made by a certain curious and refined Observer; That Sea-men have a Custom when they meet a *Whale*, to fling him out an empty *Tub*, by way of Amusement, to divert him from laying violent Hands upon the Ship. This Parable was immediately mythologiz'd; The *Whale* was interpreted to be *Hobs's Leviathan*, which tosses and plays with all other Schems of Religion and Government, whereof a great many are hollow, and dry, and empty, and noisy, and wooden, and given to Rotation. This is the *Leviathan* from whence the terrible Wits of our Age are said to borrow their Weapons. The *Ship* in danger, is easily understood to be its old Antitype the *Commonwealth*. But, how to analyze the *Tub*, was a Matter of Difficulty; when after long Enquiry and Debate, the literal Meaning was preserved: And it was decreed, that in order to prevent these *Leviathans* from tossing and sporting with the *Commonwealth*, (which of it self is too apt to *fluctuate*) they

The PREFACE.

they should be diverted from their Game by *a Tale of a Tub*. And my Genius being conceived to lye not unhappily that way, I had the Honor done me to be engaged in the Performance.

THIS is the sole Design in publishing the following Treatise, which I hope will serve for an *Interim* of some Months to employ those unquiet Spirits, till the perfecting of that great Work; into the Secret of which, it is reasonable the courteous Reader should have some little Light.

IT is intended that a large Academy be erected, capable of containing nine thousand seven hundred forty and three Persons; which by modest Computation is reckoned to be pretty near the current Number of *Wits* in this Island. These are to be disposed into the several Schools of this Academy, and there pursue those Studies to which their Genius most inclines them. The Undertaker himself will publish his Proposals with all convenient speed, to which I shall refer the curious Reader for a more particular Account, mentioning at present only a few of the principal Schools. There is, first, a large *Pedera-*
stick

stick School, with *French* and *Italian* Masters. There is also, the *Spelling* School, a very *spacious Building*: The School of *Looking-Glasses*: The School of *Swearing*: The School of *Criticks*: The School of *Salivation*: The School of *Hobby-Horses*: The School of *Poetry*: The School of *Tops*: The School of *Spleen*: The School of *Gaming*; with many others too tedious to recount. No Person to be admitted Member into any of these Schools, without an Attestation under two sufficient Persons Hands, certifying him to be a *Wit*.

But, to return. I am sufficiently instructed in the principal Duty of a Preface, if my Genius were capable of arriving at it. Thrice have I forced my Imagination to take the *Tour* of my Invention, and thrice it has returned empty; the latter having been wholly drained by the following Treatise. Not so, my more successful Brethren the *Moderns*, who will by no means let slip a Preface or Dedication, without some notable distinguishing Stroke, to surprize the Reader at the Entry, and kindle a wonderful Expectation of what is to ensue. Such was that of a most ingenious Poet, who solliciting his Brain

Brain for something new, compared himself to the *Hangman*, and his Patron to the *Patient*: This was * *Insigne, recens, indictum ore alio* When I went thro' that necessary and noble † Course of Study, I had the happiness to observe many such egregious Touches, which I shall not injure the Authors by transplanting: Because I have remarked, that nothing is so very tender as a *Modern* Piece of Wit, and which is apt to suffer so much in the Carriage. Some things are extreamly witty *to day*, or *fasting*, or *in this Place*, or *at eight a Clock*, or *over a Bottle*, or *spoken by Mr*. Whatdicall'um, or *in a Summer's Morning*: Any of which, by the smallest Transposal or Misapplication, is utterly annihilate. Thus, *Wit* has its Walks and Purlieus, out of which it may not stray the breadth of a Hair, upon peril of being lost. The *Moderns* have artfully fixed this *Mercury*, and reduced it to the Circumstances of Time, Place and Person. Such a Jest there is, that will not pass out of *Convent-Garden*; and such a one, that is no where intelligible but at *Hide-Park* Corner. Now, tho' it sometimes tenderly affects me to consider, that all the towardly Passages I shall deliver in the following

* *Hor.*

† *Reading Prefaces, &c.*

The PREFACE.

lowing Treatise, will grow quite out of date and relish with the first shifting of the present Scene; yet I must need subscribe to the Justice of this Proceeding: because, I cannot imagine why we should be at Expence to furnish Wit for succeeding Ages, when the former have made no sort of Provision for ours; wherein I speak the Sentiment of the very newest, and consequently the most Orthodox Refiners, as well as my own. However, being extreamly sollicitous that every accomplish'd Person who has got into the Taste of Wit calculated for this present Month of *August* 1697, should descend to the very *bottom* of all the *Sublime* throughout this Treatise; I hold it fit to lay down this general Maxim. Whatever Reader desires to have a thorow Comprehension of an Author's Thoughts, cannot take a better Method, than by putting himself into the Circumcumstances and Posture of Life, that the Writer was in, upon every important Passage as it flowed from his Pen; For this will introduce a Parity and strict Correspondence of Idea's between the Reader and the Author. Now, to assist the diligent Reader in so delicate an Affair, as far as brevity will permit, I have recollected,

The PREFACE.

lected, that the shrewdest Pieces of this Treatise, were conceived in Bed, in a Garrat: At other times (for a Reason best known to my self) I thought fit to sharpen my Invention with Hunger; and in general, the whole Work was begun, continued, and ended, under a long course of Physick, and a great want of Money. Now, I do affirm, it will be absolutely impossible for the candid Peruser to go along with me in a great many bright Passages, unless upon the several Difficulties emergent, he will please to capacitate and prepare himself by these Directions. And this I lay down as my principal *Postulatum*.

BECAUSE I have profess'd to be a most devoted Servant of all *Modern* Forms; I apprehend some curious *Wit* may object against me, for proceeding thus far in a Preface, without declaiming according to the Custom, against the Multitude of Writers, whereof the whole Multitude of Writers most reasonably complains. I am just come from perusing some hundreds of Prefaces, wherein the Authors do at the very beginning address the gentle Reader concerning this enormous Grievance. Of these

The PREFACE.

I have preserved a few Examples, and shall set them down as near as my Memory has been able to retain them.

One begins thus;

For a Man to set up for a Writer, when the Press swarms with, &c.

Another;

The Tax upon Paper does not lessen the Number of Scriblers, who daily pester, &c.

Another;

When every little Would-be-wit takes Pen in hand, 'tis in vain to enter the Lists, &c.

Another;

To observe what Trash the Press swarms with, &c.

Another;

SIR. It is meerly in Obedience to your Commands that I venture into the Publick; for who upon a less Consideration would be of a Party with such a Rabble of Scriblers, &c.

Now,

The PREFACE.

Now, I have two Words in my own Defence, against this Objection. First: I am far from granting the Number of Writers, a Nuisance to our Nation, having strenuously maintained the contrary in several Parts of the following Discourse. Secondly: I do not well understand the Justice of this Proceeding, because I observe many of these polite Prefaces, to be not only from the same Hand, but from those who are most voluminous in their several Productions: Upon which I shall tell the Reader a short Tale.

A *Mountebank in* Lecester-Fields *had drawn a huge Assembly about him. Among the rest, a fat unweildy Fellow, half stifled in the Press, would be every fit crying out,* Lord! what a filthy Crowd is here; Pray, good People, give way a little; Bless me! what a Devil has rak'd this Rabble together: Z----ds, what squeezing is this! Honest Friend, remove your Elbow. *At last a Weaver that stood next him could hold no longer?* A Plague confound you (*said he*) for an over-grown Sloven; and who (*in the Devil's Name*) I wonder, helps to make up the Crowd half so much as your self? Don't *you confider (with a Pox) that you take up more room with that Carcafs than any five here? Is not the Place as free for us as for you? Bring your own Guts to a reasonable Compafs (and be d----n'd) and then I'll engage we shall have room enough for us all.*

THERE are certain common Privileges of a Writer, the Benefit whereof, I hope there will be no Reason to doubt; particularly, that where I am not underftood, it fhall be concluded, that fomething very ufeful and profound is coutcht underneath: And again, that whatever Word or Sentence is printed in a different Character, fhall be judged to contain fomething extraordinary either of *Wit* or *Sublime.*

As for the Liberty I have thought fit to take of praifing my felf, upon fome Occafions or none; I am fure it will need no Excufe, if a Multitude of great Examples be allowed fufficient Authority: For, it is here to be noted, that *Praife* was originally a Penfion paid by the World; but the *Moderns* finding the Trouble and Charge too great in collecting it, have lately bought out the *Fee-Simple*; fince which time, the Right of Prefentation is wholly in our felves. For this Reafon it is, that when

an

an Author makes his own Elogy, he uses a certain Form to declare and infist upon his Title, which is commonly in these or the like Words, *I speak without Vanity*; which I think plainly shews it to be a Matter of Right and Justice. Now, I do here once for all declare, that in every Encounter of this Nature, thro' the following Treatise, the Form aforesaid is imply'd; which I mention, to save the Trouble of repeating it on so many Occasions.

'Tis a great Ease to my Conscience that I have writ so elaborate and useful a Discourse without one grain of Satyr intermixt; which is the sole Point wherein I have taken Leave to dissent from the famous Originals of our Age and Country. I have observ'd some Satyrists to use the Publick much at the rate that Pedants do a naughty Boy ready hors'd for Discipline; First expostulate the Case, then plead the Necessity of the Rod, from great Provocations, and conclude every Period with a Lash. Now, if I know any thing of Mankind, these Gentlemen might very well spare their Reproof and Correction: For, there is not through all Nature another so callous and insensible a Member as *the World's Posteriors*, whether you apply

ply to it the *Toe* or the *Birch*. Besides, most of our late Satyrists seem to lye under a sort of Mistake, that because *Nettles* have the Prerogative to Sting, therefore all *other Weeds* must do so too. I make not this Comparison out of the least Design to detract from these worthy Writers: For it is well known among *Mythologists*, that *Weeds* have the Preeminence over all other Vegetables; and therefore the first *Monarch* of this Island, whose Taste and Judgment were so acute and refined, did very wisely root out the *Roses* from the Collar of *the Order*, and plant the *Thistles* in their stead, as the nobler Flower of the two. For which Reason it is conjectured by profounder Antiquaries, that the Satyrical Itch, so prevalent in this Part of our Island, was first brought among us from beyond the *Tweed*. Here may it long flourish and abound; May it survive and neglect the Scorn of the World, with as much Ease and Contempt, as the World is insensible to the Lashes of it. May their own Dullness, or that of their Party, be no Discouragement for the Authors to proceed; but let them remember, it is with *Wits* as with *Razors*, which are never so apt to *cut* those they

are

The PREFACE.

are employ'd on, as when they have *lost their Edge:* Besides, those whose Teeth are too rotten to bite, are best of all others qualified to revenge that Defect with their Breath.

I am not like other Men, to envy or undervalue the Talents I cannot reach; for which Reason I must needs bear a true Honor to this large eminent Sect of our *British* Writers. And I hope, this little Panegyrick will not be offensive to their Ears, since it has the Advantage of being only designed for themselves. Indeed, Nature her self has taken Order, that Fame and Honor should be purchased at a better Penyworth by Satyr, than by any other Productions of the Brain; the World being soonest provoked to *Praise* by *Lashes*, as Men are to *Love*. There is a Problem in an ancient Author, why Dedications, and other Bundles of Flattery run all upon stale musty Topicks, without the smallest Tincture of any thing New; not only to the torment and nauseating of the *Christian* Reader, but (if not suddenly prevented) to the universal spreading of that pestilent Disease, the Lethargy in this Island: Whereas, there is very little

little Satyr which has not something in it untouch'd before. The Defects of the former are usually imputed to the want of Invention among those who are Dealers in that kind: But, I think, with a great deal of Injustice; the Solution being easy and natural. For, the Materials of Panegyrick being very few in Number, have been long since exhausted: For, as Health is but one Thing, and has been always the same, whereas Diseases are by thousands, besides new and daily Additions: So, all the Virtues that have been ever in Mankind, are to be counted upon a few Fingers; but his Follies and Vices are innumerable, and Time adds hourly to the Heap. Now, the utmost a poor Poet can do, is to get by heart a List of the Cardinal Virtues, and deal them with his utmost Liberality to his Hero or his Patron: He may ring the Changes as far as it will go, and vary his Phrase till he has talk'd round; but the Reader quickly finds, it is all * *Pork*, with a little variety of Sawce: For there is no inventing Terms of Art beyond our Idea's; and when Idea's are exhausted, Terms of Art must be so too.

* *Plutarch.*

BUT,

The PREFACE.

BUT, tho' the Matter for Panegyrick were as fruitful as the Topicks of Satyr, yet would it not be hard to find out a sufficient Reason, why the latter will be alway better received than the first. For, this being bestowed only upon one or a few Persons at a time, is sure to raise Envy, and consequently ill Words from the rest, who have no share in the Blessing: But Satyr being levelled at all, is never resented for an Offence by any, since every individual Person makes bold to understand it of others, and very wisely removes his particular Part of the Burthen upon the Shoulders of the World, which are broad enough, and able to bear it. To this purpose, I have sometimes reflected upon the Difference between *Athens* and *England* with respect to the Point before us. In the *Attick* * Commonwealth, it was the Priviledge and Birth-right of every Citizen and Poet, to rail aloud and in publick, or to expose upon the Stage by Name, any Person they pleased. tho' of the greatest Figure, whether a *Creon*, an *Hyperbolus*, an *Alcibiades*, or a *Demosthe-*

* *Vid. Xenoph.*

nes: But, on the other side, the least reflecting Word let fall against the *People* in general, was immediately caught up, and revenged upon the Authors, however considerable for their Quality or their Merits. Whereas, in *England* it is just the Reverse of all this. Here, you may securely display your utmost *Rhetorick* against Mankind, in the Face of the World; tell them, " *That all are gone astray;* " *That there is none that doth good, no not* " *one; That we live in the very Dregs of* " *Time; That Knavery and Atheism are* " *Epidemick as the Pox; That Honesty* " *is fled with Astræa;* with any other Common Places *equally* new and eloquent, which are furnished by the * *Splendida bilis.* And when you have done, the whole Audience, far from being offended, shall return you Thanks, as a Deliverer of precious and useful Truths. Nay further; It is but to venture your Lungs, and you may Preach in *Covent-Garden* against Foppery and Fornication, **and** *something else:* Against Pride, and Dissimulation, and Bribery, at *White-Hall*: You may expose Rapine and Injustice in the *Inns of Court* Chappel:

* Hor.

The PREFACE.

pel: And in a *City* Pulpit be as fierce as you pleafe, againſt Avarice, Hypocrify and Extortion. 'Tis but a *Ball* bandied to and fro, and every Man carries a *Racket* about Him to ſtrike it from himſelf among the the reſt of the Company. But on the other ſide, whoever ſhould miſtake the Nature of things ſo far, as to drop but a ſingle Hint in publick, How *ſuch a one* ſtarved half the Fleet, and half poyſon'd the reſt: How *ſuch a one* from a true Principle of *Love* and *Honor*, pays no Debts but for *Wenches* and *Play:* How *ſuch a one* has got a Clap, and runs out of his Eſtate: How *Paris* bribed by *Juno* and *Venus*, loath to offend either Party, ſlept out the whole Cauſe on the Bench: Or, how *ſuch an Orator* makes long Speeches in the Senate, with much Thought, little Senſe, and to no Purpoſe. Whoever, I ſay, ſhould venture to be thus particular, muſt expect to be impriſoned for *Scandalum Magnatum*; to have *Challenges* ſent him; to be ſued for *Defamation*; and to be *brought before the Bar of the Houſe*.

BUT,

BUT, I forget that I am expatiating on a Subject, wherein I have no Concern, having neither a Talent nor an Inclination for Satyr; On the other side, I am so entirely satisfied with the whole present Procedure of human Things, that I have been for some Years preparing Materials towards *A Panegyrick upon the World*; to which I intended to add a Second Part, entitled, *A Modest Defence of the Proceedings of the Rabble in all Ages.* Both these I had Thoughts to publish by way of Appendix to the following Treatise; but finding my Common-Place-Book fill much slower than I had reason to expect, I have chosen to defer them to another Occasion. Besides, I have been unhappily prevented in that Design, by a certain Domestick Misfortune, in the Particulars whereof, tho' it would be very seasonable, and much in the *Modern* way, to inform the *gentle Reader*, and would also be of great Assistance towards extending this Preface into the Size now in Vogue, which by Rule ought to be *large* in Proportion as the subsequent Volume is *small*; Yet I shall
now

now dismiss our impatient Reader from any further Attendance at the *Porch*; and having duly prepared his Mind by a preliminary Discourse, shall gladly introduce Him to the sublime Mysteries that ensue.

A TALE OF A TUB, &c.

SECT. I.

The INTRODUCTION.

WHOEVER hath an Ambition to be heard in a Crowd, muft prefs, and fqueeze, and thruft, and climb with indefatigable Pains, till he has exalted himfelf to a certain Degree of Altitude above them. Now, in all Affemblies, tho' you wedge them ever fo clofe, we may obferve this peculiar Property; that, over their Heads there is Room enough; but how to reach it, is the difficult

cult Point; It being as hard to get quit of *Number* as of *Hell*;

———— *Evadere ad auras,*
Hoc opus, hic labor eſt.————

To this End, the Philoſopher's Way in all Ages, has been by erecting certain *Edifices in the Air*; But, whatever Practice and Reputation theſe kind of Structures have formerly poſſeſſed, or may ſtill continue in; not excepting even that of *Socrates*, when he ſuſpended in a Basket to help Comtemplation; I think, with due Submiſſion, they ſeem to labor under two Inconveniencies. Firſt, that the Foundations being laid too high, they have been often out of *Sight*, and ever out of *Hearing*. Secondly, that the Materials being very tranſitory, have ſuffered much from Inclemences of Air, eſpecially in theſe North-Weſt Regions.

THEREFORE, towards the juſt Performance of this great Work, there remain but three Methods that I can think on; Whereof the Wiſdom of our Anceſtors being highly ſenſible, has, to encourage all aſpiring Adventures, thought fit to erect

INTRODUCTION. 35

rect three wooden Machines, for the Use of those Orators who desire to talk much without Interruption. These are, the *Pulpit*, the *Ladder*, and the *Stage-Itinerant*. For, as to the *Bar*, tho' it be compounded of the same Matter, and designed for the same Use, it cannot however be well allowed the Honor of a fourth, by reason of its level or inferior Situation, exposing it to perpetual Interruption from Collaterals. Neither can the *Bench* it self, tho' raised to a proper Eminency, put in a better Claim, whatever its Advocats insist on. For if they please to look into the original Design of its Erection, and the Circumstances or Adjuncts subservient to that Design, they will soon acknowledge the present Practice exactly correspondent to the Primitive Institution, and both to answer the Etymology of the Name, which in the *Phœnician* Tongue is a Word of great Signification, importing, if literally interpreted, *The Place of Sleep*; but in common Acceptation, *A Seat well bolster'd and cushion'd, for the Repose of old and gouty Limbs: Senes ut in otia tuta recedant.* Fortune being indebted to them this Part of Retaliation, that, as formerly, they have long *Talkt*, whilst others

D 2 *Slept*,

36 INTRODUCTION.

Slept, fo now they may *Sleep* as long whilſt others *Talk*.

But if no other Argument could occur to exclude the *Bench* and the *Bar* from the Liſt of Oratorial Machines, it were ſufficient, that the Admiſſion of them would overthrow a Number which I was reſolved to eſtabliſh whatever Argument it might coſt me: In imitation of that prudent Method obſerved by many other Philoſophers and great Clerks, whoſe chief Art in Diviſion has been, to grow fond of ſome proper myſtical Number, which their Imaginations have rendred Sacred, to a Degree, that they force common Reaſon to find room for it in every part of Nature ; reducing, including, and adjuſting every *Genus* and *Species* within that Compaſs, by coupling ſome againſt their Wills, and baniſhing others at any Rate. Now, among all the reſt, the profound Number *THREE* is that which hath moſt employ'd my ſublimeſt Speculations, nor ever without wonderful Delight. There is now in the Preſs, (and will be publiſh'd next Term) a Panegyrical Eſſay of mine upon this Number, wherein I have by moſt convincing Proofs, not only reduced the *Senſes* and the *Elements*

INTRODUCTION. 37

ments under its Banner, but brought over several Deserters from its two great Rivals *SEVEN* and *NINE.*

Now, the first of these Oratorial Machines in Place as well as Dignity, is the *Pulpit.* Of *Pulpits* there are in this Island several sorts; but I esteem only That made of Timber from the *Sylva Caledonia*, which agrees very well with our Climate. If it be upon its Decay, 'tis the better, both for Conveyance of Sound, and for other Reasons to be mentioned by and by. The Degree of Perfection in Shape and Size, I take to consist, in being extremely narrow, with little Ornament, and best of all without a Cover; (for by ancient Rule, it ought to be the only uncover'd *Vessel* in every Assembly where it is rightfully used) by which means, from its near Resemblance to a Pillory, it will ever have a mighty Influence on human Ears.

Of *Ladders* I need say nothing: 'Tis observed by Foreiners themselves, to the Honor of our Country, that we excel all Nations in our Practice and Understanding of this Machine. The ascending Orators do not only oblige their Audience in the agreeable Delivery, but the whole World in their *early* Publication of their Speeches; which I look upon as the choicest Treasury of our British Eloquence, and whereof I am informed, that worthy Citizen and Bookseller, Mr. *John Dunton*, hath made a faithful and a painful Collection, which he shortly designs to publish in Twelve Volumes in Folio, illustrated with Copper-Plates. A Work highly useful and curious, and altogether worthy of such a Hand.

The last Engine of Orators, is the *Stage-itinerant*, erected with much Sagacity, *sub Jove pluvio, in triviis & quadriviis.* It is the great Seminary of the two former, and its Orators are sometimes preferred to the One, and sometimes to the Other, in proportion to their Deservings, there being a strict and perpetual Intercourse between all three.

From this accurate Deduction it is manifest that for obtaining Attention in Publick, there is of necessity required *a superior Position of Place.* But, altho' this Point be generally granted, yet the Cause is little agreed in; and it seems to me, that

INTRODUCTION.

that very few Philosophers have fallen into a true, natural Solution of this *Phænomenon*. The deepest Account, and the most fairly digested of any I have yet met with, is this, That Air being a heavy Body, and therefore (according to the System of * *Epicurus*) continually descending, must needs be more so, when loaden and press'd down by Words; which are also Bodies of much Weight and Gravity, as it is manifest from those deep *Impressions* they make and leave upon us; and therefore must be delivered from a due Altitude, or else they will neither carry a good Aim, nor fall down with a sufficient Force.

* *Lucret. Lib.* 2.

> *Corpoream quoque enim vocem constare fatendum est,*
> *Et sonitum, quoniam possunt impellere Sensus.* Lucr. *Lib.* 4.

AND I am the readier to favour this Conjecture, from a common Observation; that in the several Assemblies of these Orators, Nature it self hath instructed the Hearers, to stand with their Mouths open, and erected parallel to the Horizon, so as they may be intersected by a perpendicular

40 INTRODUCTION.

cular Line from the Zenith to the Center of the Earth. In which Pofition, if the Audience be well compact, every one carries home a Share, and little or nothing is loft.

I confefs, there is fomething yet more refined in the Contrivance and Structure of our Modern Theatres. For, Firft; the Pit is funk below the Stage with due Regard to the Inftitution above deduced ; that whatever *weighty* Matter fhall be delivered thence (whether it be *Lead* or *Gold*) may fall plum into the Jaws of certain *Criticks* (as I think they are called) which ftand ready open to devour them. Then, the Boxes are built round, and raifed to a Level with the Scene, in deference to the Ladies, becaufe, That large Portion of Wit laid out in raifing Pruriences and Protuberencies, is obferved to run much upon a Line, and ever in a Circle. The whining Paffions, and little ftarved Conceits, are gently wafted up by their own extreme Levity, to the middle Region, and there fix and are frozen by the frigid Underftandings of the Inhabitants. Bombaft and Buffoonry, by Nature lofty and light, foar higheft of all, and would be loft in the Roof, if the prudent

INTRODUCTION. 41

dent Architect had not with much Foresight contrived for them a fourth Place, called *the Twelve-Peny Gallery*, and there planted a suitable Colony, who greedily intercept them in their Passage.

Now this Physico-logical Scheme of Oratorial Receptacles or Machines, contains a great Mystery, being a Type, a Sign, an Emblem, a Shadow, a Symbol, bearing Analogy to the spatious Commonwealth of Writers, and to those Methods by which they must exalt themselves to a certain Eminency above the inferior World. By the *Pulpit* are adumbrated the Writings of our *Modern Saints* in *Great Britain*, as they have spiritualized and refined them from the Dross and Grossness of *Sense* and *Human Reason*. The Matter, as we have said, is of rotten Wood, and that upon two Considerations; Because it is the Quality of rotten Wood to give *Light* in the Dark: And secondly, Because its Cavities are full of Worms: Which is a Type with a Pair of Handles, having a Respect to the two principal Qualifications of the Orator, and the two different Fates attending upon his Works.

42 INTRODUCTION.

THE *Ladder* is an adequate Symbol of *Faction* and of *Poetry*, to both of which so noble a Number of Authors are indebted for their Fame. Of *Faction*, because * * * * * * *
* * * * * *
Hiatus in * * * * * * *
MS.
* * * * * *
* * * * Of *Poetry*, because its Orators do *perorare* with a Song; and because climbing up by slow Degrees, Fate is sure to turn them off before they can reach within many Steps of the Top: And because it is a Preferment attained by transferring of Propriety, and a confounding of *Meum* and *Tuum*.

UNDER the *Stage-itinerant* are couched those Productions designed for the Pleasure and Delight of Mortal Man; such as, *Six-peny-worth of Wit*, Westminster *Drolleries*, *Delightful Tales*, *Compleat Jesters*, and the like; by which the Writers of and for GRUB-STREET, have in these later Ages so nobly triumpht over *Time*; have clipt his Wings, pared his Nails, filed his Teeth, turned back his Hour-Glass, blunted his Scythe, and drawn the Hob-Nails

out

out of his Shoes. It is under this Classis, I have presumed to list my present Treatise, being just come from having the Honor conferred upon me, to be adopted a Member of that illustrious Fraternity.

Now, I am not unaware, how the Productions of the *Grub-Street* Brotherhood, have of late Years fallen under many Prejudices; nor how it has been the perpetual Employment of two *Junior* start-up Societies, to ridicule them and their Authors, as unworthy their established Post in the Commonwealth of Wit and Learning. Their own Consciences will easily inform them, whom I mean; Nor has the World been so negligent a Looker on, as not to observe the continual Efforts made by the Societies of *Gresham* and of *Will's*, to edify a Name and Reputation upon the Ruin of Ours. And this is yet a more feeling Grief to Us upon the Regards of Tenderness as well as of Justice, when we reflect on their Proceedings, not only as unjust, but as ungrateful, undutiful, and unnatural. For, how can it be forgot by the World or themselves, (to say nothing of our own Records, which are
full

full and clear in the Point) that they both are Seminaries, not only of our *Planting*, but our *Watring* too? I am informed, Our two *Rivals* have lately made an Offer to enter into the Lists with united Forces, and challenge Us to a Comparison of Books, both as to *Weight* and *Number*. In Return to which, (with Licence from our *President*) I humbly offer two Answers: First, We say, the Proposal is like that which *Archimedes* made upon a * *smaller* Affair, including an Impossibility in the Practice; For, where can they find Scales of *Capacity* enough for the first, or an Arithmetician of *Capacity* enough for the second. Secondly, We are ready to accept the Challenge, but with this Condition, that a third indifferent Person be assigned, to whose impartial Judgment it shall be left to decide, which Society each Book, Treatise or Pamphlet do most properly belong to. This Point, God knows, is very far from being fixed at present; For, We are ready to produce a Catalogue of some Thousands, which in all common Justice ought to be entitled to Our Fraternity, but by the revolted and new-fangled Writers, most perfidiously ascribed to

the

* Viz. About moving the Earth.

INTRODUCTION. 45

the others. Upon all which, we think it very unbecoming our Prudence, that the Determination should be remitted to the Authors themselves; when our Adverſaries by Briguing and Caballing, have cauſed ſo univerſal a Defection from us, that the greateſt Part of our Society hath already deſerted to them, and our neareſt Friends begin to ſtand aloof, as if they were half aſhamed to own Us.

This is the utmoſt I am authorized to ſay upon ſo ungrateful and melancholy a Subject; becauſe We are extreme unwilling to inflame a Controverſy, whoſe Continuance may be ſo fatal to the Intereſts of Us All, deſiring much rather that Things be amicably compoſed, and We ſhall ſo far advance on our Side, as to be ready to receive the two *Prodigals* with open Arms, whenever they ſhall think fit to return from their *Husks* and their *Harlots*; which I think from the * preſent Courſe of their Studies they moſt properly may be ſaid to be engaged in; and like an indulgent Parent, continue to them our Affection and our Bleſſing.

* *Virtuoſo Experiments, and Modern Comedies.*

But

BUT the greatest Maim given to that general Reception, which the Writings of our Society have formerly received, next to the transitory State of all sublunary Things, hath been a superficial Vein among many Readers of the present Age, who will by no means be persuaded to inspect beyond the Surface and the Rind of Things; whereas, *Wisdom* is a *Fox*, who after long hunting, will at last cost you the Pains to dig out: 'Tis a *Cheese*, which by how much the richer, has the thicker, the homelier, and the courser Coat; and whereof to a judicious Palate, the *Maggots* are the best. 'Tis a *Sack-Posset*, wherein the deeper you go, you will find it the sweeter. *Wisdom* is a *Hen*, whose *Cackling* we must value and consider, because it is attended with an *Egg*; But then, lastly, 'tis a *Nut*, which unless you chuse with Judgment, may cost you a Tooth, and pay you with nothing but a *Worm*. In consequence of these momentous Truths, the *Grubæan* Sages have always chosen to convey their Precepts and their Arts, shut up within the Vehicles of Types and Fables, which having been perhaps more careful and curious in a-
dorning,

dorning, than was altogether neceffary, it has fared with thefe Vehicles after the ufual Fate of Coaches over-finely painted and gilt; that the tranfitory Gazers have fo dazzled their Eyes, and fill'd their Imaginations with the outward Luftre, as neither to regard or confider, the Perfon or the Parts of the Owner within. A Misfortune we undergo with fomewhat lefs Reluctancy, becaufe it has been common to us with *Pythagoras, Æfop, Socrates,* and other of our Predeceffors.

However, that neither the World nor our felves may any longer fuffer by fuch Mifunderftandings, I have been prevailed on, after much Importunity from my Friends, to travel in a compleat and laborious Differtation upon the prime Productions of our Society, which befides their beautiful Externals for the Gratification of fuperficial Readers, have darkly and deeply couched under them, the moft finifhed and refined Syftems of all Sciences and Arts; as I do not doubt to lay open by Untwifting or Unwinding, and either to draw up by Exantlation, or difplay by Incifion.

This

INTRODUCTION.

THIS great Work was entred upon some Years ago, by one of our most eminent Members: He began with the History of *Reynard* the *Fox*, but neither lived to publish his Essay, nor to proceed further in so useful an Attempt, which is very much to be lamented, because the Discovery he made, and communicated with his Friends, is now universally received; Nor, do I think, any of the Learned will dispute, that famous Treatise to be a compleat Body of Civil Knowlege, and the *Revelation*, or rather, the *Apocalyps* of all State *Arcana*. But the Progress I have made is much greater, having already finished my Annotations upon several Dozens: From some of which, I shall impart a few Hints to the candid Reader, as far as will be necessary to the Conclusion at which I aim.

THE first Piece I have handled is that of *Tom Thumb*, whose Author was a *Pythagorean* Philosopher. This dark Treatise contains the whole Scheme of the *Metampsycosis*, deducing the Progress of the Soul thro' all her Stages.

INTRODUCTION. 49

THE next is *Doctor Faustus*, penn'd by *Artephius*, an Author of some note, and an *Adeptus*; He published it in the * nine hundred eighty fourth Year of his Age; this Writer proceeds wholly by *Reincrudation*, or in the *via humida*: And the Marriage between *Faustus* and *Hellen*, does most conspicuously dilucidate the fermenting of the *Male* and *Female Dragon*.

* He lived a thousand.

WHITTINGTON *and his Cat*, is the Work of that Mysterious *Rabbi*, *Jehuda Hannasi*; containing a Defence of the *Guemara* of the *Jerusalem Misna*, and its just preference to that of *Babylon*, contrary to the vulgar Opinion.

THE *Hind and Panther*. This is the Master-piece of a famous Writer † now living, intended for a compleat Abstract of sixteen thousand Schoolmen from *Scotus* to *Bellarmin*.

† Viz. in the Year 1697.

Tommy Potts. Another Piece supposed by the same Hand, by way of Supplement to the former.

E   THE

INTRODUCTION.

THE *Wife Men of* Gotham, *cum Appendice.* This is a Treatise of immense Erudition, being the great Original and Fountain of those Arguments, bandied about both in *France* and *England*, for a juſt Defence of the *Modern* Learning and Wit, againſt the Preſumption, the Pride, and the Ignorance of the *Antients.* This unknown Author hath ſo exhauſted the Subject, that a penetrating Reader will eaſily diſcover, whatever hath been written ſince upon that Diſpute, to be little more than Repetition. An Abſtract of this Treatiſe hath been lately publiſhed by a *worthy Member* of our Society.

THESE Notices may ſerve to give the Learned Reader an Idea, as well as a Taſte, of what the whole Work is likely to produce: wherein I have now altogether circumſcribed my Thoughts and my Studies; and if I can bring it to a Perfection before I die, ſhall reckon I have well employ'd the poor Remains of an unfortunate Life. This indeed is more than I can juſtly expect from a Quill worn to the Pith in the Service of the State, in *Pro's* and *Con's* upon *Popiſh Plots*, and *Meal Tubs,*

INTRODUCTION.

Tubs, and *Exclusion Bills,* and *Passive Obedience,* and *Addresses of Lives and Fortunes;* and *Prerogative,* and *Property,* and *Liberty of Conscience,* and *Letters to a Friend*: From an Understanding and a Conscience, thread-bare and ragged with perpetual turning; From a Head broken in a hundred places, by the Malignants of the opposite Factions; and from a Body spent with Poxes ill cured, by trusting to Bawds and Surgeons, who, (as it afterwards appeared) were profess'd Enemies to Me and the Government, and revenged their Party's Quarrel upon my Nose and Shins. Fourscore and eleven Pamphlets have I writ under three Reigns, and for the Service of six and thirty Factions. But finding the State has no further Occasion for Me and my Ink, I retire willingly to draw it out into Speculations more becoming a Philosopher, having to my unspeakable Comfort, passed a long Life, with a *Conscience void of Offence towards God and towards Man.*

BUT to return. I am assured from the Reader's Candor, that the brief Specimen I have given, will easily clear all the rest of our Society's Productions, from an Asperfion grown, as it is manifest, out of Envy and Ignorance; That they are of little farther Use or Value to Mankind, beyond the common Entertainments of their Wit and their Style: For, these I am sure have never yet been disputed by our keenest Adversaries: In both which, as well as the more profound and mystical Part, I have throughout this Treatise closely followed the most applauded Originals. And to render all compleat, I have with much Thought and Application of Mind, so ordered, that the chief Title prefixed to it. (I mean, That under which I design it shall pass in the common Conversations of Court and Town) is modelled exactly after the Manner peculiar to *Our* Society.

I confess to have been somewhat liberal in the Business of * Titles, having observed the Humor of multiplying them. to bear great Vogue among certain Writers, whom I exceedingly Reverence. And indeed, it seems not unreasonable, that Books, the Children of the Brain, should have the Honor to be Christned with variety

* *The Title Page in the Original was so torn, that it was not possible to recover several Titles which the Author here speaks of.*

riety of Names, as well as other Infants of Quality. Our famous *Dryden* has ventured to proceed a Point farther, endeavouring to introduce also a Multiplicity of * *God-fathers*; which is an Improvement of much more Advantage, upon a very obvious Account. 'Tis a Pity this admirable Invention has not been better cultivated, so as to grow by this time into general Imitation, when such an Authority serves it for a Precedent. Nor have my Endeavours been wanting to second so useful an Example: But it seems, there is an unhappy Expence usually annexed to the Calling of a God-father, which was clearly out of my Head, as it is very reasonable to believe. Where the Pinch lay, I cannot certainly affirm; but having employ'd a World of Thoughts and Pains, to split my Treatise into forty Sections, and having entreated forty Lords of my Acquaintance, that they would do me the Honor to stand, they all made it a Matter of Conscience, and sent me their Excuses.

* *See* Virgil *translated*, &c.

SECTION II.

ONCE upon a Time, there was a Man who had three Sons by one Wife, and all at a Birth, neither could the Mid-wife tell certainly which was the Eldest. Their Father died while they were young, and upon his Death-Bed, calling the Lads to him, spoke thus.

Sons; Because I have purchased no Estate, nor was born to any, I have long considered of some good Legacies to bequeath You; And at last, with much Care as well as Expence, have provided each of you (here they are) a new Coat. Now, you are to understand, that these Coats have two Virtues contained in them: One is, that with good wearing, they will last you fresh and sound as long as you live: The other is, that they will grow in the same Proportion with your Bodies, lengthning and widening of themselves, so as to be always fit. Here, let me see them on you before I die. So, very well. Pray Children, wear them clean, and brush them often. You will find in my Will (here it is) full Instructions in every Particular concerning

concerning the Wearing and Management of your Coats; wherein you must be very exact, to avoid the Penalties I have appointed for every Transgression or Neglect, upon which your future Fortunes will entirely depend. I have also commanded in my Will, that you should live together in one House like Brethren and Friends, for then you will be sure to thrive, and not otherwise.

HERE the Story says, this good Father died, and the three Sons went altogether to seek their Fortunes.

I shall not trouble you with recounting, what Adventures they met for the first seven Years, any further than by taking notice, that they carefully observed their Father's Will, and kept their Coats in very good Order; That they travelled thro' several Countries, encountred a reasonable Quantity of Gyants, and slew certain Dragons.

BEING now arrived at the proper Age for producing themselves, they came up to Town, and fell in love with the Ladies, but especially three, who about that time were in chief Reputation: The Dutchess *d'Argent, d' Argent, Madame de Grands Titres,* and the Countefs *d' Orgueil.* On their firft Appearance, our three Adventurers met with a very bad Reception; and foon with great Sagacity guefling out the Reafon, they quickly began to improve in the good Qualities of the Town: They Writ, and Raillyed, and Rhymed, and Sung, and Said, and faid Nothing; They Drank, and Fought, and Whor'd, and Slept, and Swore, and took Snuff: They went to new Plays on the firft Night, haunted the *Chocolate-*Houfes, beat the Watch, lay on Bulks, and got Claps: They bilkt Hackney-Coachmen, ran in Debt with Shop-keepers, and lay with their Wives: They kill'd Bayliffs, kick'd Fidlers down Stairs, eat at *Lockets,* loyter'd at *Will*'s: They talk'd of the Drawing-Room and never came there, Dined with Lords they never faw; Whifper'd a Dutchefs, and fpoke never a Word; expofed the Scrawls of their Laundrefs for Billets-doux of Quality; came ever juft from Court, and were never feen in it; attended the Levee *fub dio*; Got a Lift of the Peers by heart in one Company, and with great Familiarity retailed them in another. Above all, they conftantly attended thofe Committees

mittees of Senators who are silent in the *House*, and loud in the *Coffee-House*, where they nightly adjourn to chew the Cud of Politicks, and are encompas'd with a Ring of Disciples, who lye in wait to catch up their Droppings. The three Brothers had acquired fourty other Qualifications of the like Stamp, too tedious to recount, and by consequence, were justly reckoned the most accomplish'd Persons in Town: But all would not suffice, and the Ladies aforesaid continued still inflexible: To clear up which Difficulty, I must with the Reader's good Leave and Patience, have recourse to some Points of Weight, which the Authors of that Age have not sufficiently illustrated.

For, about this Time it happened, a Sect arose, whose Tenents obtained and spread very far, especially in the *Grand Monde*, and among every Body of good Fashion. They worshipped a sort of *Idol*, who as their Doctrine delivered, did daily create Men, by a kind of Manufactury Operation. This *Idol* they placed in the highest Parts of the House, on an Altar erected about three Foot: He was shewn in the Posture of a *Persian* Emperor, sitting

ting on a *Superficies*, with his Legs interwoven under him. This God had a *Goose* for his Enfign; whence it is, that some Learned Men pretend to deduce his Original from *Jupiter Capitolinus*. At his left Hand, beneath the Altar, *Hell* seemed to open, and catch at the Animals the *Idol* was creating; to prevent which, certain of his Priests hourly flung in Pieces of the uninformed Mass, or Substance, and sometimes whole Limbs already enlivened, which that horrid Gulph infatiably swallowed, terrible to behold. The *Goose* was also held a Subaltern Divinity, or *Deus minorum gentium*, before whose Shrine was sacrificed that Creature, whose hourly Food is Human Gore, and who is in so great Renown abroad, for being the Delight and Favourite of the *Ægyptian Circopithecus*. Millions of these Animals were cruelly flaughtered every Day, to appease the Hunger of that confuming Deity. The chief *Idol* was also worshipped as the Inventor of the *Yard* and the *Needle*, whether as the God of Seamen, or on Account of certain other myftical Attributes, hath not been sufficiently cleared.

THE

THE Worshippers of this Deity had also a System of their Belief, which seemed to turn upon the following Fundamental. They held the Universe to be a large *Suit of Cloaths*, which *invests* every Thing: That the Earth is *invested* by the Air; The Air is *invested* by the Stars; and the Stars are *invested* by the *Primum Mobile*. Look on this Globe of Earth, you will find it to be a very compleat and fashionable *Dress*. What is that which some call *Land*, but a fine Coat faced with Green? or the Sea, but a Wastcoat of Water-Tabby? Proceed to the particular Works of the Creation, you will find how curious *Journey-man* Nature hath been, to trim up the *vegetable* Beaux: Observe how sparkish a Perewig adorns the Head of a *Beech*, and what a fine Doublet of white Satin is worn by the *Birch*. To conclude from all, What is Man himself but a *Micro-Coat*, or rather a compleat Suit of Cloaths with all its Trimmings. As to his Body, there can be no Dispute; but examine even the Acquirements of his Mind, you will find them all contribute in their Order, towards furnishing out an exact Dress: To instance no more; Is not Religion a *Cloak*, Honesty a *Pair of Shoes*,

worn

worn out in the Dirt, Self-love a *Surtout*, Vanity a *Shirt*, and Conscience a *Pair of Breeches*, which tho' a Cover for Lewdness as well as Nastiness, is easily slipt down for the Service of both.

These *Postulata* being admitted, it will follow in due course of Reasoning, that those Beings which the World calls improperly *Suits of Cloaths*, are in Reality the most refined Species of Animals, or to proceed higher, that they are Rational Creatures, or Men. For, is it not manifest, that They live, and move, and talk, and perform all other Offices of Human Life? Are not Beauty, and Wit, and Mien, and Breeding, their inseparable Proprieties? In short, we see nothing but them, hear nothing but them. Is it not They who walk the Streets, fill up *Parliament*—, *Coffee*—, *Play*—, *Bawdy-houses*. 'Tis true indeed, that these Animals, which are vulgarly called *Suits of Cloaths*, or *Dresses*, do according to certain Compositions receive different Appellations. If one of them be trimm'd up with a Gold Chain, and a red Gown, and a white Rod, and a great Horse, it is called a *Lord Mayor*; If certain Ermines and Furs be placed in a certain

tain Pofition, we ftile them a *Judge*, and fo, an apt Conjunction of Lawn and black Satin, we entitle a *Bifhop*.

OTHERS of thefe Profeffors, tho' agreeing in the main Syftem, were yet more refined upon certain Branches of it; and held, that Man was an Animal compounded of two *Dreffes*, the *Natural* and the *Celeftial Suit*, which were the Body and the Soul: That the Soul was the outward, and the Body the inward Cloathing; that the latter was *ex traduce*; but the former, of daily Creation and Circumfufion. This laft they proved by *Scripture*, becaufe, *in Them we Live, and Move, and have our Being*; As likewife by Philofophy, becaufe they are *All in All, and All in every Part*. Befides, faid they; Separate thefe two, and you will find the Body to be only a fenflefs unfavory Carcafs. By all which it is manifeft, that the outward Drefs muft needs be the Soul.

To this Syftem of Religion were tagged feveral fubaltern Doctrines, which were entertained with great Vogue; as particularly, the Faculties of the Mind were deduced by the Learned among them in this manner: *Embroidery,* was *Sheer Wit;* *Gold Fringe* was *agreeable Converſation*, *Gold Lace* was *Repartee,* a huge long *Perewig* was *Humor,* and a *Coat full of Powder* was very good *Raillery:* All which required abundance of *Fineſſe* and *Delicateſſe* to manage with Advantage, as well as a ſtrict Obſervance after Times and Faſhions.

I have with much Pains and Reading, collected out of antient Authors, this ſhort Summary of a Body of Philoſophy and Divinity, which ſeems to have been compoſed by a Vein and Race of Thinking, very different from any other Syſtems, either *Antient* or *Modern.* And it was not meerly to entertain or ſatisfy the Reader's Curioſity, but rather to give him Light into ſeveral Circumſtances of the following Story: that knowing the State of Diſpoſitions and Opinions in an Age ſo remote, he may better comprehend thoſe great Events which were the Iſſue of them. I adviſe therefore the courteous Reader, to peruſe with a world of Application, again and again, whatever I have written upon this Matter. And ſo leaving theſe broken Ends, I carefully gather

ther up the chief Thread of my Story, and proceed.

THESE Opinions therefore were so universal, as well as the Practices of them, among the refined Part of Court and Town, that our three Brother Adventurers, as their Circumstances then stood, were strangely at a loss. For, on the one side, the three Ladies they address'd themselves to, (whom we have named already) were ever at the very Top of the Fashion, and abhorred all that were below it, but the breadth of a Hair. On the other side, their Father's Will was very precise, and it was the main Precept in it, with the greatest Penalties annexed, not to add to, or diminish from their Coats, one Thread, without a positive Command in the Will. Now, the Coats their Father had left them, were, 'tis true, of very good Cloath, and besides, so neatly sown, you would swear they were all of a Piece, but at the same time, very plain, and with little or no Ornament; And it happened, that before they were a Month in Town, great *Shoulder-knots* came up: Strait, all the World was *Shoulder-knots*; no approaching the Ladies *Ruelles* without the *Quota* of *Shoulder-knots: That Fellow*, cries one, *has no Soul; where is his Shoulder-knot?* Our three Brethren soon discovered their Want by sad Experience, meeting in their Walks, with forty Mortifications and Indignities. If they went to the *Play-house*, the Door-keeper shewed them into the Twelvepeny Gallery. If they called a Boat, says a Water-man, *I am first Sculler:* If they stept to the *Rose* to take a Bottle, the Drawer would cry, *Friend we sell no Ale.* If they went to visit a Lady, a Footman met him at the Door with, *Pray send up your Message.* In this unhappy Case, they went immediately to consult their Father's Will, read it over and over, but not a Word of the *Shoulder-knot.* What should they do? What Temper should they find? Obedience was absolutely necessary, and yet *Shoulder-knots* appeared extreamly requisite. After much Thought, one of the Brothers who happened to be more *Book-learned* than the other two, said, he had found an Expedient. *'Tis true*, said he, *there is nothing here in this Will*, totidem verbis, *making mention of* Shoulder-knots, *but I dare conjecture, we may find them* inclusivè, *or* totidem syllabis. This Distinction was immediately approved by all;

and

and so they fell again to examine the Will. But their evil Star had so directed the Matter, that the first Syllable was not to be found in the whole Writing. Upon which Disappointment, he who found the former Evasion, took heart, and said, *Brothers, there is yet Hopes; for tho' we cannot find them* totidem verbis, *nor* totidem syllabis, *I dare engage we shall make them out* tertio modo, *or* totidem literis. This Discovery was also highly commended, upon which they fell once more to the Scrutiny, and soon pickt out *S, H, O, U, L, D, E, R*; when the same Planet, Enemy to their Repose, had wonderfully contrived, that a *K* was not to be found. Here was a weighty Difficulty! But the distinguishing Brother (for whom we shall hereafter find a Name) now his Hand was in, proved by a very good Argument, that *K* was a modern illegitimate Letter, unknown to the Learned Ages, nor any where to be found in antient Manuscripts. Tis true, said he, the Word *Calenda* hath in * *Q. V. C.* been sometimes writ with a *K*, but erroneously, for in the best Copies it is ever spelt with a *C*. And by consequence it was a gross Mistake in our

* *Quibusdam veteribus codicibus.*

our Language to spell *Knot* with a *K*, but that from henceforward, he would take care it should be writ with a *C*. Upon this, all further Difficulty vanished; *Shoulder-knots* were made clearly out, to be *Jure Paterno*, and our three Gentlemen swaggered with as large and as flanting ones as the best.

BUT; as human Happiness is of a very short Duration, so in those Days were human Fashions, upon which it entirely depends. *Shoulder-knots* had their Time, and we must now imagine them in their Decline; for a certain Lord came just from *Paris*, with fifty Yards of *Gold Lace* upon his Coat, exactly trimm'd after the Court Fashion of *that Month*. In two Days all Mankind appeared closed up in Bars of *Gold Lace:* Whoever durst peep abroad without his Compliment of *Gold Lace*, was as scandalous as a ———, and as ill received among the Women. What should our three Knights do in this momentous Affair; They had sufficiently strained a Point already, in the Affair of *Shoulder-knots:* Upon Recourse to the Will, nothing appeared there but *altum silentium*. That of the *Shoulder-knots* was a loose, flying,

ing, circumstantial Point; but this of *Gold Lace*, seemed too considerable an Alteration without better Warrant; it did *aliquo modo essentiæ adhærere*, and therefore required a positive Precept. But about this Time it fell out, that the learned Brother aforesaid, had read *Aristotelis Dialectica*, and especially that wonderful Piece *de Interpretatione*, which has the Faculty of teaching its Readers to find out a Meaning in every Thing but it self; like Commentators on the *Revelations*, who proceed Prophets without understanding a Syllable of the Text Brothers, said he, *You are to be informed, that, of Wills,* duo sunt genera, *Nuncupatory and Scriptory; that in the Scriptory Will here before us, there is no Precept or Mention about Gold Lace,* conceditur; *But,* si idem affirmetur de nuncupatorio, negatur. *For, Brothers, if you remember, we heard a Fellow say when we were Boys, that he heard my Father's Man say, that he heard my Father say, that he would advise his Sons to get* Gold Lace *on their Coats, as soon as ever they could procure Money to buy it. By G— that is very true,* cries the other; *I remember it perfectly well,* said the third. And so without more ado they got the largest *Gold Lace*

Lace in the Parish, and walkt about as fine as Lords.

   A while after, there came up *all in Fashion*, a pretty sort of *flame-coloured Satin* for Linings, and the *Mercer* brought a Pattern of it immediately to our three Gentlemen. *An please your Worships* (said he) *My Lord C——, and Sir J. W. had Linings out of this very Piece last Night, it takes wonderfully, and I shall not have a Remnant left, enough to make my Wife a Pin-cushion by to morrow Morning at ten a Clock.* Upon this they fell again to romage the Will, because the present Case also required a positive Precept, the Lining being held by Orthodox Writers to be of the Essence of the Coat. After long search, they could fix upon nothing to the Matter in hand, except a short Advice of their Father's in the Will, to take Care of *Fire,* and put out their *Candles* before they went to Sleep. This, tho' a good deal for the Purpose, and helping very far towards Self-Conviction, yet not seeming wholly of Force to establish a Command; and being resolved to avoid farther Scruple, as well as future Occasion for Scandal, says He that was the Scholar; *I remember to have*

have read in *Wills*, of a *Codicil annexed*, which is indeed a Part of the *Will*, and what it contains hath equal Authority with the rest. Now, I have been considering of this same *Will* here before us, and I cannot reckon it to be compleat for want of such a *Codicil*. I will therefore fasten one in its proper Place very dexterously; I have had it by me some Time, it was written by a *Dog-keeper* of my Grand-father's, and talks a great deal (as good Luck would have it) of this very flame-colour'd *Sattin*. The Project was immediately approved by the other two; an old Parchment Scrowl was tagged on according to Art, in the Form of a *Codicil annexed*, and the *Sattin* bought and worn.

Next Winter, a *Player*, hired for the Purpose by the Corporation of *Fringe-makers*, acted his Part in a new Comedy, all covered with Silver-Fringe, and according to the laudable Custom gave Rise to that Fashion. Upon which, the Brothers consulting their Father's Will, to their great Astonishment found these Words: Item, *I charge and command my said three Sons, to wear no Sort of* Silver Fringe *upon, or about their said Coats*, &c. with a Penalty

nalty in cafe of Difobedience, too long here to infert. However, after fome Paufe, the Brother fo often mentioned for his Erudition, who was well skill'd in Criticifms, had found in a certain Author, which he faid fhould be namelefs, that the fame Word which in the Will is called *Fringe,* does alfo fignify a *Broom-ſtick,* and doubtlefs ought to have the fame Interpretation in this Paragraph. This another of the Brothers difliked, becaufe of that Epithet, *Silver,* which could not, he humbly conceived, in Propriety of Speech be reafonably applied to a *Broom-ſtick:* But it was replied upon him, that this Epithet was underſtood in a *Mythological,* and *Allegorical* Senfe. However, he objected again, why their Father fhould forbid them to wear a *Broom-ſtick* on their Coats, a Caution that feemed unnatural and impertinent; Upon which he was taken up ſhort, as one that fpoke irreverently of a *Myſtery,* which doubtlefs was very ufeful and fignificant, but ought not to be overcurioufly pryed into, or nicely reafoned upon. And in fhort, their Father's Authority being now confiderably funk, this Expedient was allowed to ferve as a lawful

ful Dispensation, for wearing their full Proportion of *Silver Fringe.*

A while after, was revived an old Fashion, long antiquated, of *Embroidery* with *Indian Figures* of Men, Women and Children. Here they had no Occasion to examine the Will. They remembred but too well, how their Father had always abhorred this Fashion; that he made several Paragraphs on purpose, importing his utter Detestation of it, and bestowing his everlasting Curse to his Sons, whenever they should wear it. For all this, in a few Days, they appeared higher in the Fashion than any body else in Town. But they solved the Matter by saying, that these Figures were not at all the *same* with those that were formerly worn, and were meant in the Will: Besides, they did not wear them in that Sense, as forbidden by their Father, but as they were a commendable Custom, and of great Use to the Publick. That these rigorous Clauses in the Will did therefore require some *Allowance,* and a favourable Interpretation, and ought to be understood *cum grano Salis.*

But, Fashions perpetually altering in that Age, the Scholastick Brother grew weary of searching further Evasions, and solving everlasting Contradictions. Resolved therefore at all Hazards to comply with the Modes of the World, they concerted Matters together, and agreed unanimously, to lock up their Father's Will in a *Strong-Box*, brought out of *Greece* or *Italy*, (I have forgot which) and trouble themselves no further to examine it, but onely refer to its Authority whenever they thought fit. In consequence whereof, a while after, it grew a general Mode to wear an infinite Number of *Points*, most of them *tagg'd with Silver:* Upon which the Scholar pronounced *ex Cathedrâ*, that *Points* were absolutely *Jure Paterno*, as they might very well remember. 'Tis true indeed, the Fashion prescribed somewhat more than were directly named in the Will; However, that they, as Heirs general of their Father, had Power to make and add certain Clauses for publick Emolument, though not deduceable *totidem verbis* from the Letter of the Will, or else, *Multa absurda sequerentur*. This was understood for *Canonical*, and therefore on the

the following *Sunday* they came to Church all covered with *Points*.

THE Learned Brother so often mentioned, was reckoned the best Scholar in all that, or the next Street to it; insomuch, as having run something behind-hand with the World, he obtained the Favour from a *certain Lord*, to receive him into his House, and to teach his Children. A while after, the *Lord* died, and He by long Practice upon his Father's Will, found the Way of contriving a *Deed of Conveyance* of that House to Himself and his Heirs: Upon which he took Possession, turned the young Squires out, and received his Brothers in their stead.

SECT.

SECT. III.

A Digression concerning Criticks.

THO' I have been hitherto as cautious as I could, upon all Occasions, most nicely to follow the Rules and Methods of Writing, laid down by the Example of our illustrious *Moderns*; yet has the unhappy shortness of my Memory led me into an Error, from which I must immediately extricate my self, before I can decently pursue my principal Subject. I confess with Shame, it was an unpardonable Omission to proceed so far as I have already done, before I had performed the due Discourses, Expostulatory, Supplicatory, or Deprecatory with my *good Lords* the *Criticks*. Towards some Attonement for this grievous Neglect, I do here make humbly bold to present them with a short Account of Themselves and their *Art*, by looking into the Original and Pedigree of the Word, as it is generally understood among us, and very briefly considering the antient and present State thereof.

BY

concerning Criticks.

By the Word, *Critick*, at this Day so frequent in all Converſations, there have ſometime been diſtinguiſhed three very different Species of Mortal Men, according as I have read in *Antient Books and Pamphlets*. For firſt, by this Term were underſtood, ſuch Perſons as invented or drew up Rules for Themſelves and the World, by obſerving which, a careful Reader might be able to pronounce upon the Productions of the *Learned*, form his Taſte to a true Reliſh of the *Sublime* and the *Admirable*, and divide every Beauty of Matter or of Style from the Corruption that Apes it: In their common Peruſal of Books, ſingling out the Errors and Defects, the Nauſeous, the Fulſom, the Dull, and the Impertinent, with the Caution of a Man that walks thro' *Edinborough* Streets in a Morning, who is indeed as careful as he can, to watch diligently, and ſpy out the Filth in his Way, not that he is curious to obſerve the Colour and Complexion of the Ordure, or take its Dimenſions, much leſs to be padling in, or tailing it: but only with a Deſign to come out as cleanly as he may. Theſe Men ſeem, tho' very erroneouſly, to have underſtood the Appellation

pellation of *Critick* in a literal Sense; That, one principal Part of his Office was, to Praise and Acquit; and, that a *Critick* who sets up to Read, only for an Occasion of Censure and Reproof, is a Creature as barbarous, as a *Judge*, who should take up a Resolution to *hang* all Men that came before Him upon a Tryal.

AGAIN; by the Word, *Critick*, have been meant, the Restorer of Antient Learning from the Worms, and Graves, and Dust of Manuscripts.

Now, the Races of these two have been for some Ages utterly extinct; and besides, to Discourse any further of them, would not be at all to my Purpose.

THE Third, and noblest Sort, is that of the *TRUE CRITICK*, whose Original is the most Antient of all. Every *True Critick* is a Hero born, descending in a direct Line from a Celestial Stem, by *Momus* and *Hybris*, who begat *Zoilus*, who began *Tigellius*, who begat *Etcætera* the Elder, who begat B--t--ly, and *Rym--r*, and W--tt--n, and *Perrault*, and *Dennis*, who begat *Etcætera* the Younger.

AND

AND these are the *Criticks*, from whom the Commonwealth of Learning has in all Ages received such immense Benefits, that the Gratitude of their Admirers placed their Origine in Heaven, among those of *Hercules, Theseus, Perseus*, and other great Deservers of Mankind. But Heroick Virtue it self hath not been exempt from the Obloquy of evil Tongues. For it hath been objected, that those Antient Heroes, famous for their Combating so many Giants, and Dragons, and Robbers, were in their own Persons a greater Nuisance to Mankind, than any of those Monsters they subdued; And therefore, to render their Obligations more Compleat, when all *other* Vermin were destroy'd, should in Conscience have concluded with the same Justice upon themselves: as *Hercules* most generously did, and hath upon that Score, procured to himself more Temples and Votaries than the best of his Fellows. For these Reasons, I suppose it is, why some have conceived, it would be very expedient for the Publick Good of Learning, that every *True Critick*, as soon as he had finished his Task assigned, should immediately deliver himself up to Rats-bane,

bane of Hemp, or from some convenient *Altitude*, and that no Man's Pretensions to so Illustrious a Character, should by any means be received, before That Operation were performed.

Now, from this Heavenly Descent of *Criticism*, and the close Analogy it bears to *Hroick Virtue*, 'tis easy to assign the proper Employment of a *True, Antient, Genuin Critick*; Which is, to travel thro' this vast World of Writings: to pursue and hunt those Monstrous Faults bred within them: to drag out the lurking Errors like *Cacus* from his Den; to multiply them like *Hydra*'s Heads; and rake them together like *Augeas*'s Dung. Or else to drive away a sort of *dangerous Fowl*, who have a perverse Inclination, to plunder the best Branches of the *Tree of Knowledge*, like those *Stymphalian* Birds that eat up the Fruit.

These Reasonings will furnish us with an adequate Definition of a *True Critick*: that, He is *a Discoverer and Collector of Writers Faults*. Which may be further put beyond Dispute by the following Demonstration: That whoever will examine the

the Writings in all kinds, wherewith this antient Sect has honored the World, shall immediately find from the whole Thread and Tenor of them, that the Idea's of the Authors have been altogether converfant, and taken up with the Faults, and Blemishes, and Overfights, and Miftakes of other Writers; and let the Subject treated on be whatever it will, their imaginations are so entirely possefs'd and replete with the Defects of other Pens, that the very Quinteffence of what is bad, does of neceffity diftil into their own: By which means the whole appears to be nothing else, but an *Abftract* of the *Criticifms* themfelves have made.

HAVING thus briefly confidered the Original and Office of a *Critick*, as the Word is underftood in its moft noble and univerfal Acceptation, I proceed to refute the Objections of thofe who argue from the Silence and Pretermiffion of Authors; by which they pretend to prove, that the very Art of *Criticifm*, as now exercifed, and by me explained, is wholly *Modern*; and confequently, that the *Criticks* of *Great Britain* and *France*, have no Title to an Original so Antient and Illuftrious as I have deduced. Now, if I can clearly make out on the contrary, that the moſt antient Writers have particularly deſcribed, both the Perſon and the Office of a *True Critick*, agreeable to the Definition laid down by me; their grand Objection from the Silence of Authors will fall to the Ground.

I confeſs to have for a long time born a Part in this general Error; From which I ſhould never have acquitted my ſelf, but thro' the Aſſiſtance of our Noble *Moderns*, whoſe moſt edifying Volumes I turn indefatigably over Night and Day, for the Improvement of my Mind, and the Good of my Country: Theſe have with unwearied Pains made many uſeful Searches into the weak Sides of the *Antients*, and given us a comprehenſive Liſt of them.* Beſides, they have proved beyond Contradiction, that the very fineſt Things delivered of old, have been long ſince invented, and brought to Light by much later Pens, and that the nobleſt Diſcoveries thoſe *Antients* ever made of Art or of Nature, have all been produced by the tranſcending Genius of the preſent Age.

* See Wotton *of Ancient and Modern Learning*.

Age. Which clearly shews, how little Merit those *Antients* can justly pretend to; and takes off that blind Admiration paid them by Men in a Corner, who have the Unhappiness of conversing too little with *present Things*. Reflecting maturely upon all this, and taking in the whole Compass of Human Nature, I easily concluded, that these *Antients*, highly sensible of their many Imperfections, must needs have endeavoured from some Passages in their Works, to obviate, soften, or divert the Censorious Reader, by *Satyr*, or *Panegyrick* upon the *True Criticks*, in Imitation of their *Masters* the *Moderns*. Now, in the Common-*Places* of * both these, I was plentifully instructed, by a long Course of useful Study in *Prefaces* and *Prologues*; and therefore immediately resolved to try what I could discover of either, by a diligent Perusal of the most Antient Writers, and especially those who treated of the earliest Times. Here I found to my great Surprise, that although they all entred, upon Occasion, into particular Descriptions of the *True Critick*, according as they were governed by their Fears or their Hopes: yet whatever they toucht of that kind, was

* *Satyr, and Panegyrick upon Criticks.*

with

with abundance of Caution, adventuring no farther than *Mythology* and *Hieroglyphick.* This, I suppose, gave ground to superficial Readers, for urging the Silence of Authors, against the Antiquity of the *True Critick*; tho' the *Types* are so apposite, and the Applications so necessary and natural, that it is not easy to conceive, how any Reader of a *Modern Eye* and *Taste* could over-look them. I shall venture from a great Number to produce a few, which I am very confident, will put this Question beyond Dispute.

It well deserves considering, that these *Antient Writers* in treating Enigmatically upon this Subject, have generally fixed upon the very *same Hieroglyph*, varying only the Story according to their Affections or their Wit. For first; *Pausanias* is of Opinion, that the Perfection of Writing correct, was entirely owing to the Institution of *Criticks*; and, that he can possibly mean no other than the *True Critick*, is, I think, manifest enough from the following Description. He says, *They were a Race of Men, who delighted to nibble at the Superfluities, and Excrescencies of Books; which the Learned at length observing, took Warning*

Warning of their own Accord, to lop the *Luxurient,* the *Rotten,* the *Dead,* the *Sapless,* and the *Overgrown Branches from their Works.* But now, all this he cunningly shades under the following Allegory; *That the* * Nauplians *in* Argia, *learned the Art of pruning their Vines, by obferving, that when an* ASS *had browfed upon one of them, it thrived the better, and bore fairer Fruit.* But † *Herodotus* holding the very fame Hieroglyph, speaks much plainer, and almost *in terminis.* He hath been so bold to tax the *True Criticks,* of Ignorance and Malice; telling us openly, for I think nothing can be plainer, that *in the Weftern Part of* Libya, *there were* ASSES *with* HORNS: Upon which Relation * *Ctefias* yet refines, mentioning the very fame Animal about *India;* adding, *That whereas all other* ASSES *wanted a Gall, thefe horned ones were fo redundant in that Part, that their Flefh was not to be eaten, becaufe of its extream* Bitterness.

* Lib. ----

† Lib. 4.

* Vide excerpta ex eo apud Photium.

Now, the Reafon why thofe Antient Writers treated this Subject only by Types and Figures, was, becaufe they durſt not make open Attacks againſt a Party ſo Potent and ſo Terrible, as the *Criticks* of thoſe Ages were: whoſe very Voice was ſo Dreadful, that a Legion of Authors would tremble, and drop their Pens at the Sound; For ſo *Herodotus* tells us expreſly in another Place, how *a vaſt Army of* Scythians *was put to flight in a Panick Terror, by the Braying of an* ASS. From hence it is conjectured by certain profound *Philologers*, that the great Awe and Reverence paid to a *True Critick*, by the Writers of *Britain*, have been derived to Us, from thoſe our *Scythian* Anceſtors. In ſhort, this Dread was ſo univerſal, that in proceſs of Time, thoſe Authors who had a mind to publiſh their Sentiments more freely, in deſcribing the *True Criticks* of their ſeveral Ages, were forced to leave off the uſe of the former Hieroglyph, as too nearly approaching the *Prototype*, and invented other Terms inſtead thereof, that were more cautious and myſtical; ſo † *Diodorus* ſpeaking to the ſame purpoſe, ventures no farther than to ſay, that *in the Mountains of* Helicon *there grows a certain* Weed, *which bears a Flower of ſo damned a Scent, as to poiſon*

* Lib. 4.
† Lib.

poison those who offer to smell it. *Lucretius* gives exactly the same Relation.

Est etiam in magnis Heliconis montibus arbos,
Floris odore hominem retro consueta necare. Lib. 6.

But *Ctesias*, whom we lately quoted, hath been a great deal bolder; He had been used with much severity by the *True Criticks* of his own Age, and therefore could not forbear to leave behind him, at least one deep Mark of his Vengeance, against the whole Tribe. His Meaning is so near the Surface, that I wonder how it possibly came to be overlookt by those who deny the Antiquity of the *True Criticks*. For pretending to make a Description of many strange Animals about *India*, he hath set down these remarkable Words. *Among the rest,* says he, *there is a* Serpent *that wants* Teeth, *and consequently cannot bite, but if its* Vomit *(to which it is much addicted) happens to fall upon any Thing, a certain Rottenness or Corruption ensues:* These Serpents *are generally found among the Mountains where* Jewels *grow, and they frequently emit a* poisonous Juice, *whereof*

whereof, whoever drinks, that *Person's* Brains flies out of his *Nostrils*.

THERE was also among the *Antients* a sort of *Critick*, not distinguisht in *specie* from the Former, but in Growth or Degree, who seem to have been only the *Tyro's* or junior Scholars; yet because of their differing Employments, they are frequently mentioned as a Sect by themselves. The usual exercise of these younger Students, was to attend constantly at Theatres, and learn to spy out the *worst Parts* of the Play, whereof they were obliged carefully to take Note, and render a rational Account, to their Tutors. Flesht at these smaller Sports, like young Wolves, they grew up in Time, to be nimble and strong enough for hunting down large Game. For it hath been observed both among Antients and Moderns, that a *True Critick* hath one Quality in common with a *Whore* and an *Alderman*, never to change his Title or his Nature; that a *Grey Critick* has been certainly a *green* one, the Perfections and Acquirements of his Age being only the improved Talents of his Youth; like *Hemp*, which some Naturalists inform us, is bad for *Suffocations*, tho' taken

taken but in the *Seed.* I esteem the Invention, or at least the Refinement of *Prologues,* to have been owing to these younger Proficients, of whom *Terence* makes frequent and honourable mention, under the Name of *Malevoli.*

Now, 'tis certain, the Institution of the *True Criticks,* was of absolute Necessity to the Commonwealth of Learning. For all Human Actions seem to be divided like *Themistocles* and his Company; One Man can *Fiddle,* and another can make a *small Town a great City;* and he that cannot do either one or the other, deserves to be kick'd out of the Creation The avoiding of which Penalty, has doubtless given the first Birth to the Nation of *Criticks,* and withal, an Occasion for their secret Detractors to report; that a *True Critick* is a sort of Mechanick, set up with a a Stock and Tools for his Trade, at as little Expence as a *Taylor;* and that there is much Analogy between the Utensils and Abilities of both: That the *Taylor's Hell* is the Type of a Critick's *Common-place-Book,* and his Wit and Learning held forth by the *Goose:* That it requires at least as many of these, to the making up of

of one Scholar, as of the others to the
Compofition of a Man: That the Valor
of both is equal, and their *Weapons* near
of a Size. Much may be faid in anfwer
to thefe invidious Reflections; and I can
pofitively affirm the firft to be a Falfhood:
For, on the contrary, nothing is more
certain, than that it requires greater Lay-
ings out, to be free of the *Critick*'s Company, than of any other you can name.
For, as to be a *true Beggar*, it will coft the
richeft Candidate every Groat he is worth;
fo, before one can commence a *True Critick*, it will coft a Man all the good Qualities of his Mind; which, perhaps, for a
lefs Purchafe, would be thought but an indifferent Bargain.

Having thus amply proved the Antiquity of *Criticifm*, and defcribed the Primitive State of it; I fhall now examine the
prefent Condition of this Empire, and fhew
how well it agrees with its
antient felf. * A certain
Author whofe Works have
many Ages fince been en-
tirely loft, does in his fifth
Book and eighth Chapter, fay of *Criticks*,
that *their Writings are the Mirrors of
Learning*.

* *A Quotation after the manner of a great Author. Vide Bently's Differtation, &c.*

Learning. This I underſtand in a literal Senſe, and ſuppoſe our Author muſt mean, that whoever deſigns to be a perfect Writer, muſt inſpect into the Books of *Criticks*, and correct his Invention there as in a Mirror. Now, whoever conſiders, that the *Mirrors* of the Ancients were made of *Braſs*, and *fine Mercurio*, may preſently apply the two principal Qualifications of a *True Modern Critick*, and conſequently, muſt needs conclude, that theſe have always been, and muſt be for ever the ſame. For, *Braſs* is an Emblem of Duration, and when it is skilfully burniſhed, will caſt *Reflections* from its own *Superficies*, without any Aſſiſtance of *Mercury* from behind. All the other Talents of a *Critick* will not require a particular Mention, being included, or eaſily deduceable to theſe. However, I ſhall conclude with three Maxims, which may ſerve both as Characteriſticks to diſtinguiſh a *True Modern Critick* from a Pretender, and will be alſo of admirable Uſe to thoſe worthy Spirits, who engage in ſo uſeful and honorable an Art.

THE firſt is, That *Criticiſm*, contrary to all other Faculties of the Intellect, is ever held the trueſt and beſt, when it is the very *firſt* Reſult of the *Critick*'s Mind: As Fowlers reckon the firſt Aim for the sureſt, and ſeldom fail of miſſing the Mark, if they ſtay for a Second.

SECONDLY; The *True Criticks* are known by their Talent of ſwarming about the nobleſt Writers, to which they are carried meerly by Inſtinct, as a Rat to the beſt Cheeſe, or a Waſp to the faireſt Fruit. So, when the *King* is a Horſe-back, he is ſure to be the *dirtieſt* Perſon of the Company, and they that make their Court beſt, are ſuch as *beſpatter* him moſt.

LASTLY; A *True Critick*, in the Peruſal of a Book, is like a *Dog* at a Feaſt, whoſe Thoughts and Stomach are wholly ſet upon what the Gueſts *fling away*, and conſequently, is apt to *Snarl* moſt, when there are the feweſt *Bones*.

THUS

THUS much, I think, is sufficient to serve by way of Address to my Patrons, the *True Modern Criticks*, and may very well atone for my past Silence, as well as That which I am like to observe for the future. I hope, I have deserved so well of their whole *Body*, as to meet with generous and tender Usage at their *Hands*. Supported by which Expectation, I go on boldly to pursue those Adventures already so happily begun.

SECT.

SECT. IV.
A TALE of a TUB.

I HAVE now with much Pains and Study, conducted the Reader to a Period, where he must expect to hear of great Revolutions. For no sooner had Our *Learned Brother*, so often mentioned, got a warm House of his own over his Head, than he began to look big, and to take mightily upon him; insomuch, that unless the Gentle Reader out of his great Candor, will please a little to exalt his Idea, I am afraid he will henceforth hardly know the *Hero* of the Play, when he happens to meet Him; his Part, his Dress, and his Mien being so much altered.

HE told his Brothers, he would have them to know, that he was their Elder, and consequently his Father's sole Heir; Nay, a while after, he would not allow them to call Him, *Brother*, but Mr. *PETER*; And then he must be styled, *Father* Peter; and sometimes, *My Lord* Peter. To support this Grandeur, which he soon began to consider, could not be maintained without

out a Better *Fonde* than what he was born to; After much Thought, he caſt about at laſt, to turn *Projector* and *Virtuoſo*; wherein he ſo well ſucceded, that many famous Diſcoveries, Projects, and Machines, which bear great Vogue and Practice at preſent in the World, are owing entirely to *Lord Peter's* Invention. I will deduce the beſt Account I have been able to collect of the Chief amongſt them, without conſidering much the Order they came out in; becauſe, I think, Authors are not well agreed as to that Point.

I hope, when this Treatiſe of mine ſhall be tranſlated into Forein Languages, (as I may without Vanity affirm, That the Labor of collecting, the Faithfulneſs in recounting, and the great Uſefulneſs of the Matter to the Publick, will amply deſerve that Juſtice) that the worthy Members of the ſeveral *Academies* abroad, eſpecially thoſe of *France* and *Italy*, will favourably accept theſe humble Offers, for the Advancement of Univerſal Knowledge. I do alſo advertiſe the moſt Reverend Fathers the *Eaſtern* Miſſionaries, that I have purely for their ſakes, made uſe of ſuch Words and Phraſes, as will beſt admit

mit an eafy Turn into any of the *Oriental* Languages, efpecially the *Chinefe*. And fo I proceed with great Content of Mind, upon reflecting, how much Emolument this whole Globe of Earth is like to reap by my Labors.

The firft Undertaking of *Lord Peter*, was to purchafe a large Continent, lately faid to have been difcovered in *Terra Auftralis incognita*. This Tract of Land he bought at a very great Penny-worth from the Difcoverers themfelves, (tho' fome pretended to doubt whether they had ever been there) and then retailed it into feveral Cantons to certain Dealers, who carried over Colonies, but were all Ship-wreckt in the Voyage. Upon which, *Lord Peter* fold the faid Continent to other Cuftomers *again*, and *again*, and *again*, and *again*, with the fame Succefs.

The fecond Project I fhall mention, was his Sovereign Remedy of the *Worms*, efpecially thofe in the *Spleen*. The Patient was to eat nothing after Supper for three Nights: As foon as he went to Bed, he was carefully to lye on one Side, and when he grew weary, to turn upon the other:

other: He muſt alſo duly confine his two Eyes to the ſame Object; and by no means break Wind at both Ends together, without manifeſt Occaſion. Theſe Preſcriptions diligently obſerved, the *Worms* would void inſenſibly by Perſpiration, aſcending thro' the *Brain*.

A third Invention, was the erecting of a *Whiſpering-Office*, for the Publick Good and Eaſe of all ſuch as were Hypocondriacal, or troubled with the Cholick; as likewiſe of all Eves-droppers, Phyſicians, Midwives, ſmall Politicians, Friends fallen out, Repeating Poets, Lovers Happy or in Deſpair, Bawds, Privy-Counſellors, Pages, Paraſites, and Buffoons; In ſhort, of all ſuch as are in Danger of burſting with too much *Wind*. An *Aſs*'s Head was placed ſo conveniently, that the Party affected might eaſily with his Mouth accoſt either of the Animal's Ears; which he was to apply cloſe for a certain Space, and by a ſugetive Faculty, peculiar to the Ears of that Animal, receive immediate Benefit, either by Eructation, or Expiration, or Evomition.

ANOTHER very beneficial Project of *Lord Peter*'s, was an *Office of Enſurance*, for Tobacco-Pipes, Martyrs of the Modern Zeal, Volumes of Poetry, Shadows, - - - - - - - - and Rivers: That theſe, nor any of theſe ſhall receive Damage by *Fire*. From whence our *Friendly Societies* may plainly find themſelves, to be only Tranſcribers from this Original; tho' the one and the other have been of *great* Benefit to the Undertakers, as well as of *equal* to the Publick.

Lord Peter was alſo held the Original Author of *Puppets* and *Raree-Shows*; the great Uſefulneſs whereof being ſo generally known, I ſhall not enlarge further upon this Particular.

BUT, another Diſcovery for which he was much renowned, was his famous univerſal *Pickle*. For having remarkt how your common *Pickle* in uſe among Huſwives, was of no further Benefit than to preſerve dead Fleſh, and certain kinds of Vegetables; *Peter*, with great Coſt as well as Art, had contrived a *Pickle* proper
for

for Houses, Gardens, Towns, Men, Women, Children, and Cattle; wherein he could preserve them as Sound as Insects in Amber. Now, this *Pickle* to the Taste, the Smell, and the Sight, appeared exactly the same, with what is in common Service for Beef, and Butter, and Herrings, (and has been often that way applied with great Success) but for its many Sovereign Virtues was quite a different Thing. For *Peter* would put in a certain Quantity of his *Powder Pimperlim-pimp*, after which it never failed of Success. The Operation was performed by *Spargefaction* in a proper Time of the Moon. The Patient who was to be *pickled*, if it were a House, would infallibly be preserved from all Spiders, Rats, and Weazels; If the Party affected were a Dog, he should be exempt from Mange, and Madness, and Hunger. It also infallibly took away all Scabs and Lice, and scall'd Heads from Children never hindring the Patient from any Duty, either at Bed or Board.

But of all *Peter's* Rarities, he most valued a certain Set of *Bulls*, whose Race was by great Fortune preserved in a lineal Descent from those that guarded the *Golden-Fleece*.

Fleece. Tho' some who pretended to observe them curiously, doubted the Breed had not been kept entirely chaste; because they had degenerated from their Ancestors in some Qualities, and had acquired others very extraordinary, but a Forein Mixture. The *Bulls* of *Colchos* are recorded to have *brazen Feet*; But whether it happened by ill Pasture and Running, by an Allay from Intervention of other Parents, from stolen Intrigues; Whether a Weakness in their Progenitors had impaired the seminal Virtue; Or by a Decline necessary thro' a long Course of Time, the Originals of Nature being depraved in these latter sinful Ages of the World; Whatever was the Cause, 'tis certain that *Lord Peter*'s *Bulls* were extremely vitiated by the Rust of Time in the Metal of their Feet, which was now sunk into common *Lead*. However, the terrible *roaring* peculiar to their Lineage, was preserved; as likewise that Faculty of breathing out *Fire* from their Nostrils; which notwithstanding, many of their Detractors took to be a Feat of Art, and to be nothing so terrible as it appeared; proceeding only from their usual Course of Dyet, which was of *Squibs* and *Crackers*. However, they had

two

two peculiar Marks which extreamly diſtinguiſhed them from the *Bulls* of *Jaſon*, and which I have not met together in the Deſcription of any other Monſter, beſide that in *Horace*;

Varias inducere plumas,

and

Atrum definit in piſcem.

For, theſe had *Fiſhes Tails*, yet upon Occaſion, could *out-fly* any Bird in the Air. *Peter* put theſe *Bulls* upon ſeveral Employs. Sometimes he would ſet them a *roaring* to fright *Naughty Boys*, and make them quiet. Sometimes he would ſend them out upon Errands of great Importance; where it is wonderful to recount, and perhaps the cautious Reader may think much to believe it; An *Appetitus ſenſibilis*, deriving it ſelf thro' the whole Family, from their Noble Anceſtors, Guardians of the *Golden Fleece*; they continued ſo extremely fond of *Gold*, that if *Peter* ſent them abroad, though it were only upon a Compliment; they would *Roar*, and *Spit*, and *Belch*, and *Piſs*, and *Fart*, and *Snivle* out *Fire*, and keep a perpetual

petual Coyl, till you flung them a Bit of Gold; but then *Pulveris exigui jactu,* they would grow calm and quiet as Lambs. In short, whether by secret Connivance, or Encouragement from their Master, or out of their own liquorish Affection to Gold, or both; it is certain they were no better than a sort of sturdy, swaggering Beggars; and where they could not prevail to get an Alms, would make Women miscarry, and Children fall into Fits; who, to this very Day, usually call Sprites and Hobgoblins by the Name of *Bull-Beggars.* They grew at last so very troublesome to the Neighbourhood, that some Gentlemen of the *North-West,* got a Parcel of right *English Bull-Dogs,* and baited them so terribly, that they felt it ever after.

I must needs mention one more of *Lord Peter's* Projects, which was very extraordinary, and discovered him to be Master of a high Reach, and profound Invention. Whenever it happened that any Rogue of *Newgate* was condemned to be hang'd, *Peter* would offer him a Pardon for a certain Sum of Money, which when the poor Caitiff had made all Shifts to scrape up and send; *His Lordship*

ship would return a Piece of Paper in this Form.

TO all Mayors, Sheriffs, Jaylors, Constables, Bayliffs, Hangmen, &c. Whereas we are informed that A. B. remains in the Hands of you, or any of you, under the Sentence of Death. We will and command you upon Sight hereof, to let the said Prisoner depart to his own Habitation, whether he stands condemned for Murder, Sodomy, Rape, Sacrilege, Incest, Treason, Blasphemy, &c. for which this shall be your sufficient Warrant: And if you fail hereof, G--- d---mn You and Yours to all Eternity. And so we bid you heartily Farewel.

Your most Humble

Man's Man,

EMPEROR PETER.

THE Wretches trusting to this, lost their Lives and Money too.

I desire of those whom the *Learned* among Posterity will appoint for Commentators upon this elaborate Treatise; that they will proceed with great Caution upon certain dark Points, wherein all who are not *Verè adepti*, may be in Danger to form rash and hasty Conclusions, especially in some mysterious Paragraphs, where certain *Arcana* are joyned for Brevity sake, which in the Operation must be divided. And, I am certain, that future Sons of Art, will return large Thanks to my Memory, for so grateful, so useful an *Innuendo*.

IT will be no difficult Part to perswade the Reader, that so many worthy Discoveries met with great Success in the World: tho' I may justly assure him, that I have related much the smallest Number; My Design having been only to single out such, as will be of most Benefit for Publick Imitation, or which best served to give some Idea of the Reach and Wit of the Inventor. And therefore it need not be wondred, if by this Time, *Lord Peter* was become exceeding Rich. But alas, he had kept his Brain so long, and so violently

lently upon the Rack, that at laſt it *ſhook it ſelf*, and began to *turn round* for a little Eaſe. In ſhort, what with Pride, Projects, and Knavery, poor *Peter* was grown diſtracted, and conceived the ſtrangeſt Imaginations in the World. In the Height of his Fits (as it is uſual with thoſe who run Mad out of Pride) He would call Himſelf *God Almighty*, and ſometimes, *Monarch of the Univerſe*. I have ſeen him, (ſays my Author) take three old *high-crown'd Hats*, and clap them all on his Head, three Story high, with a huge Bunch of *Keys* at his Girdle, and an *Angling-Rod* in his Hand. In which Guiſe, whoever went to take him by the Hand in the Way of Salutation, *Peter* with much Grace, like a well educated Spaniel, would preſent them with his *Foot*, and if they refuſed his Civility, then he would raiſe it as high as their Chops, and give them a damn'd Kick on the Mouth, which hath ever ſince been call'd a *Salute*. Whoever walkt by, without paying him their Compliments, having a wonderful ſtrong Breath, he would blow their Hats off into the Dirt. Mean time, his Affairs at home went upſide down; and his two Brothers had a wretched Time; Where his firſt *Boutade* was, to kick both their *Wives* one Morning out of Doors, and his own too, and in their stead, gave Orders to pick up the first three Strolers could be met with in the Streets. A while after, he nail'd up the Cellar Door, and would not allow his Brothers a Drop of *Drink* to their Victuals. Dining one Day at an Alderman's in the City, *Peter* observed him expatiating after the manner of his Brethren, in the Praises of his Surloyn of Beef. *Beef*, said the Sage Magistrate, *is the King of Meat; Beef comprehends in it the Quintessence of Partridge, and Quail, and Venison, and Pheasant, and Plum-pudding, and Custard.* When *Peter* came home, he would needs take the Fancy of cooking up this Doctrine into use, and apply the Precept in default of a Sirloyn, to his brown Loaf: *Bread*, says he, *Dear Brothers, is the Staff of Life; in which Bread is contained inclusive the Quintessence of Beef, Mutton, Veal, Venison, Partridge, Plum-pudding, and Custard: And to render all compleat, there is intermingled a due Quantity of Water, whose Crudities are also corrected by Yeast or Barm, thro' which means it becomes a wholsome fermented Liquor, diffused thro' the Mass of the Bread.* Upon the Strength of these Conclusions,

clusions, next Day at Dinner was the brown Loaf served up in all the Formality of a City Feast. *Come Brothers,* said *Peter, fall to, and spare not; here is excellent good Mutton; or hold, now my Hand is in, I'll help you.* At which word, in much Ceremony, with Fork and Knife, he carves out two good Slices of the Loaf, and presents each on a Plate to his Brothers. The Elder of the two, not suddenly entring into Lord *Peter*'s Conceit, began with very civil Language to examine the Mystery. *My Lord,* said he, *I doubt, with great Submission, there may be some Mistake. What,* says *Peter, you are pleasant; Come then, let us hear this Jest, your Head is so big with. None in the World, my Lord; but unless I am very much deceived, your Lordship was pleased a while ago, to let fall a Word about Mutton, and I would be glad to see it with all my Heart. How,* said *Peter,* appearing in great Surprize, *I do not comprehend this at all——* Upon which, the younger interposing, to set the Business right; *My Lord,* said he, *My Brother, I suppose, is hungry, and longs for the Mutton, your Lordship hath promised us to Dinner. Pray,* said Peter, *take me along with you, either you are both Mad, or disposed to be merrier than I*

approve

approve of; If You *there, do not like your Piece, I will carve you another, tho' I should take that to be the choice Bit of the whole Shoulder.* What then, my Lord, replied the firſt, *it ſeems this is a Shoulder of Mutton all this while.* Pray, Sir, ſays Peter, *eat your Vittels and leave off your Impertinence, if you pleaſe, for I am not diſpoſed to reliſh it at preſent:* But the other could not forbear, being over provoked at the affected Seriouſneſs of *Peter's* Countenance. By G—, *My Lord,* ſaid he, *I can only ſay, that to my Eyes, and Fingers, and Teeth, and Noſe, it ſeems to be nothing but a Cruſt of Bread.* Upon which, the ſecond put in his Word; *I never ſaw a Piece of Mutton in my Life, ſo nearly reſembling a Slice from a Twelve-peny Loaf.* Look ye, Gentlemen, cries *Peter* in a Rage, *to convince you, what a couple of blind, poſitive, ignorant, wilful Puppies you are, I will uſe but this plain Argument; By G—, it is true, good, natural Mutton as any in* Leaden-Hall *Market; and G— confound you both eternally, if you offer to believe otherwiſe.* Such a thundring Proof as this, left no further Room for Objection: The two Unbelievers began to gather and pocket up their Miſtake as haſtily as they could. *Why, truly,* ſaid
the

the firſt, *upon more mature Conſideration*—*Ay,* ſays the other, interrupting him, *now I have thought better on the Thing, your Lordſhip ſeems to have a great deal of Reaſon.* Very well, ſaid Peter. *Here Boy, fill me a Beer-Glaſs of Claret. Here's to you both with all my Heart.* The two Brethren much delighted to ſee him ſo readily appeas'd returned their moſt humble Thanks, and ſaid, they would be glad to pledge His Lordſhip. *That you ſhall,* ſaid Peter, *I am not a Perſon to refuſe you any Thing that is reaſonable; Wine moderately taken, is a Cordial; Here is a Glaſs a piece for you; 'Tis true natural Juice from the Grape; none of your damn'd* Vintner's Brewings. Having ſpoke thus, he preſented to each of them another large dry Cruſt, bidding them drink it off, and not be baſhful, for it would do them no Hurt. The two Brothers, after having performed the uſual Office in ſuch delicate Conjunctures, of ſtaring a ſufficient Period at *Lord Peter,* and each other; and finding how Matters were like to go, reſolved not to enter on a new Diſpute, but let him carry the Point as he pleaſed; for he was now got into one of his mad Fits, and to Argue or Expoſtulate further, would only ſerve to to render him a hundred times more untractable.

I have chosen to relate this worthy Matter in all its Circumstances, because it gave a principal Occasion to that great and famous *Rupture*, which happened about the same time among these Brethren, and was never afterwards made up. But, of That, I shall treat at large in another Section.

HOWEVER, it is certain, that *Lord Peter*, even in his lucid Intervals, was very lewdly given in his common Conversation, extream wilful and positive, and would at any time rather argue to the Death, than allow himself to be once in an Error. Besides, he had an abominable Faculty of telling huge palpable *Lies* upon all Occasions; and swearing, not only to the Truth, but cursing the whole Company to Hell, if they pretended to make the least Scruple of believing Him. One time, he swore, he had a *Cow* at home, which gave as much Milk at a Meal, as would fill three thousand Churches; and what was yet more extraordinary, would never turn Sower. Another time, he was telling of an old *Sign-Post*
that

that belonged to his *Father*, with Nails and Timber enough on it, to build fixteen large Men of War. Talking one Day of *Chinese* Waggons, which were made so light as to sail over Mountains: *Z — nds,* said *Peter, where's the Wonder of that? By G——, I saw a large House of Lime and Stone travel over Sea and Land (granting that it stopt sometimes to bait) above two thousand* German *Leagues.* And that which was the good of it, he would swear desperately all the while, that he never told a Lye in his Life; And at every Word; *By G——, Gentlemen, I tell you nothing but the Truth; And the D——l broil them eternally that will not believe me.*

IN short, *Peter* grew so scandalous, that all the Neighbourhood began in plain Words to say, he was no better than a Knave. And his two Brothers long weary of his ill Usage, resolved at last to leave him; but first, they humbly desired a Copy of their Father's *Will,* which had now lain by neglected, time out of Mind. Instead of granting this Request, he called them *damn'd Sons of Whores, Rogues, Traytors,* and the rest of the vile Names he could muster up. However, while he was
abroad

abroad one Day upon his Projects, the two Youngſters watcht their Opportunity, made a Shift to come at the *Will*, and took a *Copia vera*, by which they preſently ſaw how groſly they had been abuſed: Their Father having left them equal Heirs, and ſtrictly commanded, that whatever they got, ſhould lye in common among them all. Purſuant to which, their next Enterpriſe was to break open the Cellar-Door, and get a little good *Drink* to ſpirit and comfort their Hearts. In copying the *Will*, they had met another Precept againſt Whoring, Divorce, and ſeparate Maintenance; Upon which, their next Work was to diſcard their Concubines, and ſend for their Wives. Whilſt all this was in agitation, there enters a Sollicitor from from *Newgate*, deſiring *Lord Peter* would pleaſe to procure a *Pardon* for a *Thief* that was to be *hanged* to morrow. But the two Brothers told him, he was a Coxcomb to ſeek Pardons from a Fellow, who deſerv'd to be hang'd much better than his Client; and diſcovered all the Method of that Impoſture, in the ſame Form I delivered it a while ago, adviſing the Sollicitor to put his Friend upon obtaining *a Pardon from the King.* In the

the midst of all this Clutter and Revolution, in comes *Peter* with a File of Dragoons at his Heels, and gathering from all Hands what was in the Wind, He and his Gang, after several Millions of Scurrilities and Curses, not very important here to repeat, by main Force, very fairly kicks them both out of Doors, and would never let them come under his Roof from that Day to this.

SECT.

SECT. V.

A Digression in the Modern Kind.

WE whom the World is pleased to honor with the Title of *Modern Authors*, should never have been able to compass our great Design of an everlasting Remembrance, and never dying Fame, if our Endeavours had not been so highly serviceable to the general Good of Mankind. This, *O Universe*, is the adventurous Attempt of me thy Secretary;

—————— *Quemvis perferre laborem*
Suadet, & inducit noctes vigilare serenas.

To this End, I have some Time since, with a World of Pains and Art, dissected the Carcass of *Human Nature,* and read many useful Lectures upon the several Parts, both *Containing* and *Contained*; till at last it *smelt* so strong, I could preserve it no longer. Upon which, I have been at a great Expence to fit up all the Bones with exact Contexture, and in due Symmetry;

Symmetry; so that I am ready to shew a very compleat Anatomy thereof to all curious *Gentlemen and others*. But not to Digress farther in the midst of a Digression, as I have known some Authors inclose Digressions in one another, like a Nest of Boxes; I do affirm, that having carefully cut up *Human Nature*, I have found a very strange, new, and important Discovery; That the Publick Good of Mankind is performed by two Ways, *Instruction*, and *Diversion*. And I have farther proved in my said several Readings, (which, perhaps, the World may one day see, if I can prevail on any Friend to steal a Copy, or on certain Gentlemen of my Admirers, to be very Importunate) that, as Mankind is now disposed, he receives much greater Advantage by being *Diverted* than *Instructed*; His Epidemical Diseases being *Fastidiosity, Amorphy*, and *Oscitation*; whereas in the present universal Empire of Wit and Learning, there seems but little Matter left for *Instruction*. However, in Compliance with a Lesson of great Age and Authority, I have attempted carrying the Point in all its Heights; and accordingly throughout this Divine Treatise, have skilfully kneaded

I up

up both together with a *Layer* of *Utile*, and a *Layer* of *Dulce*.

WHEN I consider how exceedingly ou Illustrious *Moderns* have eclipsed the weak glimmering Lights of the *Antients*, and turned them out of the Road of all fashionable Commerce, to a degree, that our choice Town Wits of most refined Accomplishments, are in grave Dispute, whether there have been ever any *Antients* or no: In which Point we are like to receive wonderful Satisfaction from the most useful Labours and Lucubrations of that Worthy *Modern*, Dr. B---tly. I say, when I consider all this, I cannot but bewail, that no famous *Modern* hath ever yet attempted an universal System in a small portable Volume, of all Things that are to be Known, or Believed, or Imagined, or Practised in Life. I am, however, forced to acknowledge, that such an Enterprise was thought on some Time ago by a great Philosopher of *O Brazile*. The Method he proposed, was by a certain curious *Receipt*, a *Nostrum*, which after his untimely Death, I found among his Papers; and do here out of my great Affection to the *Modern Learned*, present them with it, not doubting,

ing, it may one Day encourage some worthy Undertaker.

You take fair correct Copies, well bound in Calf's Skin, and Lettered at the Back, of all Modern Bodies of Arts and Sciences whatsoever, and in what Language you please. These you distil in baineo Mariæ, *infusing* Quintessence of Poppy Q. S. *together with three Pints of* Lethe, *to be had from the Apothecaries. You cleanse away carefully the* Sordes *and* Caput mortuum, *letting all that is volatile evaporate. You preserve onely the first Running, which is again to be distilled seventeen times, till what remains will amount to about two Drams. This you keep in a Glass Vial* Hermetically *sealed, for one and twenty Days. Then you begin your Catholick Treatise, taking every Morning fasting, (first shaking the Vial) three Drops of this* Elixir, *snuffing it strongly up your Nose. It will dilate it self about the Brain (where there is any) in fourteen Minutes, and you immediately perceive in your Head an infinite Number of* Abstracts, Summaries, Compendiums, Extracts, Collections, Medulla's, Excerpta quædam's, Florilega's *and the like, all disposed into great Order, and reduceable upon Paper.*

I must needs own, it was by the Assistance of this *Arcanum*, that I, tho' otherwise *impar*, have adventured upon so daring an Attempt; never atchieved or undertaken before, but by a certain Author called *Homer*, in whom, tho' otherwise a Person not without some Abilities, and *for an Antient*, of a tolerable Genius; I have discovered many gross Errors, which are not to be forgiven his very Ashes, if by chance any of them are left. For whereas, we are assured, he design'd his Work for a * compleat Body of all Knowledge Human, Divine, Political, and Mechanick; it is manifest, he hath wholly neglected some, and been very imperfect in the rest. For, first of all, as eminent a *Cabalist* as his Disciples would represent Him, his Account of the *Opus magnum* is extreamly poor and deficient; he seems to have read but very superficially, either *Sendivogus*, *Behmen*, or *Anthroposophia Theomagica*. He is also quite mistaken about the *Sphæra Pyroplastica*, a neglect not to be atoned for; and (if the Reader will admit so severe a Censure) *Vix crederem Autorem hunc,*

* *Homerus omnes res humanas Poematis complexus est.* Xenoph. in Conviv.

lunæ, unquam audivisse ignis vocem. His Failings are not less prominent in several Parts of the *Mechanicks*. For, having read his Writings with the utmost Application usual among *Modern Wits*, I could never yet discover the least Direction about the Structure of that useful Instrument, a *Save-all*. For want of which, if the *Moderns* had not lent their Assistance, we might yet have wandred *in the Dark*. But I have still behind, a Fault far more notorious to tax this Author with; I mean, his gross Ignorance in the *Common Laws of this Realm*, and in the Doctrine as well as Discipline of the Church of *England*. A Defect indeed, for which both he and all the Antients stand most justly censured by my worthy and ingenious Friend Mr. *W--tt--n*, Batchellor of Divinity, in his incomparable Treatise of *Antient and Modern Learning*; A Book never to be sufficiently valued, whether we consider the happy Turns and Flowings of the Author's Wit, the great Usefulness of his sublime Discoveries upon the Subject of *Flies* and *Spittle*, or the laborious Eloquence of his Stile. And I cannot forbear doing that Author the Justice of my publick Acknowledgments, for the great *Helps* and *Liftings* I

I 3   had

had out of his incomparable Piece, while I was penning this Treatise.

BUT, besides these Omissions in *Homer* already mentioned, the curious Reader will also observe several Defects in that Author's Writings, for which he is not altogether so accountable. For whereas every Branch of Knowledge has received such wonderful Acquirements since his Age, especially within these last three Years, or thereabouts; it is almost impossible, he could be so very perfect in Modern Discoveries, as his Advocates pretend. We freely acknowledge Him to be the Inventor of the *Compass*, of *Gun-powder*, and the *Circulation of the Blood*: But, I challenge any of his Admirers to shew me in all his Writings, a compleat Account of the *Spleen*; Does he not also leave us wholly to seek in the Art of *Political Wagering*? What can be more defective and unsatisfactory than his long Dissertation upon *Tea*? and as to his Method of *Salivation without Mercury*, so much celebrated of late, it is to my own Knowledge and Experience, a Thing very little to be relied on.

IT was to supply such momentous Defects, that I have been prevailed on after long Sollicitation, to take Pen in Hand; and I dare venture to Promise, the Judicious Reader shall find nothing neglected here, that can be of Use upon any Emergency of Life. I am confident to have included and exhausted all that Human Imagination can *Rise* or *Fall* to. Particularly, I recommend to the Perusal of the Learned, certain Discoveries that are wholly untoucht by others; whereof I shall only mention among a great many more; *My New Help of Smatterers*, or the *Art of being Deep learned, and Shallow read. A curious Invention about Mouse-Traps. An Universal Rule of Reason*, or *Every Man his own Carver*; Together with a most useful Engine for *catching of Owls*. All which the judicious Reader will find largely treated on, in the several Parts of this Discourse.

I hold my self obliged to give as much Light as is possible, into the Beauties and Excellencies of what I am writing, because it is become the Fashion and Humor most applauded among the first Authors

thors of this Polite and Learned Age, when they would correct the ill Nature of Critical, or inform the Ignorance of Courteous Readers. Besides, there have been several famous Pieces lately published both in Verse and Prose; wherein, if the Writers had not been pleased, out of their great Humanity and Affection to the Publick, to give us a nice Detail of the *Sublime*, and the *Admirable* they contain; it is a thousand to one, whether we should ever have discovered one Grain of either. For my own particular, I cannot deny, that whatever I have said upon this Occasion, had been more proper in a Preface, and more agreeable to the Mode, which usually directs it there. But I here think fit to lay hold on that great and honorable Privilege of being the *Last Writer*; I claim an absolute Authority in Right, as the *freshest Modern*, which gives me a Despotick Power over all Authors before me. In the Strength of which Title, I do utterly disapprove and declare against that pernicious Custom, of making the Preface a Bill of Fare to the Book. For I have always lookt upon it as a high Point of Indiscretion in *Monster-mongers* and other *Retailers of strange Sights*; to hang

out

out a fair large Picture over the door, drawn after the Life, with a most eloquent description underneath: This hath saved me many a Threepence, for my Curiosity was fully satisfied, and I never offered to go in, tho' often invited by the urging and attending Orator, with his last *moving* and *standing* Piece of Rhetorick; *Sir, Upon my Word, we are just going to begin.* Such is exactly the Fate, at this Time, of *Prefaces, Epistles, Advertisements, Introductions, Prolegomena's, Apparatus's, To-the-Readers's.* This Expedient was admirable at first; Our Great *Dryden* has long carried it as far as it would go, and with incredible Success. He has often said to me in Confidence, that the world would have never suspected him to be so great a Poet, if he had not assured them so frequently in his Prefaces, that it was impossible they could either doubt or forget it. Perhaps it may be so; However, I much fear, his Instructions have edify'd out of their Place, and taught Men to grow wiser in certain Points, where he never intended they should: For it is lamentable to behold, with what a lazy Scorn, many of the yawning Readers in our Age, do now-a-days twirl over forty or fifty

Pages

Pages of *Preface* and *Dedication*, (which is the usual *Modern* Stint) as if it were so much *Latin*. Tho' it must be also allowed on the other Hand, that a very considerable Number is known to proceed *Criticks* and *Wits*, by reading nothing else. Into which two Factions, I think, all present Readers may justly be divided. Now, for my self, I profess to be of the former Sort; and therefore having the *Modern* Inclination to expatiate upon the Beauty of my own Productions, and display the bright Parts of my Discourse; I thought best to do it in the Body of the Work, where, as it now lies, it makes a very considerable Addition to the Bulk of the Volume, *a Circumstance by no means to be neglected by a skilful Writer.*

HAVING thus paid my due Deference and Acknowledgment to an established Custom of our newest Authors, by *a long Digression unsought for*, and *an universal Censure unprovoked*; By forcing into the Light, with much Pains and Dexterity, my own Excellencies and other Mens Defaults, with great Justice to my self and Candor to them; I now happily resume my Subject, to the infinite Satisfaction both of the Reader and the Author. SECT

SECT. VI.

A TALE of a TUB.

WE left *Lord Peter* in open Rupture with his two Brethren; both for ever discarded from his House, and resigned to the wide World, with little or nothing to trust to. Which are Circumstances that render them proper Subjects for the Charity of a Writer's Pen to work on; Scenes of Misery ever affording the fairest Harvest for great Adventures. And in this, the World may perceive the Difference between the Integrity of a generous Author, and that of a common Friend. The latter is observed to adhere close in Prosperity, but on the Decline of Fortune, to drop suddenly off. Whereas, the generous Author, just on the contrary, finds his Hero on the Dunghil, from thence by gradual Steps, raises Him to a Throne, and then immediately withdraws, expecting not so much as Thanks for his Pains: In imitation of which Example, I have placed *Lord Peter* in a Noble House, given Him a
Title

Title to wear, and Money to spend. There I shall leave Him for some Time; returning where common Charity directs me, to the Assistance of his two Brothers, at their lowest Ebb. However, I shall by no means forget my Character of an Historian, to follow the Truth step by step, whatever happens, or wherever it may lead me.

THE two Exiles so nearly united in Fortune and Interest, took a Lodging together; Where, at their first Leisure, they began to reflect on the numberless Misfortunes and Vexations of their Life past, and cou'd not tell, of the sudden, to what Failure in their Conduct they ought to impute them; When, after some Recollection, they called to Mind the Copy of their Father's *Will*, which they had so happily recovered. This was immediately produced, and a firm Resolution taken between them, to alter whatever was already amiss, and reduce all their future Measures to the strictest Obedience prescribed therein. The main Body of the *Will* (as the Reader cannot easily have forgot) consisted in certain admirable Rules about the wearing of their Coats;

in

in the Perusal whereof, the two Brothers at every Period duly comparing the Doctrine with the Practice, there was never seen a wider Difference between two Things; horrible down-right Transgressions of every Point. Upon which, they both resolved without farther Delay, to fall immediately upon reducing the Whole, exactly after their Father's Model.

But, here it is good to stop the hasty Reader, ever impatient to see the End of an Adventure, before We Writers can duly prepare him for it. I am to record, that these two Brothers began to be distinguished at this Time, by certain Names. One of them desired to be called *MARTIN*, and the other took the Appellation of *JACK*. These two had lived in much Friendship and Agreement under the Tyranny of their Brother *Peter*, as it is the Talent of Fellow-Sufferers to do; Men in Misfortune, being like Men in the Dark, to whom all Colours are the same: But when they came forward into the World, and began to display themselves to each other, and to the Light, their Complexions appear'd extremely different; which the present Posture of their Affairs gave

gave them sudden Opportunity to discover.

But, here the severe Reader may justly tax me as a Writer of short Memory a Deficiency to which a true *Modern* cannot but of Necessity be a little subject. Because, *Memory* being an Employment of the Mind upon things past, is a Faculty, for which the Learned, in our Illustrious Age, have no manner of Occasion, who deal entirely with *Invention*, and strike all Things out of themselves, or at least, by Collision, from each other: Upon which Account, we think it highly reasonable to produce our great Forgetfulness, as an Argument unanswerable for our great Wit. I ought in Method, to have informed the Reader about fifty Pages ago, of a Fancy *Lord Peter* took, and infused into his Brothers, to wear on their Coats whatever Trimmings came up in Fashion; never pulling off any, as they went out of the Mode, but keeping on all together; which amounted in time to a Medley, the most Antick you can possibly conceive; and this to a Degree, that upon the Time of their Falling out, there was hardly a Thread of the Original Coat to be be seen, but an infinite Quantity of *Lace*, and *Ribbands*, and *Fringe*, and *Embroidery*, and *Points*; (I mean, only those *tagg'd with Silver*, for the rest fell off.) Now, this material Circumstance, having been forgot in due Place; as good Fortune hath ordered, comes in very properly here, when the two Brothers are just going to reform their Vestures into the Primitive State, prescribed by their Father's *Will*.

THEY both unanimously entred upon this great Work, looking sometimes on their Coats, and sometimes on the *Will*. *Martin* laid the first Hand; at one Twitch brought off a large Handful of *Points*, and with a second Pull, stript away ten dozen Yards of *Fringe*. But when He had gone thus far, he demurred a while: He knew very well, there yet remained a great deal more to be done; however, the first Heat being over, his Violence began to cool, and he resolved to proceed more moderately in the rest of the Work; having already very narrowly scap'd a swinging Rent in pulling of the *Points*, which being *tagged with Silver* (as we have observed before) the judicious Workman min had with much Sagacity, double-down, to preserve them from *falling*. Resolving therefore to rid his Coat of a huge Quantity of *Gold Lace*; he pickt up the Stitches with much Caution, and diligently gleaned out all the loose Threads as he went, which proved to be a Work of Time. Then he fell about the embroidered *Indian* Figures of Men, Women and Children; against which, as you have heard in its due Place, their Father's Testament was extremely exact and severe: These, with much Dexterity and Application, were after a while, quite eradicated, or utterly defaced. For the rest, where he observed the Embroidery to be workt so close, as not to be got away without damaging the Cloth, or where it served to hide or strengthned any Flaw in the Body of the Coat, contracted by the perpetual tampering of Workmen upon it; he concluded, the wisest Course was to let it remain, resolving in no Case whatsoever, that the Substance of the Stuff should suffer Injury; which he thought the best Method for serving the true Intent and Meaning of his Father's *Will*. And this is the nearest Account I have been able to collect, of

Martin's

Martin's Proceedings upon this great Revolution.

But, his Brother *Jack*, whose Adventures will be so extraordinary, as to furnish a great Part in the Remainder of this Discourse; entred upon the Matter with other Thoughts, and a quite different Spirit. For, the Memory of *Lord Peter*'s Injuries, produced a Degree of Hatred and Spight, which had a much greater Share of inciting Him, than any Regards after his Father's Commands, since these appeared at best, only Secondary and Subservient to the other. However, for this Meddly of Humor, he made a Shift to find a very plausible Name, honoring it with the Title of *Zeal*; which is, perhaps, the most significant Word that hath been ever yet produced in any Language: As, I think, I have fully proved in my excellent *Analytical* Discourse upon that Subject; wherein I have deduced a *Histori-theo-physi-logical* Account of *Zeal*, shewing how it first proceeded from a *Notion* into a *Word*, and from thence in a hot Summer, ripened into a *tangible Substance*. This Work containing three large Volumes in Folio, I design very shortly to publish-

publish by the *Modern* way of *Subscription*, not doubting but the Nobility and Gentry of the Land will give me all possible Encouragement, having already had such a Taste of what I am able to perform.

I record therefore, that Brother *Jack*, brim-full of this miraculous Compound, reflecting with Indignation upon *PETER*'s Tyranny, and further provoked by the Despondency of *Martin*; prefaced his Resolutions to this purpose. *What?* said he; *A Rogue that lockt up his Drink, turned away our Wives, cheated us of our Fortunes; paumed his damned Crusts upon us for Mutton; and at last kickt us out of Doors; must we be in His Fashions with a Pox? a Rascal, besides that all the Street cries out against.* Having thus kindled and enflamed himself as high as possible, and by Consequence, in a delicate Temper for beginning a Reformation, he set about the Work immediately, and in three Minutes, made more Dispatch than *Martin* had done in as many Hours. For, (Courteous Reader) you are given to understand, that *Zeal* is never so highly obliged, as when you set it a *Tearing*; and *Jack,*

Jack, who doated on that Quality in himself, allowed it at this Time its full Swinge. Thus it happened, that stripping down a Parcel of *Gold Lace*, a little too hastily, he rent the *main Body* of his *Coat* from Top to Bottom; and whereas his Talent was not of the happiest in *taking up a Stitch*, he knew no better way, than to dern it again with *Packthread* and a *Scewer*. But the Matter was yet infinitely worse (I record it with Tears) when he proceeded to the *Embroidery:* For, being Clumsy by Nature, and of Temper, Impatient; withal, beholding Millions of Stitches, that required the nicest Hand, and sedatest Constitution, to extricate; in a great Rage, he tore off the whole Piece, Cloth and all, and flung it into the Kennel, and furiously thus continuing his Career; *Ah, Good Brother* Martin, said he, *do as I do, for the Love of God; Strip, Tear, Pull, Rent, Flay off all, that we may appear as unlike that Rogue* Peter, *as it is possible: I would not for a hundred Pounds carry the least Mark about me, that might give Occasion to the Neighbours, of suspecting I was related to such a Rascal.* But *Martin*, who at this Time happened to be extremely flegmatick and sedate, begged his Brother, of all *Love*, not to damage his *Coat* by any *Means*; for he never would get such another: Desired him *to consider, that it was not their Business to form their Actions by any Reflection upon* Peter's, *but by observing the Rules prescribed in their Father's* Will. That he should remember, Peter *was still their Brother, whatever Faults or Injuries he had committed; and therefore they should by all means avoid such a Thought, as that of taking Measures for Good and Evil, from no other Rule, than of Opposition to Him.* That it *was true, the Testament of their good Father was very exact in what related to the wearing of their* Coats ; *yet was it no less penal and strict in prescribing Agreement, and Friendship, and Affection between them. And therefore, if straining a Point were at all dispensable, it would certainly be so, rather to the Advance of Unity, than Increase of Contradiction.*

Martin had still proceeded as gravely as he began; and doubtless, would have delivered an admirable Lecture of Morality, which might have exceedingly contributed to my Reader's *Repose,* both of *Body* and *Mind* : (the true ultimate End of *Ethicks*;) But *Jack* was already gone

gone a Flight-fhot beyond his Patience. And as in Scholaftick Difputes, nothing ferves to rouze the Spleen of him that *Oppofes*, fo much as a kind of Pedantick affected Calmnefs in the *Refpondent*; Difputants being for the moft part like unequal Scales, where the *Gravity* of one Side advances the *Lightnefs* of the Other, and caufes it to fly up and kick the Beam; So it happened here, that the *Weight* of *Martin's* Arguments exalted *Jack's Levity*, and made him fly out and fpurn againft his Brother's Moderation. In fhort, *Martin's Patience* put *Jack* in a *Rage*; but that which moft afflicted him was, to obferve his Brother's Coat fo well reduced into the State of Innocence; while his own was either wholly rent to his Shirt; or thofe Places which had fcaped his cruel Clutches, were ftill in *Peter's* Livery. So that he looked like a drunken *Beau*, half rifled by *Bullies*; Or like a Frefh Tenant of *Newgate*, when he has refufed the Payment of *Garnifh*; Or like a difcovered *Shoplifter*, left to the Mercy of *Exchange-Women*; Or like a *Bawd* in her old Velvet Petticoat, refigned into the fecular Hands of the *Mobile*. Like any, or like all of thefe, a

Meddley

Meddley of *Rags*, and *Lace*, and *Rents*, and *Fringes*, unfortunate *Jack* did now appear: He would have been extreamly glad to see his Coat in the Condition of *Martin*'s, but infinitely gladder to find that of *Martin*'s in the same Predicament with his. However, since neither of these was likely to come to pass, he thought fit to lend the whole Business another Turn, and to dress up Necessity into a Virtue. Therefore, after as many of the *Fox*'s Arguments, as he could muster up, for bringing *Martin* to *Reason*, as he called it; or, as he meant it, into his own ragged, bobtail'd Condition; and observing he said all to little purpose; what, alas, was left for the forlorn *Jack* to do, but after a Million of Scurrilities against his Brother, to run mad with Spleen, and Spight, and Contradiction. To be short, here began a mortal Breach between these two. *Jack* went immediately to *New Lodgings*, and in a few Days it was for certain reported, that he had run out of his Wits. In a short time after, he appeared abroad, and confirmed the Report, by falling into the oddest Whimsies that ever a sick Brain conceived.

AND

AND now the little Boys in the Streets began to falute him with feveral Names. Sometimes they would call Him, *Jack the Bald*; fometimes, *Jack with a Lanthorn*; fometimes, *Dutch Jack*; fometimes, *French Hugh*; fometimes *Tom the Beggar*; and fometimes, *Knocking Jack of the North*. And it was under one, or fome, or all of thefe Appellations (which I leave the Learned Reader to determine) that he hath given Rife to the moft Illuftrious and Epidemick Sect of *Æolifts*; who with honourable Commemoration, do ftill acknowledge the Renowned *JACK* for their Author and Founder. Of whofe Originals, as well as Principles, I am now advancing to gratify the World with a very particular Account.

────── *Mellæo contingens cuncta Lepore.*

SECT. VII.

A Digreſſion in Praiſe of Digreſſions.

I HAVE ſometimes *heard* of an *Iliad* in a *Nut-ſhell*; but it hath been my Fortune to have much oftner *ſeen* a *Nut-ſhell* in an *Iliad*. There is no doubt, that Human Life has received moſt wonderful Advantages from both; but to which of the two the World is chiefly indebted, I ſhall leave among the Curious, as a Problem worthy of their utmoſt Enquiry. For the Invention of the latter, I think the Commonwealth of Learning is chiefly obliged to the great *Modern* Improvement of *Digreſſions*: The late Refinements in Knowledge, running parallel to thoſe of Dyet in our Nation, which among Men of a judicious Taſte, are dreſt up in various Compounds, conſiſting in *Soups* and *Ollioes*, *Fricaſſees* and *Ragouſts*.

'TIS true, there is a ſort of moroſe, detracting, ill-bred People, who pretend utterly to diſreliſh theſe polite Innovations: And as to the Similitude from Dyet

Dyet, they allow the Parallel, but are so bold to pronounce the Example it self, a Corruption and Degeneracy of Taste. They tell us, that the Fashion of jumbling fifty Things together in a Dish, was at first introduced in Compliance to a depraved and *debauched Appetite*, as well as to a *crazy Constitution*; And to see a Man hunting thro' an *Ollio*, after the *Head* and *Brains* of a *Goose*, a *Wigeon*, or a *Woodcock*, is a Sign, he wants a Stomach and Digestion for more substantial Victuals. Further, they affirm, that *Digressions* in a Book, are like *Forein Troops* in a *State*, which argue the Nation to want a *Heart* and *Hands* of its own, and often, either *subdue* the *Natives*, or drive them into the most *unfruitful Corners*.

BUT, after all that can be objected by these supercilious Censors; 'tis manifest, the Society of Writers would quickly be reduced to a very inconsiderable Number, if Men were put upon making Books, with the fatal Confinement of delivering nothing beyond what is to the Purpose. 'Tis acknowledged, that were the Case the same among Us, as with the *Greeks* and *Romans*, when Learning
was

was in its *Cradle*, to be reared and fed, and cloathed by *Invention*; it would be an easy Task to fill up Volumes upon particular Occasions, without further exspatiating from the Subject, than by moderate Excursions, helping to advance or clear the main Design. But with *Knowledge*, it has fared as with a numerous Army, encamped in a fruitful Country; which for a few Days maintains it self by the Product of the Soyl it is on; Till Provisions being spent, they send to forrage many a Mile, among Friends or Enemies it matters not. Mean while, the neighbouring Fields trampled and beaten down, become barren and dry, affording no Sustenance but Clouds of Dust.

T H E whole Course of Things being thus entirely changed between *Us* and the *Antients*; and the *Moderns* wisely sensible of it, we of this Age have discovered a shorter, and more prudent Method, to become *Scholars* and *Wits*, without the Fatigue of *Reading* or of *Thinking*. The most accomplisht Way of using Books at present, is twofold: Either first, to serve them as some Men

do

do *Lords*, learn their *Titles* exactly, and then brag of their Acquaintance. Or Secondly, which is indeed the choicer, the profounder, and politer Method, to get a thorough Insight into the *Index*, by which the whole Book is governed and turned, like *Fishes* by the *Tail*. For, to enter the Palace of Learning at the *great Gate*, requires an Expence of Time and Forms; therefore Men of much Haste and little Ceremony, are content to get in by the *Back-Door*. For, the Arts are all in a *flying* March, and therefore more easily subdued by attacking them in the *Rear*. Thus Physicians discover the State of the whole Body, by consulting only what comes from *Behind*. Thus Men catch Knowledge by throwing their *Wit* on the *Posteriors* of a Book, as Boys do Sparrows with flinging *Salt* upon their *Tails*. Thus Human Life is best understood by the wise man's Rule of *Regarding the End*. Thus are the Sciences found like *Hercules*'s Oxen, by *tracing them backwards*. Thus are *old Sciences* unravelled like *old Stockins*, by beginning at the *Foot*.

BESIDES all this, the Army of the Sciences hath been of late with a world of Martial Discipline, drawn into its *close Order*, so that a View, or a Muster may be taken of it with abundance of Expedition. For this great Blessing we are wholly indebted to *Systems* and *Abstracts*, in which the *Modern* Fathers of Learning, like prudent Usurers, spent their Sweat for the Ease of Us their Children. For *Labor* is the Seed of *Idleness*, and it is the peculiar Happiness of our Noble Age to gather the *Fruit*.

Now the Method of growing Wise, Learned, and *Sublime*, having become so regular an Affair, and so established in all its Forms; the Number of Writers must needs have encreased accordingly, and to a Pitch that has made it of absolute Necessity for them to interfere continually with each other. Besides, it is reckoned, that there is not at this present, a sufficient Quantity of new Matter left in Nature, to furnish and adorn any one particular Subject to the Extent of a Volume. This I am told by a very skilful *Computer*, who hath given
a full

a full Demonstration of it from Rules of *Arithmetick.*

THIS, perhaps, may be objected against, by those, who maintain the Infinity of Matter, and therefore, will not allow that any *Species* of it can be exhausted. For Answer to which, let us examine the noblest Branch of *Modern* Wit or Invention, planted and cultivated by the present Age, and, which of all others, hath born the most, and the fairest Fruit. For tho' some Remains of it were left us by the *Antients*, yet have not any of those, as I remember, been translated or compiled into Systems for *Modern* Use. Therefore We may affirm, to our own Honor, that it has in some sort, been both invented, and brought to a Perfection by the same Hands. What I mean, is that highly celebrated Talent among the *Modern* Wits, of deducing Similitudes, Allusions, and Applications, very Surprizing, Agreeable, and Appofite, from the *Genitals* of either Sex, together with *their proper Uses*. And truly, having observed how little Invention bears any Vogue, besides what is derived into these *Channels*, I have sometimes had a Thought, That the happy
Genius

Genius of our Age and Country, was prophetically held forth by that antient * typical Description of the *Indian* Pygmies; *whose Stature did not exceed above two Foot; Sed quorum pudenda crassa, & ad talos usque pertingentia.* Now, I have been very curious to inspect the late Productions, wherein the Beauties of this kind have most prominently appeared. And altho' this *Vein* hath bled so freely, and all Endeavours have been used in the Power of Human Breath, to dilate, extend, and and keep it open: Like the Scythians, † *who had a Custom, and an Instrument, to blow up the Privities of their Mares, that they might yield the more Milk*; Yet I am under an Apprehension, it is near growing dry, and past all Recovery; And that either some new *Fonde* of Wit should, if possible, be provided, or else that we must e'en be content with Repetition here, as well as upon all other Occasions.

* *Ctesiæ fragm. apud Photium.*

† *Herodot. L. 4.*

This will stand as an uncontestable Argument, that our *Modern* Wits are not to reckon upon the Infinity of Matter, for a constant Supply. What remains therefore,

in Praise of Digressions.

therefore, but that our laſt Recourſe muſt be had to large *Indexes*, and little *Compendiums*; *Quotations* muſt be plentifully gathered, and bookt in Alphabet; To this End, tho' Authors need be little conſulted, yet *Criticks*, and *Commentators*, and *Lexicons* carefully muſt. But above all, thoſe judicious Collectors of *bright Parts*, and *Flowers*, and *Obſervanda's*, are to be nicely dwelt on; by ſome called the *Sieves* and *Boulters* of Learning; tho' it is left undetermined, whether they dealt in *Pearls* or *Meal*; and conſequently, whether we are more to value that which *paſſed thro'*, or what *ſtaid behind*.

By theſe Methods, in a few Weeks, there ſtarts up many a Writer, capable of managing the profoundeſt, and moſt univerſal Subjects. For, what though his *Head* be empty, provided his *Common-place-Book* be full: And if you will bate him but the Circumſtances of *Method*, and *Style*, and *Grammar*, and *Invention*; allow him but the common Priviledges, of tranſcribing from others, and digreſſing from himſelf, as often as he ſhall ſee Occaſion; He will deſire no more ingredients towards fitting up a Treatiſe, that ſhall make

make a very comely Figure on a Book-seller's Shelf, there to be preserved neat and clean, for a long Eternity, adorn'd with the Heraldry of its Title, fairly inscribed on a Label; never to be thumb'd or greas'd by Students, nor bound to everlasting Chains of Darkness in a Library: But when the Fulness of Time is come, shall haply undergo the Tryal of Purgatory, in order *to ascend the Sky.*

WITHOUT these Allowances, how is it possible, we *Modern* Wits should ever have an Opportunity to introduce our Collections, listed under so many thousand Heads of a different Nature? for want of which, the Learned World would be deprived of infinite Delight, as well as Instruction, and we our selves buried beyond Redress in an inglorious and undistinguisht Oblivion.

FROM such Elements as these, I am alive to behold the Day, wherein the Corporation of Authors can out-vie all its Brethren in the *Field.* A Happiness derived to us with a great many others, from our *Scythian* Ancestors; among whom, the Number of *Pens* was so infinite,

in Praise of Digressions. 145

finite, that the *Grecian* Eloquence had no other way of
expressing it, than by saying, *That in the
Regions, far to the* North, *it was hardly possible for a Man to travel, the very Air was
so replete with* Feathers.

*Herodot. L. 4.

THE Necessity of this Digression, will
easily excuse the Length; and I have chosen for it as proper a Place as I could readily
find. If the judicious Reader can assign
a fitter, I do here empower him to remove
it into any other Corner he please. And
so I return with great Alacrity to pursue
a more important Concern.

L   SECT.

SECT. VIII.

A TALE of a TUB.

THE Learned *Æolists*, maintain the Original Cause of all Things, to be *Wind*, from which Principle this whole Universe was at first produced, and into which it must at last be resolved; that the same Breath which had kindled, and blew *up* the Flame of Nature, should one Day blow it *out*.

Quod procul à nobis flectat Fortuna gubernans.

THIS is what the *Adepti* understand by their *Anima Mundi*; that is to say, the *Spirit*, or *Breath*, or *Wind* of the World: Or Examine the whole System by the Particulars of Nature, and you will find it not to be disputed. For, whether you please to call the *Forma informans* of Man, by the Name of *Spiritus, Animus, Afflatus,* or *Anima*; what are all these, but several Appellations for *Wind*? which is the ruling Element in every Compound, and into

into which they all resolve upon their Corruption. Farther, what is Life it self, but as it is commonly called, the *Breath of our Nostrils?* Whence it is very justly observed by Naturalists, that *Wind* still continues of great Emolument in *certain Mysteries* not to be named, giving Occasion for those happy Epithets of *Turgidus*, and *Inflatus*, apply'd either to the *Emittent*, or *Recipient* Organs.

By what I have gathered out of antient Records, I find, the *Compass* of their Doctrine took in two and thirty Points; wherein it would be tedious to be very particular. However, a few of their most important Precepts, deduceable from it, are by no means to be omitted; among which, the following Maxim was of much Weight; That since *Wind* had the Master Share, as well as Operation in every Compound, by Consequence, those Beings must be of chief Excellence, wherein that *Primordium* appears most prominently to abound; and therefore, *Man* is in highest Pefection of all created Things, as having by the great Bounty of Philosophers, been endued with three distinct *Anima's* or *Winds*, to which the Sage *Æolists*, with much

much Liberality, have added a fourth, of equal Necessity, as well as Ornament with the other three; by this *quartum Principium*, taking in the four Corners of the World. Which gave Occasion to that Renowned *Cabalist, Bumbastus*, of placing the Body of Man, in due position to the four Cardinal Points.

IN Consequence of this, their next Principle was, that, *Man* brings with Him into the World a peculiar Portion, or Grain of *Wind*, which may be called a *Quinta essentia*, extracted from the other four. This *Quintessence* is of Catholick Use upon all Emergencies of Life, is improveable into all Arts and Sciences, and may be wonderfully refined, as well as enlarged by certain Methods in Education. This, when *blown* up to its Perfection, ought not to be covetously hoarded up, stifled, or hid under a Bushel, but freely communicated to Mankind. Upon these Reasons, and others of equal Weight, the Wise *Æolists*, affirm the Gift of BELCHING, to be the noblest Act of a Rational Creature. To cultivate which Art, and render it more serviceable to Mankind, they made Use of several Methods. At certain Seasons

sons of the Year, you might behold the Priests amongst them in vast Numbers, with their *Mouths gaping wide against a Storm.* At other Times were to be seen, several Hundreds link'd together in a circular Chain, with every Man a Pair of Bellows appled to his Neighbour's Breech, by which they blew up each other to the Shape and Size of a *Tun*; and for that Reason, with great Propriety of Speech, did usually call their Bodies, their *Vessels.* When, by these and the like Performances, they were grown sufficiently replete, they would immediately depart, and disembogue for the Publick Good, a plentiful Share of their Acquirements into their Disciples Chaps. For we must here observe, that all Learning was esteemed among them, to be compounded from the same Principle. Because, First, it is generally affirm'd, or confess'd, that Learning *puffeth Men up*: And Secondly, they proved it by the following Syllogism; *Words are but Wind*; *and Learning is nothing but Words*; Ergo, *Learning is nothing but Wind.* For this Reason, the Philosophers among them, did in their Schools, deliver to their Pupils, all their Doctrines and Opinions by *Eructation,* wherein they had acquired a wonderful Eloquence, and of incredible Variety. But the great Charaæteriftick, by which their chief Sages were beft diftinguifhed, was a certain Pofition of Countenance, which gave undoubted Intelligence to what Degree or Proportion, the Spirit agitated the inward Mafs. For, after certain Gripings, the *Wind* and Vapors iffuing forth; having firft by their Turbulence and Convulfions within, caufed an Earthquake in Man's little World; diftorted the Mouth, bloated the Cheeks, and gave the Eyes a terrible kind of *Relievo*. At which Junctures, all their *Belches* were received for Sacred, the Sourer the better, and fwallowed with infinite Confolation by their meager Devotes. And to render thefe yet more compleat, becaufe the Breath of Man's Life is in his Noftrils, therefore, the choiceft, moft edifying, and moft enlivening *Belches*, were very wifely conveyed thro' that Vehicle, to give them a Tincture as they paffed.

Their Gods were the four *Winds*, whom they worfhipped, as the Spirits that pervade and enliven the Univerfe, and as thofe from whom alone all *Infpiration* can
properly

properly be said to proceed. However, the Chief of these, to whom they performed the Adoration of *Latria*, was the *Almighty North*. An Antient Deity, whom the Inhabitants of *Megalopolis* in *Greece*, had likewise in highest Reverence.
**Omnium deorum Boream ma-*   * *Pausan.* L. 8. *xime celebrant.* This God, tho' endued with Ubiquity, was yet supposed by the profounder *Æolists*, to possess one peculiar Habitation, or (to speak in Form) a *Cælum Empyræum*, wherein he was more intimately present. This was situated in a certain Region, well known to the Antient *Greeks*, by them call'd, Σκοτία, or the *Land of Darkness*. And altho' many Controversies have arisen upon that Matter; yet so much is undisputed, that from a Region of the *like Denomination*, the most refined *Æolists* have borrowed their Original, from whence, in every Age, the zealous among their Priesthood, have brought over their choicest *Inspiration*, fetching it with their own Hands, from the Fountain Head, in certain *Bladders*, and disploding it among the Sectaries in all Nations, who did, and do, and ever will, daily Gasp and Pant after it.

L 4   Now,

Now, their Mysteries and Rites were performed in this Manner. 'Tis well known among the Learned, that the Virtuoso's of former Ages, had a Contrivance for carrying and preserving *Winds* in Casks or Barrels, which was of great Assistance upon long Sea Voyages; And the Loss of so useful an Art at present, is very much to be lamented, tho' I know not how, with great Negligence omitted by *Pancirollus*. It was an Invention ascribed to *Æolus* himself, from whom this Sect is denominated, and who in Honor of their Founder's Memory, have to this Day preserved great Numbers of those *Barrels,* whereof they fix one in each of their Temples, first beating out the Top. Into this *Barrel,* upon Solemn Days, the Priest enters; where, having before duly prepared himself by the Methods already described, a secret Funnel is also convey'd from his Posteriors, to the Bottom of the Barrel, which admits new Supplies of Inspiration from a *Northern* Chink or Cranny. Whereupon, You behold him swell immediately to the Shape and Size of his *Vessel*. In this Posture he disembogues whole Tempests upon his Auditory, as the

the Spirit from beneath gives him Utterance; which issuing *ex adytis*, and *penetralibus*, is not performed without much Pain and Gripings. And the *Wind* in breaking forth, deals with his Face, as it does with that of the Sea; first *blackning*, then *wrinkling*, and at last, *bursting it into a Foam*. It is in this Guise, the Sacred *Æolist* delivers his oracular *Belches* to his panting Disciples; Of whom, some are greedily gaping after the sanctified Breath; others are all the while hymning out the Praises of the *Winds*; and gently wafted to and fro by their own Humming, do thus represent the soft Breezes of their Deities appeased.

IT is from this Custom of the Priests, that some Authors maintain these *Æolists*, to have been very antient in the World. Because, the Delivery of their Mysteries, which I have just now mentioned, appears exactly the same with that of other Antient Oracles, whose Inspirations were owing to certain subterraneous *Effluviums* of *Wind*, delivered with the *same* Pain to the Priest, and much about the *same* Influence on the People. It is true indeed, that these were frequently managed and

directed

directed by *Female* Officers, whose Organs were understood to be better disposed for the Admission of those Oracular *Gusts*, as entring, and passing up thro' a Receptacle of greater Capacity, and causing also a Pruriency by the Way, such as with due Management, hath been refined from Carnal, into a Spiritual Extasie. And to strengthen this profound Conjecture, it is further insisted, that this Custom of *Female* Priests is kept up still in certain refined Colleges of our *Modern Æolists*, who are agreed to receive their Inspiration, derived thro' the Receptacle aforesaid, like their Ancestoss, the *Sybils*.

AND, whereas the Mind of Man, when he gives the Spur and Bridle to his Thoughts, doth never stop, but naturally sallies out into both extreams of High and Low, of Good and Evil; His first Flight of Fancy, commonly transports Him to Idea's of what is most Perfect, finished, and exalted; till having soared out of his own Reach and Sight, not well perceiving how near the Frontiers of Height and Depth, border upon each other; With the same Course and Wing, he falls down plum into the lowest Bottom of Things; like one who travels the *East* into the *West*;
or

or like a strait Line drawn by its own Length into a Circle. Whether a Tincture of Malice in our Natures, makes us fond of furnishing every bright Idea with its Reverse; Or, whether Reason reflecting upon the Sum of Things, can like the Sun, serve only to enlighted one half of the Globe, leaving the other half, by Necessity, under Shade and Darkness: Or, whether Fancy, flying up to the Imagination of what is Highest and Best, becomes over-short, and spent, and weary, and suddenly falls like a dead Bird of Paradise, to the Ground. Or, whether after all these *Metaphysical* Conjectures, I have not entirely missed the true Reason; The Proposition, however, which hath stood me in so much Circumstance, is altogether true; That, as the most uncivilized Parts of Mankind, have some way or other, climbed up into the Conception of a *God*, or Supream Power, so they have seldom forgot to provide their Fears with certain ghastly Notions, which instead of better, have served them pretty tolerably for a *Devil*. And this Proceeding seems to be natural enough; For it is with Men, whose Imaginations are lifted up very high, after the same Rate, as with those, whose

whose Bodies are so; that, as they are delighted with the Advantage of a nearer Contemplation upwards, so they are equally terrified with the dismal Prospect of the Precipice below. Thus, in the Choice of a *Devil*, it hath been the usual Method of Mankind, to single out some Being, either in Act, or in Vision, which was in most Antipathy to the God they had framed. Thus, also, the Sect of *Æolists*, possessed themselves with a Dread, and Horror, and Hatred of two Malignant Natures, betwixt whom, and the Deities they adored, perpetual Enmity was established. The first of these, was the *Camelion*, sworn Foe to *Inspiration*, who in Scorn, devoured large Influences of their God, without refunding the smallest Blast by *Eructation*. The other was a huge terrible Monster, called *Moulinavent*, who with four strong Arms, waged eternal Battel with all their Divinities, dextrously turning to avoid their Blows, and repay them with Interest.

THUS furnisht, and set out with *Gods*, as well as *Devils*, was the renowned Sect of *Æolists*; which makes at this Day so illustrious a Figure in the World, and whereof

whereof, that Polite Nation of *Laplanders*, are beyond all Doubt, a moſt Authentick Branch; Of whom, I therefore cannot, without Injuſtice, here omit to make honourable Mention; ſince they appear to be ſo cloſely allied in Point of Intereſt, as well as Inclinations, with their Brother *Æoliſts* among Us, as not only to buy their *Winds* by wholeſale from the *ſame* Merchants, but alſo to retail them after the *ſame* Rate and Method, and to Cuſtomers much alike.

No w, whether the Syſtem here delivered, was wholly compiled by *Jack*, or, as ſome Writers believe, rather copied from the Original at *Delphos*, with certain Additions and Emendations ſuited to Times and Circumſtances, I ſhall not abſolutely determine. This I may affirm, that *Jack* gave it at leaſt a new Turn, and formed it into the ſame Dreſs and Model, as it lies deduced by me.

I have long ſought after this Opportunity, of doing Juſtice to a Society of Men, for whom I have a peculiar Honor,

nor, and whofe Opinions, as well as Practices, have been extremely mifreprefented, and traduced by the Malice or Ignorance of their Adverfaries. For, I think it one of the greateft, and beft of humane Actions, to remove Prejudices, and place Things in their trueft and faireft Light; which I therefore boldly undertake without any Regards of my own befide the Confcience, the Honor, and the Thanks.

SECT.

SECT. IX.

A Digression concerning the Original, the Use, and Improvement of Madness *in a Commonwealth.*

NOR shall it any ways detract from the just Reputation of this famous Sect, that its Rise and Institution are owing to such an Author as I have described *Jack* to be; A Person whose Intellectuals were overturned, and his Brain shaken out of its natural Position; which we commonly suppose to be a Distemper, and call by the Name of *Madness* or *Phrenzy*. For, if we take a Survey of the greatest Actions that have been performed in the World, under the Influence of Single Men; which are, *The Establishment of New Empires by Conquest; The Advance and Progress of New Schemes in Philosophy; and the contriving, as well as the propagating of New Religions:* We shall find the Authors of them all, to have been Persons, whose natural Reason hath admitted great Revolutions from their Dyet, their Education, the Prevalency

valency of some certain Temper, together with the particular Influence of Air and Climate. Besides, there is something Individual in human Minds, that easily kindles at the accidental Approach ad Collision of certain Circumstances, which tho' of paltry and mean Appearance, do often flame out into the greatest Emergencies of Life. For, great Turns are not always given by strong Hands, but by lucky Adaption, and at proper Seasons; and it is of no import, where the Fire was kindled, if the Vapor has once got up into the Brain. For, the *upper Region* of Man, is furnished like the *middle Region* of the Air; The Materials are formed from Causes of the widest Difference, yet produce at last the same Substance and Effect. Mists arise from the Earth, Steams from Dunghils, Exhalations from the Sea, and Smoak from Fire; yet all Clouds are the same in Composition, as well as Consequences: And the Fumes issuing from a Jakes, will furnish as comely and useful a Vapor, as Incense from an Altar. Thus far, I suppose, will easily be granted me: And then it will follow; that as the Face of Nature never produces Rain, but when it is overcast and disturbed; so Human Under-

Understanding, seated in the Brain, must be troubled and over-spread by Vapors, ascending from the lower Faculties, to water the Invention, and render it fruitful. Now, altho' these Vapors (as it hath been already said) are of as various Original, as those of the Skies, yet the Crop they produce, differs both in Kind and Degree, meerly according to the Soil. I will produce two Instances to prove and Explain what I am now advancing.

A certain Great Prince raised a mighty Army, filled his Coffers with infinite Treasures, provided an invincible Fleet; and all this, without giving the least Part of his Design to his greatest Ministers, or his nearest Favorites. Immediately the whole World was alarmed; the neighbouring Crowns, in trembling Expectation, towards what Point the Storm would burst; the small Politicians, every where forming profound Conjectures. Some believed he had laid a Scheme for Universal Monarchy: Others, after much Insight, determined the Matter to be a Project for pulling down the *Pope*, and setting up the *Reformed* Religion, which had once been his own. Some, again, of a deeper Sagacity, sent him into *Asia*

Asia to subdue the *Turk*, and recover *Palestine*. In the midst of all these Projects and Preparations; a certain *State-Surgeon*, gathering the Nature of the Disease by these Symptoms, attempted the Cure, at own Blow performed the Operation, broke the Bag, and out flew the *Vapor*; nor did any thing want to render it a compleat Remedy, only, that the Prince unfortunately happened to Die in the Performance. Now, is the Reader exceeding curious to learn, from whence this *Vapor* took its Rise, which had so long set the Nations at a Gaze? What secret Wheel, what hidden Spring could put into Motion so wonderful an Engine? It was afterwards discovered, that the Movement of this whole Machine had been directed by an absent *Female*, whose Eyes had raised a Protuberancy, and before Emission, she was removed into an Enemy's Country. What should an unhappy Prince do in such ticklish Circumstances as these? He tried in vain the Poet's never-failing Receipt of *Corpora quæque*; For,

> *Idque petit corpus mens unde est saucia amore;*
> *Unde feritur, eo tendit, gestitq; coire.* Lucr.

HAVING

A Digression, &c.

HAVING to no purpose used all peaceable Endeavors, the collected Part of the *Semen*, raised and enflamed, became adust, converted to Choler, turned head upon the spinal Duct, and ascended to the Brain. The very same Principle that influences a *Bully* to break the Windows of a Whore, who has jilted Him, naturally stirs up a Great Prince to raise Mighty Armies, and dream of nothing, but Sieges, Battles, and Victories.

———*Cunnus teterrima belli*
Causa ——— ———

THE other Instance is, what I have read somewhere, in a very antient Author, of a Mighty King, who for the space of above thirty Years, amused himself to take and lose Towns; beat Armies, and be beaten; drive Princes out of their Dominions; fright Children from their Bread and Butter; burn, lay waste, plunder, dragoon, massacre, Subject and Stranger, Friend and Foe, Male and Female. 'Tis recorded, that the Philosophers of each Country were in grave Dispute, upon Causes Natural, Moral, and Political,

tical, to find out where they should assign an original Solution of this *Phænomenon*. At last the *Vapor* or *Spirit*, which animated the Hero's Brain, being in perpetual Circulation, seised upon that Region of Human Body, so renowned for furnishing the *Zibeta Occidentalis*, and gathering there into a Tumor, left the rest of the World for that Time in Peace. Of such mighty Consequence it is, where those Exhalations fix, and of so little, from whence they proceed. The same Spirits which in their superior Progress would conquer a Kingdom, descending upon the *Anus*, conclude in a *Fistula*.

Let us next examine the great Introducers of new Schemes in Philosophy, and search till we can find, from what Faculty of the Soul, the Disposition arises in mortal Man, of taking it into his Head, to advance new Systems with such an eager Zeal, in Things agreed on all Hands impossible to be known : From what Seeds this Disposition springs, and to what Quality of human Nature these Grand Innovators have been indebted for their Number of Disciples. Because, it is plain, that several of

A Digreſſion &c.

of the Chief among them, both *Antient* and *Modern*, were uſually miſtaken by their Adverſaries, and indeed, by all except their own Followers, to have been Perſons crazed, or out of their Wits, having generally proceeded in the common Courſe of their Words and Actions, by a Method very different from the vulgar Dictates of *unrefined* Reaſon: agreeing for the moſt Part in their ſeveral Models, with their preſent undoubted Succeſſors in the *Academy* of *Modern Bedlam* (whoſe Merits and Principles I ſhall further examine in due Place.) Of this Kind were *Epicurus, Diogenes, Apollonius, Lucretius, Paracelſus, Des Cartes*, and others; who, if they were now in the World, tied faſt, and ſeparate from their Followers, would in this our undiſtinguiſhing Age, incur manifeſt Danger of *Phlebotomy*, and *Whips*, and *Chains*, and dark *Chambers*, and *Straw*. For, what Man in the natural State, or Courſe of Thinking, did ever conceive it in his Power, to reduce the Notions of all Mankind, exactly to the ſame Length, and Breadth, and Height of his own? Yet this is the firſt humble and civil Deſign of all Innovators in the Empire of Reaſon. *Epicurus*, modeſtly

modestly hoped, that one Time or other, a certain Fortuitous Concourse of all Mens Opinions, after perpetual Justlings, the Sharp with the Smooth, the Light and the Heavy, the Round and the Square, would by certain *Clinamina*, unite in the Notions of *Atoms* and *Void*, as these did in the Originals of all Things. *Cartesius* reckoned to see before he died, the Sentiments of all Philosophers, like so many lesser Stars in his *Romantick* System, rapt and drawn within his own *Vortex*. Now, I would gladly be informed, how it is possible to account for such Imaginations as these in particular Men, without Recourse to my *Phænomenon* of *Vapors*, ascending from the lower Faculties to over-shadow the Brain, and thence distilling into Conceptions, for which the Narrowness of our Mother-Tongue has not yet assigned any other Name, beside that of *Madness* or *Phrenzy*. Let us therefore now conjecture how it comes to pass, that none of these great Prescribers, do ever fail providing themselves and their Notions, with a Number of implicite Disciples. And, I think, the Reason is easie to be assigned: For, there is a peculiar *String* in the Harmony of Human Understanding, which in
several

several Individuals is exactly of the same Tuning. This, if you can dextrously screw up to its right Key, and then strike gently upon it; Whenever you have the good Fortune to light among those of the same Pitch, they will by a secret necessary Sympathy, strike exactly at the same Time. And in this one Circumstance, lyes all the Skill or Luck of the Matter; for if you chance to jar the String among those who are either above or below your own Height, instead of subscribing to your Doctrine, they will tie you fast, call you Mad, and feed you with Bread and Water. It is therefore a Point of the nicest Conduct to distinguish and adapt this noble Talent, with respect to the Differences of Persons and of Times. *Cicero* understood this very well, when writing to a Friend in *England*, with a Caution, among other Matters, to beware of being cheated by our *Hackney-Coachmen* (who, it seems, in those Days, were as arrant Rascals, as they are now) has these remarkable Words. * *Est quod gaudeas te in ista loca venisse, ubi aliquid sapere viderere.* For to speak a bold Truth, it is a fatal Miscarriage, so ill to order Affairs, as to pass

* *Epist. ad Fam. Trebat.o.*

for a *Fool* in one Company, when in another, you might be treated as a *Philosopher.* Which I defire *fome certain Gentlemen of my Acquaintance,* to lay up in their Hearts, as a very feafonable *Innuendo.*

THIS, indeed, was the Fatal Miftake of that worthy Gentleman, my moft ingenious Friend, Mr. *W--tt--n*: A Perfon, in appearance, ordain'd for great Defigns, as well as Performances; whether you will confider his *Notions* or his *Looks.* Surely, no Man ever advanced into the Publick, with fitter Qualifications of Body and Mind, for the Propogation of a new Religion. Oh, had thofe happy Talents mifapplied to vain Philofophy, been turned into their proper Channels of *Dreams* and *Vifions,* where *Diftortion* of Mind and Countenance, are of fuch Sovereign Ufe; the bafe detracting World would not then have dared to report, that fomething is amifs, that his Brain hath undergone an unlucky Shake; which, even his Brother *Modernifts* themfelves, like Ungrates, do whifper fo loud, that it reaches up to the very *Garrat* I am writing in.

LASTLY,

LASTLY, Whoever pleases to look into the Fountains of *Enthusiasm*, from whence, in all Ages, have eternally proceeded such fatning Streams, will find the Spring Head to have been as *troubled* and *muddy* as the Current; Of such great Emolument, is a Tincture of this *Vapor*, which the World calls *Madness*, that without its Help, the World would not only be deprived of those two great Blessings, *Conquests* and *Systems*, but even all Mankind would unhappily be reduced to the same Belief in Things Invisible. Now, the former *Postulatum* being held, that it is of no Import, from what Originals this *Vapor* proceeds, but either in what *Angles* it strikes and spreads over the Understanding, or upon what *Species* of Brain it ascends; It will be a very delicate Point, to cut the Feather, and divide the several Reasons to a nice and curious Reader, how this numerical Difference in the Brain, can produce Effects of so vast a Difference from the same Vapor, as to be the sole Point of Individuation between *Alexander the Great*, *Jack* of *Leyden*, and Monsieur *Des Cartes*. The present Argument, is the most abstracted that ever I engaged

engaged in, it ſtrains my Faculties to their higheſt Stretch; and I deſire the Reader to attend with utmoſt Perpenſity; For, I now proceed to unravel this knotty Point.

T H E R E is in Mankind a certain * *
* * * * * * * * * * * *
* * * * * * * *
Hic multa * * * * * * * * *
deſiderantur.
* * * * * * * *
* * * * * * * * * * *
* * * * * And this I take to be a clear Solution of the Matter.

H A V I N G therefore ſo narrowly paſt thro' this intricate Difficulty, the Reader will, I am ſure, agree with me in the Concluſion; that if the *Moderns* mean by *Madneſs*, only a Diſturbance or Tranſpoſition of the Brain, by Force of certain *Vapors* iſſuing up from the lower Faculties; Then has this *Madneſs* been the Parent of all thoſe mighty Revolutions, that have happened in *Empire*, in *Philoſophy*, and in *Religion*. For, the Brain in its natural Poſition and State of Serenity, diſpoſeth its Owner to paſs his Life in the common Forms, without any Thought of
ſubduing

subduing Multitudes to his own *Power*, his *Reasons*, or his *Visions*; And the more he shapes his Understanding by the Pattern of Human Learning, the less he is inclined to form Parties after his particular Notions; Because that instructs him in his private Infirmities, as well as in the stubborn Ignorance of the People. But when a Man's Fancy gets *astride* on his Reason, when Imagination is at Cuffs with the Senses, and common Understanding as well as common Sense, is kickt out of Doors; the first Proselyte he makes, is Himself, and when that is once compass'd, the Difficulty is not so great in bringing over others; A strong Delusion always operating from *without*, as vigorously as from *within*. For, Cant and Vision are to the Ear and the Eye, the same that Tickling is to the Touch. Those Entertainments and Pleasures we most value in Life, are such as *Dupe* and play the Wag with the Senses. For, if we take an Examination of what is generally understood by *Happiness*, as it has Respect, either to the Understanding, or the Senses; we shall find all its Properties and Adjuncts, will herd under this short Definition: That, *it is a perpetual Possession of being well Deceived.*

Deceived. And firſt, with Relation to the Mind or Underſtanding; 'tis manifeſt, what mighty Advantages Fiction has over Truth; and the Reaſon is juſt at our Elbow; becauſe Imagination can build nobler Scenes, and produce more wonderful Revolutions than Fortune or Nature will be at Expence to furniſh. Nor is Mankind ſo much to blame in his Choice, thus determining him, if we conſider that the Debate meerly lyes between *Things paſt*, and *Things conceived*; And ſo the Queſtion is only this; Whether Things that have Place in the *Imagination*, may not as properly be ſaid to *Exiſt*, as thoſe that are ſeated in the *Memory*; which may be juſtly held in the Affirmative, and very much to the Advantage of the former, ſince This is acknowledged to be the *Womb* of Things, and the Other allowed to be no more than the *Grave*. Again, if we take this Definition of Happineſs, and examine it with Reference to the Senſes, it will be acknowledged wonderfully adapt. How fade and inſipid do all Objects accoſt us, that are not convey'd in the Vehicle of *Deluſion?* How ſhrunk is every Thing, as it appears in the Glaſs of Nature? ſo, that if it were not for the Aſſiſtance of artificial

cial *Mediums*, falſe Lights, refracted Angles, Verniſh, and Tinſel; there would be a mighty Level in the Felicity and Enjoyments of Mortal Men. If this were ſeriouſly conſidered by the World, as I have a certain Reaſon to ſuſpect it hardly will; Men would no longer reckon among their high Points of Wiſdom, the Art of expoſing weak Sides, and publiſhing Infirmities; an Employment in my Opinion, neither better nor worſe than that of *Unmasking*, which, I think, has never been allowed fair Uſage, either in the *World* or the *Play-houſe*.

In the Proportion that Credulity is a more peaceful Poſſeſſion of the Mind, than Curioſity, ſo far preferable is that Wiſdom, which converſes about the Surface, to that pretended Philoſophy which enters into the Depth of Things, and then comes gravely back with Informations and Diſcoveries, that in the Inſide they are good for nothing. The two Senſes, to which all Objects firſt Addreſs themſelves, are the Sight and the Touch; Theſe never examine further than the Color, the Shape, the Size, and whatever other Qualities dwell, or are drawn by Art upon the Outward

ward of Bodies; and then comes Reason officiously, with Tools for cutting, and opening, and mangling, and piercing, offering to demonstrate, that they are not of the same consistence quite thro'. Now, I take all this to be the last Degree of perverting Nature; one of whose eternal Laws it is, to put her best Furniture forward. And therefore, in order to save the Charges of all such expensive Anatomy for the Time to come; I do here think fit to inform the Reader, that in such Conclusions as these, Reason is certainly in the Right; And that in most Corporeal Beings, which have fallen under my Cognizance, the Outside hath been infinitely preferable to the *In* : Whereof I have been further convinced from some late Experiments. Last Week I saw a Woman *flay'd*, and you will hardly believe, how much it altered her Person for the worse. Yesterday I ordered the Carcass of a *Beau* to be stript in my Presence; when we were all amazed to find so many unsuspected Faults under one Suit of Cloaths : Then I laid open his *Brain*, his *Heart*, and his *Spleen*; But, I plainly perceived at every Operation, that the farther we proceeded, we found the De-

fects

A Digreſſion, &c.

fects encreaſe upon us in Number and Bulk: From all which, I juſtly formed this Concluſion to my ſelf. That whatever Philoſopher or Projector can find out an Art to ſodder and patch up the Flaws and Imperfections of Nature, will deſerve much better of Mankind, and teach us a more uſeful Science, than that ſo much in preſent Eſteem, of widening and expoſing them (like him who held *Anatomy* to be the ultimate End of *Phyſick*.) And he, whoſe Fortunes and Diſpoſitions have placed him in a convenient Station to enjoy the Fruits of this noble Art; He that can with *Epicurus,* content his Idea's with the *Films* and *Images* that fly off upon his Senſes from the *Superficies* of Things; Such a Man truly Wiſe, creams off Nature, leaving the Sower and the Dregs, for Philoſophy and Reaſon to lap up. This is the ſublime and refined Point of Felicity, called, *the Poſſeſſion of being well deceived*; The Serene peaceful State of being a Fool among Knaves.

But to return to *Madneſs*. It is certain, that according to the Syſtem I have above deduced; every *Species* thereof proceeds from a Redundancy of *Vapor*; therefore,

fore, as some Kinds of *Phrenzy* give double Strength to the Sinews, so there are of other *Species*, which add Vigor, and Life, and Spirit to the Brain: Now, it usually happens, that these active Spirits, getting Possession of the Brain, resemble those that haunt other Waste and Empty Dwellings, which for want of Business, either vanish, and carry away a Piece of the House, or else stay at home, and fling it all out of the Windows. By which are mystically display'd the two principal Branches of *Madness*; and which some Philosophers not considering so well as I, have mistook to be different in their Causes, over-hastily assigning the first to Deficiency, and the other to Redundance.

I think it therefore manifest, from what I have here advanced, that the main Point of Skill and Address, is to furnish Employment for this Redundancy of *Vapor*, and prudently to adjust the Seasons of it; by which Means, it may certainly become of cardinal and catholick Emolument in a Commonwealth. Thus, one Man chusing a proper Juncture, leaps into a Gulph, from thence proceeds a Hero, and is called the Saver of his Country;
Another

Another atchieves the same Enterprise, but unluckily timing it, has left the Brand of *Madness*, fixt as a Reproach upon his Memory; Upon so nice a Distinction are we taught to repeat the Name of *Curtius* with Reverence and Love; that of *Empedocles*, with Hatred and Contempt. Thus, also it is usually conceived, that the Elder *Brutus* only personated the *Fool* and *Madman*, for the Good of the Publick: but this was nothing else, than a Redundancy of the same *Vapor*, long misapplied, called by the *Latins*, * *Ingenium par negotiis*: Or, (to translate it as nearly as I can) a sort of *Phrenzy*, never in its right Element, till you take it up in Business of the State.

* *Tacit.*

UPON all which, and many other Reasons of equal Weight, though not equally curious; I do here gladly embrace an Opportunity I have long sought for, of Recommending it as a very noble Undertaking, to Sir E——d S——r, Sir C——r M————ve, Sir J——n B——ls, J——n H—— Esq; and other Patriots concerned, that they would move for Leave to bring in a Bill, for appointing Commissioners to Inspect into *Bedlam*, and the Parts adjacent; who shall be empowered to *send for Persons, Papers, and Records:* to examine into the Merits and Qualifications of every Student and Professor; to observe with utmost Exactness their several Dispositions and Behaviour; by which means, duly distinguishing and adapting their Talents, they might produce admirable Instruments for the several Offices in a State, * * * * * * *Civil* and *Military*; proceeding in such Methods, as I shall here humbly propose. And, I hope, the Gentle Reader will give some Allowance to my great Solicitudes in this important Affair, upon Account of that high Esteem I have ever born that honourable Society, whereof I had some Time the Happiness to be an unworthy Member.

Is any Student tearing his Straw in piece-meal, Swearing and Blaspheming, biting his Grate, foaming at the Mouth, and emptying his Pispot in the Spectator's Faces? Let the Right Worshipful, the *Commissioners of Inspection*, give him a Regiment of Dragoons, and send him into *Flanders* among the *rest.* Is another eternally talking, sputtering, gaping, bawling, in a Sound without Period or Article?
What

What wonderful Talents are here mislaid! Let him be furnished immediately with a green Bag and Papers, and * *three Pence* in his Pocket, and away with Him to *Westminster-Hall.*

A Lawyer's Coach-hire.

You will find a Third, gravely taking the Dimensions of his Kennel; A Person of Foresight and Insight, tho' kept quite in the Dark; for why, like *Moses, Ecce cornuta erat ejus facies.* He walks duly in one Pace, intreats your Penny with due Gravity and Ceremony; talks much of hard Times, and Taxes, and the *Whore of Babylon*; Bars up the woodden of his Cell constantly at eight a Clock: Dreams of *Fire,* and *Shop-lifters,* and *Court-Customers,* and *Priviledg'd Places.* Now, what a Figure would all these Acquirements amount to, if the Owner were sent into the *City* among his Brethren! Behold a Fourth, in much and deep Conversation with himself, biting his Thumbs at proper Junctures; His Countenance chequered with Business and Design; sometimes walking very fast, with his Eyes nailed to a Paper that he holds in his Hands: A great Saver of Time, somewhat thick of Hearing, very short of Sight, but more of Memory. A Man ever in Haste, a great

great Hatcher and Breeder of Business, and excellent at the Famous Art of *whispering Nothing*. A huge Idolater of Monosyllables and Procrastination; so ready to *Give* his Word to every Body, that he never *keeps* it. One that has forgot the common *Meaning* of Words, but an admirable Retainer of the *Sound*. Extreamly subject to the *Looseness*, for his *Occasions* are perpetually *calling him away*. If you approach his Grate in his familiar Intervals; *Sir*, says he, *Give me a Penny, and I'll sing you a Song : But give me the Penny first*. (Hence comes the common Saying, and commoner Practice of parting with Money for a *Song*.) What a compleat System of *Court-Skill* is here described in every Branch of it, and all utterly lost with wrong Application? Accost the Hole of another Kennel, first stopping your Nose, you will behold a surley, gloomy, nasty, slovenly Mortal, raking in his own Dung, and dabling in his Urine. The best Part of his Diet, is the Reversion of his own Ordure, which exspiring into Steams, whirls perpetually about, and at last reinfunds. His Complexion is of a dirty Yellow, with a thin scattered Beard, exactly agreeable to that of his Dyet upon its first Declination;

like

like other Infects, who having their Birth and Education in an Excrement, from thence borrow their Color and their Smell. The Student of this Apartment is very sparing of his Words, but somewhat over-liberal of his Breath; He holds his Hand out ready to receive your Penny, and immediately upon Receipt, withdraws to his former Occupations. Now, is it not amazing to think, the Society of *Warwick-Lane*, should have no more Concern, for the Recovery of so useful a Member, who, if one may judge from these Appearances, would become the greatest Ornament to that Illustrious Body? Another Student struts up fiercely to your Teeth, puffing with his Lips, half squeezing out his Eyes, and very graciously holds you out his Hand to kiss. The *Keeper* desires you not to be afraid of this Professor, for he will do you no Hurt: To him alone is allowed the Liberty of the Anti-Chamber, and the *Orator* of the Place gives you to understand, that this solemn Person is a *Taylor* run mad with Pride. This considerable Student is adorned with many other Qualities, upon which, at present, I shall not further enlarge. - - - -

Hark in your Ear - - - - - - -
I am strangely mistaken, if all his Address, his Motions, and his Airs, would not then be very natural, and in their proper Element.

I shall not descend so minutely, as to insist upon the vast Number of *Beaux*, *Fidlers*, *Poets*, and *Politicians*, that the World might recover by such a Reformation; But what is more material, beside the clear Gain redounding to the Commonwealth, by so large an Acquisition of Persons to employ, whose Talents and Acquirements, if I may be so bold to affirm it, are now buried, or at least misapplied: It would be a mighty Advantage accruing to the Publick from this Enquiry, that all these would very much excel, and arrive at great Perfection in their several Kinds; which, I think, is manifest from what I have already shewn; and shall inforce by this one plain Instance; That even, I my self, the Author of these momentous Truths, am a Person, whose Imaginations are hard-mouth'd, and exceedingly disposed to run away with his *Reason*, which I have observed from long Experience, to be a very light Rider,

Rider, and eafily fhook off; upon which Account, my Friends will never truft me alone, without a folemn Promife, to vent my Speculations in this, or the like manner, for the univerfal Benefit of Human kind; which, perhaps, the gentle, courteous, and candid Reader, brimful of that *Modern* Charity and Tendernefs, ufually annexed to his *Office*, will be very hardly perfuaded to believe.

SECT. X.

A TALE of a TUB.

IT is an unanfwerable Argument of a very refined Age, the wonderful Civilities that have paffed of late Years, between the Nation of *Authors*, and that of *Readers*. There can hardly pop out a *Play*, a *Pamphlet*, or a *Poem*, without a Preface full of Acknowledgements to the World, for the general Reception and Applaufe they have given it, which the Lord knows where, or when, or how, or from whom it received. In due Deference to fo laudable a Cuftom, I do here return my humble Thanks to *His Majefly*, and both Houfes of *Parliament*; To the *Lords* of the King's moft honourable Privy-Council, to the Reverend the *Judges:* To the *Clergy*, and *Gentry*, and *Yeomantry* of this Land : But in a more efpecial manner, to my worthy Brethren and Friends at *Will's Coffee-Houfe*, and *Grefham-College*, and *Warwick-Lane*, and *Moor-Fields*, and *Scotland-Yard*, and *Weftminfter-Hall*, and *Guild-Hall*; In fhort, to all Inhabitants and

and Retainers whatsoever, either in Court, or Church, or Camp, or City, or Country; for their generous and universal Acceptance of this Divine Treatise. I accept their Approbation, and good Opinion with extream Gratitude, and to the utmost of my poor Capacity, shall take hold of all Opportunities to return the Obligation.

I am also happy, that Fate has flung me into so blessed an Age for the mutual Felicity of *Bookfellers* and *Authors*, whom I may safely affirm to be at this Day the two only satisfied Parties in *England*. Ask an *Author* how his last Piece hath succeeded; *Why, truly he thanks his Stars, the World has been very favourable, and he has not the least Reason to complain: And yet, By G——, He writ it in a Week at Bits and Starts, when he could steal an Hour from his urgent Affairs*; as, it is a hundred to one, you may see further in the Preface; To which he refers you, and for the rest, to the Bookseller. There you go as a Customer, and make the same Question: *He blesses his God, the Thing takes wonderful, he is just printing a Second Edition, and has but three left in his Shop. You beat down the Price: Sir, we*

shall

shall not differ; and in hopes of your Custom another Time, lets you have it as reasonable as you please; *And, pray send as many of your Acquaintance as you will, I shall upon your Account furnish them all at the same Rate.*

Now, it is not well enough consider'd, to what Accidents and Occasions the World is indebted for the greatest Part of those noble Writings, which hourly start up to entertain it. If it were not for a *rainy Day, a drunken Vigil, a Fit of the Spleen, a Course of Physick, a sleepy Sunday, an ill Run at Dice, a long Taylor's Bill, a Beggar's Purse, a factious Head, a hot Sun, costive Dyet, Want of Books, and a just Contempt of Learning.* But for these Events, I say, and same Others too long to recite, (especially *a prudent Neglect of taking Brimstone inwardly*,) I doubt, the Number of *Authors*, and of *Writings*, would dwindle away to a Degree most woful to behold. To confirm this Opinion, hear the Words of the famous *Troglodyte* Philosopher: *'Tis certain* (said he) *some Grains of Folly are of course annexed, as Part in the Composition of Human Nature, only the Choice is left us, whether we please to wear them* Inlaid *or* Embossed;

Embossed; *And we need not go very far to seek how That is usually determined, when we remember, it is with Human Faculties as with Liquors, the lightest will be ever at the Top.*

THERE is in this famous Island of *Britain* a certain paultry *Scribbler*, very voluminous, whose Character the Reader cannot wholly be a Stranger to. He deals in a pernicious Kind of Writings, called *Second Parts,* and usually passes under the Name of *The Author of the First*. I easily foresee, that as soon as I lay down my Pen, this nimble *Operator* will have stole it, and treat me as inhumanly as he hath already done Dr. *Bl——re, L——ge,* and many others who shall here be nameless. I therefore fly for Justice and Relief, into the Hands of that great *Rectifier of Saddles,* and *Lover of Mankind,* Dr. *B——tly,* begging he will take this enormous Grievance into his most *Modern* Consideration: And if it should so happen, that the *Furniture of an Ass,* in the Shape of a *Second Part,* must for my Sins, be clapt by a Mistake, upon my Back, that he will immediately please, in the Presence of the World, to lighten me of the Burther.

then, and take it home to *his own House*, till the *true Beast* thinks fit to call for it.

I N the mean time I do here give this publick Notice, that my Resolutions are, to circumscribe within this Discourse the whole Stock of Matter I have been so many Years providing. Since my *Vein* is once opened, I am content to exhaust it all at a Running, for the peculiar Advantage of my dear Country, and for the universal Benefit of Mankind. Therefore, hospitably considering the Number of my Guests, they shall have my whole Entertainment at a Meal; And I scorn to set up the *Leavings* in the Cupboard. What the *Guests* cannot eat may be given to the *Poor*, and the *Dogs* under the Table may gnaw the *Bones*; This I understand for a more generous Proceeding, than to turn the Company's Stomachs, by inviting them again to morrow to a scurvy Meal of *Scraps*.

I F the Reader fairly considers the Strength of what I have advanced in the foregoing Section, I am convinced it will produce a wonderful Revolution in his
Notions

Notions and Opinions; And he will be abundantly better prepared to receive and to relish the concluding Part of this miraculous Treatise. Readers may be divided into three Classes, the *Superficial,* the *Ignorant,* and the *Learned:* And I have with much Felicity fitted my Pen to the Genious and Advantage of each. The *Superficial* Reader will be strangely provoked to *Laughter;* which clears the Breast and the Lungs, is Soverain against the *Spleen,* and the most innocent of all *Dinreticks.* The *Ignorant* Reader (between whom and the former, the Distinction is extreamly nice) will find himself disposed to *Stare;* which is an admirable Remedy for ill Eyes, serves to raise and enliven the Spirits, and wonderfully helps *Perspiration.* But the Reader truly *Learned,* chiefly for whose Benefit, I wake, when others sleep, and sleep when others wake, will here find sufficient Matter to employ his Speculations for the rest of his Life. It were much to be wisht, and I do here humbly propose for an Experiment, that every Prince in *Christendom* will take seven of the *deepest Scholars* in his Dominions, and shut them up close for *seven* Years, in *seven* Chambers,

with

with a Command to write *seven* ample Commentaries on this comprehensive Discourse. I shall venture to affirm, that whatever Difference may be found in their several Conjectures, they will be all without the least Distortion, manifestly deduceable from the Text. Mean time, it is my earnest Request, that so useful an Undertaking may be entered upon (if their Majesties please) with all convenient speed; because, I have a strong Inclination, before I leave the World, to taste a Blessing, which we *mysterious* Writers can seldom reach, till we have got into our Graves. Whether it is, that *Fame* being a Fruit grafted on the Body, can hardly grow, and much less ripen, till the *Stock* is in the Earth: Or, whether she be a Bird of Prey, and is lured among the rest, to pursue after the Scent of a *Carcass*: Or, whether she conceives, her Trumpet sounds best and farthest, when she stands on a *Tomb*, by the Advantage of a rising Ground, and the Echo of a hollow Vault.

'Tis true, indeed, the Republick of *dark* Authors, after they once found out this excellent Expedient of *Dying*, have been

been peculiarly happy in the Variety, as well as Extent of their Reputation. For, *Night* being the univerſal Mother of Things, wiſe Philoſophers hold all Writings to be *fruitful* in the Proportion they are *dark*; And therefore, the * *true Illuminated* (that is to ſay, the *Darkeſt* of all) have met with ſuch numberleſs Commentators, whoſe *Scholiaſtick* Midwifry hath deliver'd them of Meanings, that the Authors themſelves, perhaps, never conceived, and yet may very juſtly be allowed the Lawful Parents of them: The Words of ſuch Writers being like Seed, which, however ſcattered at random, when they light upon a fruitful Ground, will multiply far beyond either the Hopes or Imagination of the Sower.

* *A Name of the* Roſycrucians.

AND therefore in order to promote ſo uſeful a Work, I will here take Leave to glance a few *Innuendo's*, that may be of great Aſſiſtance to thoſe ſublime Spirits, who ſhall be appointed to labor in a univerſal Comment upon this wonderful Diſcourſe. And Firſt, I have couched a very profound Myſtery in the Number of O's multiply'd by *Seven*, and divided by *Nine*.

Alſo,

Alſo, if a devout Brother of the *Roſy-croſs* will pray fervently for ſixty three Mornings, with a lively Faith, and then tranſpoſe certain Letters and Syllables according to Preſcription, in the ſecond and fifth Section; they will certainly reveal into a full Receit of the *Opus Magnum*. Laſtly, Whoever will be at the Pains to calculate the whole Number of each Letter in this Treatiſe, and ſum up the Difference exactly between the ſeveral Numbers, aſſigning the true natural Cauſe for every ſuch Difference; the Diſcoveries in the Product, will plentifully reward his ›Labor. But then he muſt beware of *Bythas* and *Sigè*, and be ſure not to forget the Qualities of *Acamoth*; *A cujus lacrymis humecta prodit Subſtantia, à riſu lucida, à triſtitiâ ſolida, & à timore mobilis*, wherein * *Eugenius Philalethes* hath committed an unpardonable Miſtake.

* *Vid. A-nima magica abſcondita.*

SECT.

SECT. XI.

A TALE of a TUB.

AFTER so wide a Compass as I have wandred, I do now gladly overtake, and close in with my Subject, and shall henceforth hold on with it an even Pace to the End of my Journey, except some beautiful Prospect appears within sight of my Way; whereof, tho' at present I have neither Warning nor Expectation, yet upon such an Accident, come when it will, I shall beg my Readers Favour and Company, allowing me to conduct him thro' it along with my self. For in *Writing*, it is as in *Travelling*: If a Man is in haste to be at home, (which I acknowledge to be none of my Case, having never so little Business, as when I am there) if his *Horse* be tired with long Riding, and ill Ways, or be naturally a Jade, I advise him clearly to make the straitest and the commonest Road, be it ever so dirty; But, then surely, we must own such a Man to be a scurvy Companion at best; He *spatters* himself and his Fellow-Travellers at every Step: All their Thoughts, and Wishes, and Conversation turn entirely upon the Subject of their Journey's End; and at every Splash, and Plunge, and Stumble, they heartily wish one another at the Devil.

ON the other side, when a Traveller and his *Horse* are in Heart and Plight, when his Purse is full, and the Day before him; he takes the Road only where it is clean or convenient; entertains his Company there as agreeably as he can; but upon the first Occasion, carries them along with Him to every delightful Scene in View, whether of Art, of Nature, or of both; and if they chance to refuse out of Stupidity or Weariness; let them jog on by themselves, and be d—n'd; He'll overtake them at the next Town; at which arriving, he Rides furiously thro', the Men, Women, and Children run out to gaze, a hundred *noisy Curs* run *barking* after him, of which, if he honors the boldest with a *Lash of his Whip*, it is rather out of Sport than Revenge: But should some *sourer Mungrel* dare too near an Approach, he receives a *Salute* on the Chaps by an accidental Stroak from the Courser's Heels,

(nor

(nor is any Ground loſt by the Blow) which ſends him yelping and limping home.

I now proceed to ſum up the ſingular Adventures of my renowed *Jack*; the State of whoſe Diſpoſitions and Fortunes, the careful Reader does no doubt, moſt exactly remember, as I laſt parted with them in the Concluſion of a former Section. Therefore, his next Care muſt be from two of the foregoing, to extract a Scheme of Notions, that may beſt fit his Underſtanding for a true Reliſh of what is to enſue.

JACK had not only calculated the firſt Revolutions of his Brain ſo prudently, as to give Riſe to that Epidemick Sect of *Æoliſts*, but ſucceeding alſo into a new and ſtrange Variety of Conceptions, the Fruitfulneſs of his Imagination led him into certain Notions, which, altho' in Appearance very unaccountable, were not without their Myſteries and their Meanings, nor wanted Followers to countenance and improve them. I ſhall therefore be extremely careful and exact in recounting ſuch material Paſſages of this Nature.

Nature, as I have been able to collect, either from undoubted Tradition, or indefatigable Reading; and shall describe them as graphically as it is possible, and as far as Notions of that Height and Latitude can be brought within the Compass of a Pen. Nor do I at all question, but they will furnish Plenty of noble Matter for such, whose converting Imaginations dispose them to reduce all Things into *Types*; who can make *Shadows*, no thanks to the Sun; and then mold them into Substances, no thanks to Philosophy; whose peculiar Talent lies in fixing Tropes and Allegories to the *Letter*, and refining what is Literal into Figure and Mystery.

J A C K had provided a fair Copy of his Father's *Will*, engrossed in Form upon a large Skin of Parchment; and resolving to act the Part of a most dutiful Son, he became the fondest Creature of it imaginable. For, altho', as I have often told the Reader, it consisted wholly in certain plain, easy Directions about the management and wearing of their Coats, with Legacies and Penalties, in case of Obedience or Neglect; yet He began to entertain a Fancy, that the Matter was *deeper*

and

and *darker*, and therefore muſt needs have a great deal more of Myſtery at the Bottom. *Gentlemen,* ſaid he, *I will prove this very Skin of Parchment to be Meat, Drink, and Cloth, to be the Philoſopher's Stone, and the Univerſal Medicine.* In conſequence of which Raptures, he reſolved to make uſe of it in the moſt neceſſary, as well as the moſt paltry Occaſions of Life. He had a Way of working it into any Shape he pleaſed; ſo that it ſerved him for a Night-cap when he went to Bed, and for an Umbrello in rainy Weather. He would lap a Piece of it about a ſore Toe, or when he had Fitts, burn two Inches under his Noſe; or if any Thing lay heavy on his Stomach, ſcrape off, and ſwallow as much of the Powder as would lye on a ſilver Penny, they were all infallible Remedies. With Analogy to theſe Refinements, his common Talk and Converſation, ran wholly in the Phraſe of his Will, and he circumſcribed the utmoſt of his Eloquence within that Compaſs, not daring to let ſlip a Syllable without Authority from thence. Once at a ſtrange Houſe, he was ſuddenly taken ſhort, upon an urgent Juncture, whereon it may not be allowed too particularly to dilate;

and being not able to call to mind, with that Suddenness, the Occasion required, an Authentick Phrase for demanding the Way to the Backside; he chose rather as the more prudent Course, to incur the Penalty in such Cases usually annexed. Neither was it possible for the united Rhetorick of Mankind to prevail with him to make himself clean again: Because having consulted the Will upon this Emergency, he met with a Passage near the Bottom (whether foisted in by the Transcriber, is not known) which seemed to forbid it.

H E made it a Part of his Religion, never to say Grace to his Meat, nor could all the World persuade him, as the common Phrase is, to eat his Victuals *like a Christian.*

H E bore a strange kind of Appetite to *Snap-Dragon,* and to the livid Snuffs of a burning Candle, which he would catch and swallow with an Agility, wonderful to conceive; and by this Procedure, maintained a perpetual Flame in his Belly, which issuing in a glowing Steam from both his Eyes, as well as his Nostrils,

and

and his Mouth; made his Head appear in a dark Night, like the Scull of an Ass, wherein a roguish Boy hath conveyed a Farthing Candle, *to the Terror of His Majesty's Liege Subjects.* Therefore, he made use of no other Expedient to light himself home, but was wont to say, That *a Wise Man was his own Lanthorn.*

He would shut his Eyes as he walked along the Streets, and if he happened to bounce his Head against a Post, or fall into the Kennel (as he seldom missed either to do one or both) he would tell the gibing Prentices, who looked on, that *he submitted with entire Resignation, as to a Trip, or a Blow of Fate, with whom he found, by long Experience, how vain it was either to wrestle or to cuff;* and whoever durst undertake to do either, would be sure to come off with a swinging Fall, or a bloody Nose. *It was ordained,* said he, *some few Days before the Creation, that my Nose and this very Post should have a Rencounter; and therefore, Providence thought fit to send us both into the World in the same Age, and to make us Country-men and Fellow-Citizens. Now, had my Eyes been open, it is very likely, the Business might have been a great deal worse:*

worse ; *For, how many a confounded Slip is daily got by Man, with all his Foresight about him? Besides, the Eyes of the Understanding see best, when those of the Senses are out of the way; and therefore, blind Men are observed to tread their Steps with much more Caution, and Conduct, and Judgment, than those who rely with too much Confidence, upon the Virtue of the visual Nerve, which every little Accident shakes out of Order, and a Drop, or a Film, can wholly disconcert; like a Lanthorn among a Pack of roaring Bullies, when they scower the Streets; exposing its Owner, and it self, to outward Kicks and Buffets, which both might have escap'd, if the Vanity of Appearing would have suffered them to walk in the Dark. But, further; if we examine the* Conduct *of these boasted Lights, it will prove yet a great deal worse than their* Fortune : *'Tis true, I have broke my Nose against this Post, because Providence either forgot, or did not think it convenient to twitch me by the Elbow, and give me notice to avoid it. But, let not this encourage either the present Age or Posterity, to trust their* Noses *into the keeping of their* Eyes, *which may prove the fairest Way of losing them for good and all. For, O ye Eyes, Ye blind Guides ; miserable Guar-*

dians

dians are Ye of our frail Noses; Ye, I say, who fasten upon the first Precipice in view, and then tow our wretched willing Bodies after You, to the very Brink of Destruction: But, alas, that Brink is rotten, our Feet slip, and we tumble down prone into a Gulph, without one hospitable Shrub in the Way to break the Fall; a Fall, to which not any Nose of mortal Make is equal, except that of the Giant * Laurcalco, *who was Lord of the* Silver Bridge. *Most properly, therefore, O Eyes, and with great Justice, may You be compared to those foolish Lights, which conduct Men thro' Dirt and Darkness, till they fall into a deep Pit, or a noisom Bog.*

* Vide Don Quixot.

THIS I have produced, as a Scantling of *Jack's* great Eloquence, and the Force of his Reasoning upon such abstruse Matters.

HE was besides, a Person of great Design and Improvement in Affairs of *Devotion*, having introduced a new Deity, who hath since met with a vast Number of Worshippers; by some called *Babel*, by others, *Chaos*; who had an antient Temple of *Gothick* Structure upon *Salisbury* Plain;

Plain; famous for its Shrine, and Celebration by Pilgrims.

WHEN he had some Roguish Trick to play, he would down with his Knees, up with his Eyes, and fall to Prayers, tho' in the midst of the Kennel. Then it was that those who understood his Pranks, would be sure to get far enough out of his Way; And whenever Curiosity attracted Strangers to Laugh, or to Listen; he would of a sudden, with one Hand out with his *Gear*, and piss full in their Eyes, and with the other, all to-bespatter them with Mud.

IN Winter he went always loose and unbuttoned, and clad as thin as possible, to let *in* the ambient Heat; and in Summer, lapt himself close and thick to keep it *out*.

IN all Revolutions of Government, he would make his Court for the Office of *Hangman* General; and in the Exercise of that Dignity, wherein he was very dextrous, would make use of no other *Vizard* than a *long Prayer*.

HE

He had a Tongue so Musculous and Subtil, that he could twist it up into his Nose, and deliver a strange Kind of Speech from thence. He was also the first in these Kingdoms, who began to improve the *Spanish* Accomplishment of *Braying*: and having large Ears, perpetually exposed and arrect, he carried his Art to such a Perfection, that it was a Point of great Difficulty to distinguish either, by the View or the Sound, between the *Original* and the *Copy*.

He was troubled with a Disease, reverse to that called the Stinging of the *Tarantula*; and would run Dog-mad, at the Noise of *Musick*, especially a *Pair of Bag-Pipes*. But he would cure himself again, by taking two or three Turns in *Westminster-Hall*, or *Billinsgate*, or in a *Boarding-School*, or the *Royal-Exchange*, or a *State Coffee-House*.

He was a Person that *feared* no *Colours* but mortally *hated* all, and upon that Account, bore a cruel Aversion to *Painters*, insomuch, that in his Paroxisms, as he walked the Streets, he would have

have his Pockets loaden with Stones, to pelt at the *Signs*.

Having from his manner of Living, frequent Occasions to *wash* himself, he would often leap over Head and Ears into the Water, tho' it were in the midst of the Winter, but was always observed to come out again much *dirtier*, if possible, than he went in.

He was the first that ever found out the Secret of contriving a *Soporiferous* Medicine to be convey'd in at the *Ears*; It was a Compound of *Sulphur* and *Balm of Gilead*, with a little *Pilgrim's Salve*.

He wore a large Plaister of artificial *Causticks* on his Stomach, with the Fervor of which, he could set himself a *groaning*, like the famous *Board* upon Application of a red hot Iron.

He would stand in the Turning of a Street, and calling to those who passed by, would cry to One; *Worthy Sir, do me the Honor of a good Slap in the Chaps*: To another, *Honest Friend, pray, favour me*

*me with a handsom Kick on the Arse:
Madam, shall I entreat a small Box in the
Ear, from your Ladyship's fair Hands?
Noble Captain, Lend a reasonable Thwack,
for the Love of God, with that Cane of
yours, over the poor Shoulders.* And when
he had by such earnest Sollicitations,
made a shift to procure a Basting sufficient to swell up his Fancy and his Sides;
He would return home extremely comforted, and full of terrible Accounts of
what he had undergone for the *Publick
Good. Observe this Stroak,* (said he, shewing his bare Shoulders) *a plaguy* Janisary
*gave it me this very Morning at seven a
Clock, as, with much ado, I was driving off
the* Great Turk. *Neighbours mine, this
broken Head deserves a Plaister ; had poor*
Jack *been tender of his Noddle, you would
have seen the* Pope, *and the* French King,
*long before this time of Day, among your Wives
and your Ware-houses. Dear* Christians, *the*
Great Mogul *was come as far as* White-
Chappel, *and you may thank these poor
Sides that he hath not (God bless us)
already swallowed up Man, Woman, and
Child.*

I T

IT was highly worth obferving, the fingular Effects of that Averfion, or Antipathy, which *Jack* and his Brother *Peter* feemed, even to an Affectation, to bear towards each other. *Peter* had lately done *fome Rogueries*, that forced him to abfcond; and he feldom ventured to ftir out before Night, for fear of Bayliffs. Their Lodgings were at the two moft diftant Parts of the Town, from each other; and whenever their Occafions, or Humors called them abroad, they would make Choice of the oddeft unlikely Times, and moft uncouth Rounds they could invent; that they might be fure to avoid one another: Yet after all this, it was their perpetual Fortune to meet. The Reafon of which, is eafy enough to apprehend: For, the Phrenzy and the Spleen of both, having the fame Foundation, we may look upon them as two Pair of Compaffes, equally extended, and the fixed Foot of each, remaining in the fame Center; which, tho' moving contrary Ways at firft, will be fure to encounter fomewhere or other in the Circumference. Befides, it was among the great Misfortunes of *Jack*, to bear a huge Perfonal sonal Resemblance with his Brother *Peter*. Their Humors and Dispositions were not only the same, but there was a close Analogy in their Shape, their Size, and their Mien. Insomuch, as nothing was more frequent than for a Bayliff to seize *Jack* by the Shoulders, and cry; *Mr.* Peter, *You are the King's Prisoner.* Or, at other Times, for one of *Peter's* nearest Friends, to accost *Jack* with open Arms, *Dear* Peter, *I am glad to see thee, pray send me one of your best Medicines for the Worms.* This we may suppose, was a mortifying Return of those Pains and Proceedings, *Jack* had labored in so long; And finding, how directly opposite all his Endeavors had answered to the sole End and Intention, which he had proposed to himself; How could it avoid having terrible Effects upon a Head and Heart so furnished as his? However, the poor Remainders of his *Coat* bore all the Punishment; The orient Sun never entred upon his diurnal Progress, without missing a Piece of it. He hired a Taylor to stitch up the Collar so close, that it was ready to choak him, and squeezed out his Eyes at such a Rate, as one could see nothing but the White.

What

What little was left of the main Substance of the Coat, he rubbed every Day for two hours, against a rough-cast Wall, in order to grind away the Remnants of *Lace* and *Embroidery*; but at the same time went on with so much Violence, that he proceeded a *Heathen Philosopher*. Yet after all he could do of this kind, the Success continued still to disappoint his Expectation. For, as it is the Nature of Rags, to bear a kind of mock Resemblance to Finery; there being a sort of fluttering Appearance in both, which is not to be distinguished at a Distance, in the Dark, or by short-sighted Eyes: So, in those Junctures, it fared with *Jack* and his Tatters, that they offered to the first View, a ridiculous Flanting, which assisting the Resemblance in Person and Air, thwarted all his Projects of Separation, and left so near a Similitude between them, as frequently deceived the very Disciples and Followers of both. * * * * * * *
* * * * * * * * * * *
* * * * * * * * *
Desunt nonnulla. * * * * * * * * *
* * * * * * * *
* * * * * * * *

THE

The old *Sclavonian* Proverb said well, That *it is with Men, as with Asses; whoever would keep them fast, may find a very good Hold at their Ears.* Yet, I think, we may affirm, and it hath been verified by repeated Experience, that,

Effugiet tamen hæc sceleratus vincula Proteus.

It is good therefore, to read the Maxims of our Ancestors, with great Allowances to Times and Persons: For, if we look into Primitive Records, we shall find, that no Revolutions have been so great, or so frequent, as those of human *Ears.* In former Days, there was a curious Invention to catch and keep them; which, I think, we may justly reckon among the *Artes perditæ*: And how can it be otherwise, when in these latter Centuries, the very Species is not only diminished to a very lamentable Degree, but the poor Remainder is also degenerated so far, as to mock our skilfullest *Tenure?* For, if the only slitting of one *Ear* in a Stag, hath been found sufficient to propagate the Defect thro' a whole Forest;

Why should we wonder at the greatest Consequences, from so many Loppings and Mutilations, to which the *Ears* of our Fathers and our own, have been of late so much exposed? 'Tis true, indeed, that while this *Island* of ours, was under the *Dominion of Grace,* many Endeavours were made to improve the Growth of *Ears* once more among us. The Proportion of Largeness, was not only lookt upon as an Ornament of the *Outward* Man, but as a Type of Grace in the *Inward*. Besides, it is held by Naturalists, that if there be a Protuberancy of Parts in the *Superior* Region of the Body, as in the *Ears* and *Nose*, there must be a Parity also in the *Inferior:* And therefore in that truly pious Age, the *Males* in every Assembly, according as they were gifted, appeared very forward in exposing their *Ears* to view, and the Regions about them; because * *Hippocrates* tells us, that *when the Vein behind the* Ear *happens to be cut, a Man becomes an Eunuch:* And the *Females* were nothing backwarder in beholding and edifying by them: Whereof those who had already *us'd the Means,* lookt about them with great Concern, in hopes

Lib. de aere locis & aquis.

hopes of conceiving a fuitable Offspring by fuch a Profpect: Others, who ftood Candidates for *Benevolence*, found there a plentiful Choice, and were fure to fix upon fuch as difcovered the largeft *Ears*, that the Breed might not dwindle between them. Laftly, the devouter Sifters, who lookt upon all extraordinary Dilatations of that Member, as Protrufions of Zeal, or fpiritual Excrefcencies, were fure to honor every Head they fat upon, as if they had been *cloven Tongues*; but, efpecially, that of the Preacher, whofe *Ears* were ufually of the prime Magnitude: which upon that Account, he was very frequent and exact in expofing with all Advantages to the People; in his Rhetorical *Paroxyfms*, turning fometimes to *hold forth* the one, and fometimes to *hold forth* the other: From which Cuftom, the whole Operation of Preaching is to this very Day among their Profeffors, ftyled by the Phrafe of *Holding forth*.

Such was the Progrefs of the *Saints*, for advancing the Size of that Member; And it is thought, the Succefs would have been every way anfwerable, if in Procefs of time, a cruel King had not arofe, who raifed a bloody Perfecution againft all *Ears*, above a certain Standard: Upon which, some were glad to hide their flourishing Sprouts in a black Border, others crept wholly under a Perewig: some were flit, others cropt, and a great Number sliced off to the Stumps. But of this, more hereafter, in my *general History of Ears*; which I design very speedily to bestow upon the Publick.

FROM this brief Survey of the falling State of *Ears*, in the last Age, and the small Care had to advance their antient Growth in the present, it is manifest, how little Reason we can have to rely upon a Hold so short, so weak, and so slippery; and that, whoever desires to catch Mankind fast, must have Recourse to some other Methods. Now, he that will examine Human Nature with Circumspection enough, may discover several Handles, whereof the * *Six* Senses afford one apiece, beside a great Number that are screwed to the Passions, and some few riveted to the Intellect. Among these last, *Curiosity* is one, and of all others, affords the firmest Grasp; *Curiosity*, that Spur in the side, that Bridle in the Mouth, that

* *Including Scaliger's.*

Ring

Ring in the Nofe, of a lazy, an impatient, and a grunting Reader. By this *Handle* it is, that an Author fhould feize upon his Readers; which as foon as he hath once compaft, all Refiftance and ftruggling are in vain; and they become his Prifoners as clofe as he pleafes, till Wearinefs or Dullnefs force him to let go his Gripe.

AND therefore, I the Author of this miraculous Treatife, having hitherto, beyond Expectation, maintained by the aforefaid *Handle*, a firm Hold upon my gentle Readers; it is with great Reluctance, that I am at length compelled to remit my Grafp; leaving them in the Perufal of what remains, to that natural *Ofcitancy* inherent in the Tribe. I can only affure thee, Courteous Reader, for both our Comforts, that my Concern is altogether equal to thine, for my Unhappinefs in lofing, or miflaying among my Papers the remaining Part of thefe Memoirs; which confifted of Accidents, Turns, and Adventures, both New, Agreeable, and Surprizing; and therefore, calculated in all due Points, to the delicate Tafte of this our noble Age. But, alas,

alas, with my utmost Endeavours, I have been able only to retain a few of the Heads. Under which, there was a full Account, how *Peter* got a *Protection* out of the *King's-Bench*; And of a Reconcilement between *Jack* and Him, upon a Design they had in a certain *rainy Night*, to trepan Brother *Martin* into a *Spunging-house*, and there strip him to the Skin. How *Martin*, with much ado, shew'd them both a fair pair of Heels. How a *new Warrant* came out against *Peter*; upon which, how *Jack* left him in the lurch, *stole his Protection, and made use of it himself.* How *Jack*'s Tatters came into Fashion in *Court* and *City*: How *he got upon a great Horse, and eat Custard.* But the Particulars of all these, with several others, which have now slid out of my Memory, are lost beyond all Hopes of Recovery. For, which Misfortune, leaving my Readers to condole with each other, as far as they shall find it to agree with their several Constitutions; but conjuring them by all the Friendship that hath passed between Us, from the Title-Page to this, not to proceed so far as to injure their Healths, for an Accident past Remedy; I now go on to the Ceremonial Part of an accomplish'd plish'd Writer, and therefore, by a Courtly *Modern*, least of all others to be omitted.

The CONCLUSION.

GOING *too long* is a Cause of Abortion as effectual, tho' not so frequent, as *Going too short*; and holds true especially in the *Labors* of the Brain. Well fare the Heart of that Noble * *Jesuit*, who first adventur'd to confess in Print, that Books must be suited to their several Seasons, like Dress, and Dyet, and Diversions: And better fare our noble Nation, for refining upon this, among other *French* Modes. I am living fast, to see the Time, when a *Book* that misses its Tide, shall be neglected, as the *Moon* by Day, or like *Mackarel* a Week after the Season. No Man hath more nicely observed our Climat, than the Bookseller who bought the Copy of this Work; He knows to a Tittle, what Subjects will best go off in a *dry*

* *Per: a' Orleans.*

Year,

Year, and which it is proper to expose foremost, when the Weather-glass is fallen to *much Rain*. When he had seen this Treatise, and consulted his *Almanack* upon it; he gave me to understand, that he had maturely considered the two Principal Things, which were the *Bulk* and the *Subject*; and found, it would never *take*, but after a long Vacation, and then only, in case it should happen to be a hard Year for Turnips. Upon which I desired to know, *considering my urgent Necessities*, what he thought might be acceptable this Month. He lookt *Westward*, and said, *I don't we shall have a Fit of bad Weather; However, if you could prepare some pretty little* Banter (*but not in Verse*) *or a small Treatise upon the* —— *it would run like Wild-Fire. But,* if it hold up, *I have already hired an Author to write something against Dr.* B—tl—y, *which, I am sure, will turn to Account.*

At length we agreed upon this Expedient; That when a Customer comes for one of these, and desires in Confidence to know the Author; he will tell him very privately, as a Friend, naming which ever of the Wits shall happen to be be that Week in the Vogue; and if *Durfy*'s laſt Play ſhould be in Courſe, I had as lieve he may be the Perſon as *Congreve*. This I mention, becauſe I am wonderfully well acquainted with the preſent Reliſh of Courteous Readers; and have often obſerved, with ſingular Pleaſure, that a *Fly* driven from a *Honey-pot*, will immediately, with very good Appetite alight, and finiſh his Meal on an *Excrement*.

I have one Word to ſay upon the Subject of *Profound Writers*, who are grown very numerous of late; And, I know very well, the judicious World is reſolved to liſt me in that Number. I conceive therefore, as to the Buſineſs of being *Profound*, that it is with *Writers*, as with *Wells*; A Perſon with good Eyes may ſee to the Bottom of the deepeſt, provided any *Water* be there; and, that often, when there is nothing in the world at the Bottom, beſides *Dryneſs* and *Dirt*, tho' it be but a Yard and half under Ground, it ſhall paſs, however, for wondrous *Deep*, upon no wiſer a Reaſon than becauſe it is wondrous *Dark*.

I am now trying an Experiment very frequent among Modern Authors; which is, to *write upon Nothing*: When the Subject is utterly exhausted, to let the Pen still move on; by some called, the Ghost of Wit, delighting to walk after the Death of its Body. And to say the Truth, there seems to be no Part of Knowledge in fewer Hands, than That of Discerning *when to have Done*. By the Time that an Author has writ out a Book, he and his Readers are become old Acquaintance, and grow very loath to part: So that I have sometimes known it to be in Writing, as in Visiting, where the Ceremony of taking Leave, has employ'd more Time than the whole Conversation before. The Conclusion of a Treatise, resembles the Conclusion of Human Life, which hath sometimes been compared to the End of a Feast; where few are satisfied to depart, *ut plenus vitæ conviva:* For Men will sit down after the fullest Meal, tho' it be only to *doze*, or to *sleep* out the rest of the Day. But, in this latter, I differ extreamly from other Writers; and shall be too proud, if by all my Labors, I can have any ways contributed

buted to the *Repose* of Mankind, in Times so turbulent and unquiet as these. Neither, do I think such an Employment so very alien from the Office of a *Wit*, as some would suppose. For among a very polite Nation in * *Greece*, there were the *same* Temples built and consecrated to *Sleep* and the *Muses*, between which two Deities, they believed the strictest Friendship was established.

* *Trœzenii. Pausan. l. 2.*

I have one concluding Favour, to request of my Reader; that he will not expect to be equally diverted and informed by every Line, or every Page of this Discourse; but give some Allowance to the Author's Spleen, and short Fits or Intervals of Dullness, as well as his own; And lay it seriously to his Conscience, whether, if he were walking the Streets, in dirty Weather, or a rainy Day; he would allow it fair Dealing in Folks at their Ease from a Window, to Critick his Gate, and ridicule his Dress at such a Juncture.

IN my Disposure of Employments of the Brain, I have thought fit to make

Invention

Invention the *Master*, and to give *Method* and *Reason*, the Office of its *Lacquays*. The Cause of this Distribution was, from observing it my peculiar Case, to be often under a Temptation of being *Witty*, upon Occasions, where I could be neither *Wise* nor *Sound*, nor any thing to the Matter in hand. And, I am too much a Servant of the *Modern* Way, to neglect any such Opportunities, what ever Pains or Improprieties I may be at, to introduce them. For, I have observed, that from a laborious Collection of Seven Hundred Thirty Eight *Flowers*, and *shining Hints* of the best *Modern* Authors, digested with great Reading, into my Book of *Common-Places*; I have not been able after five Years to draw, hook, or force into common Conversation, any more than a Dozen. Of which Dozen, the one Moiety failed of Success, by being dropt among unsuitable Company; and the other cost me so many Strains, and Traps, and *Ambages* to introduce, that I at length resolved to give it over. Now, this Disappointment, (to discover a Secret) I must own, gave me the first Hint of setting up for an *Author*; and, I have since found among some particular
Friends,

Friends, that it is become a very general Complaint, and has produced the same Effects upon many others. For, I have remarked many a *towardly Word*, to be wholly neglected or despised in *Discourse*, which hath passed very smoothly, with some Consideration and Esteem, after its Preferment and Sanction in *Print*. But, now, since by the Liberty and Encouragement of the Press, I am grown absolute Master of the Occasions and Opportunities, to expose the Talents I have acquired; I already discover, that the *Issues* of my *Observanda* begin to grow too large for the *Receipts*. Therefore, I shall here pause awhile, till I find, by feeling the World's Pulse, and my own, that it will be of absolute Necessity for us both, to resume my Pen.

F I N I S.

A
Full and True Account
OF THE
BATTEL
Fought laſt *FRIDAY*,

Between the

Antient and the *Modern*
BOOKS
IN
St. *JAMES*'s
LIBRARY.

LONDON:
Printed in the Year, MDCCIV.

THE BOOKSELLER TO THE READER.

THE following Difcourfe, as it is unqueftionably of the fame Author, fo it feems to have been written about the fame Time with the former, I mean, the Year 1697. when the famous Difpute was on Foot, about *Antient and Modern Learning*. The Controverfy took its Rife from an Effay of Sir *William Temple's*, upon that Subject; which was anfwer'd by *W. Wotton*, B. D. with an Appendix by Dr *Bently*, endeavouring to deftroy the Credit of *Æfop* and *Phalaris*, for Authors, whom, Sir *William Temple* had in the Effay before mentioned, highly commended. In that Appendix, the Doctor falls hard upon a new Edition of *Phalaris*, put out by the Honorable *Charles Boyle*, (now *Earl* of *Orrery*) to which, Mr. *Boyle* replyed

The Bookseller *to the* Reader.

replyed at large, with great Learning and Wit; and the Doctor, voluminously, rejoyned. In this Dispute, the Town highly resented to see a Person of Sir *William Temple*'s Character and Merits, roughly used by the two reverend Gentlemen aforesaid, and without any manner of Provocation. At length, there appearing no End of the Quarrel, our Author tells us, that the BOOKS in St. *James*'s Library, looking upon themselves as Parties principally concerned, took up the Controversy, and came to a decisive Battel; But, the Manuscript, by the Injury of Fortune, or Weather, being in several Places imperfect, we cannot learn to which side the Victory fell.

I must warn the Reader, to beware of applying to Persons what is here meant, only of Books in the most literal Sense. So, when *Virgil* is mentioned, we are not to understand the Person of a famous Poet, call'd by that Name, but only certain Sheets of Paper, bound up in Leather, containing in Print, the Works of the said Poet, and so of the rest.

THE

THE PREFACE OF THE AUTHOR.

SATYR is a sort of Glass, wherein Beholders do generally discover every body's Face but their own; which is the chief Reason for that kind of Reception it meets in the World, and that so very few are offended with it. But if it should happen otherwise, the Danger is not great; and, I have learned from long Experience, never to apprehend Mischief from those Understandings, I have been able to provoke; For, Anger and Fury, though they add Strengh to the Sinews of the Body, yet are found to relax those of the Mind, and to render all its Efforts feeble and impotent.

The Preface of the Author.

There is a Brain *that will endure but one* Scumming: *Let the Owner gather it with Discretion, and manage his little Stock with Husbandry; but of all things, let him beware of bringing it under the* Lash *of his* Betters; *because, That will make it all bubble up into Impertinence, and he will find no new Supply:* Wit, *without Knowledge, being a Sort of* Cream, *which gathers in a Night to the Top, and by a skilful Hand, may be soon whipt into* Froth; *but once scumm'd away, what appears underneath will be fit for nothing, but to be thrown to the Hogs.*

A Full and True

ACCOUNT

OF THE

BATTEL

Fought laſt FRIDAY, &c.

WHOEVER examins with due Circumſpection into the * Annual Records of *Time*, will find it remarked, that *War is the Child of Pride*, and *Pride the Daughter of Riches*; The former of which Aſſertions may be ſoon granted; but one cannot ſo eaſily ſubſcribe to the latter: For *Pride* is nearly related to Beggary and *Want*, either by Father or Mother, and ſometimes by both; And, to ſpeak naturally, it very ſeldom happens among Men

* *Riches produceth Pride; Pride is War's Ground,* &c. Vid. Ephem. de Mary Clarke; opt. Edit.

Men to fall out, when all have enough: Invasions usually travelling from *North* to *South*, that is to say, from Poverty upon Plenty. The most antient and natural Grounds of Quarrels, are *Lust* and *Avarice*; which, tho' we may allow to be Brethren or collateral Branches of *Pride*, are certainly the Issues of *Want*. For, to speak in the Phrase of Writers upon the Politicks, we may observe in the Republick of *Dogs*, (which in its Original seems to be an Institution of the *Many*) that the whole State is ever in the profoundest Peace, after a full Meal; and, that Civil Broils arise among them, when it happens for one great *Bone* to be seized on by some *leading Dog*, who either divides it among the *Few*, and then it falls to an *Oligarchy*, or keeps it to Himself, and then it runs up to a *Tyranny*. The same Reasoning also, holds Place among them, in those Dissensions we behold upon a Turgescency in any of their Females. For, the Right of Possession lying in common (it being impossible to establish a Property in so delicate a Case) Jealousies and Suspicions do so abound, that the whole Commonwealth of that Street, is reduced to a manifest *State of War*, of every *Citizen* against

gainst every *Citizen*; till some One of more Courage, Conduct, or Fortune than the rest, seizes and enjoys the Prize: Upon which, naturally arises Plenty of Heartburning, and Envy, and Snarling against the *Happy Dog*. Again, if we look upon any of these Republicks engaged in a Forein War, either of Invasion or Defence, we shall find, the same Reasoning will serve, as to the Grounds and Occasions of each; and, that *Poverty*, or *Want*, in some Degree or other, (whether Real, or in Opinion, which makes no Alteration in the Case) has a great Share, as well as *Pride*, on the Part of the Aggressor.

Now, whoever will please to take this Scheme, and either reduce or adapt it to an Intellectual State, or Commonwealth of Learning, will soon discover the first Ground of Disagreement between the two great Parties at this Time in Arms; and may form just Conclusions upon the Merits of either Cause. But the Issue or Events of this War are not so easy to conjecture at: For, the present Quarrel is so enflamed by the warm Heads of either Faction, and the Pretensions *somewhere or other* so exorbitant, as not to admit the least Overtures of Accommodation: This Quarrel firſt began (as I have heard it affirmed by an old Dweller in the Neighbourhood) about a ſmall Spot of Ground, *lying* and *being*, upon one of the two Tops of the Hill *Parnaſſus*; the higheſt and largeſt of which, had it ſeems, been time out of Mind, in quiet Poſſeſſion of certain Tenants, call'd the *Antients*; And the other was held by the *Moderns*. But, theſe diſliking their preſent Station, ſent certain Ambaſſadors to the *Antients*, complaining of a great Nuiſſance, how, the Height of that Part of *Parnaſſus*, quite ſpoiled the Proſpect of theirs, eſpecially towards the *Eaſt*; and therefore, to avoid a War, offered them the Choice of this Alternative; either that the *Antients* would pleaſe to remove themſelves and their Effects down to the lower Summity, which the *Moderns* would graciouſly ſurrender to them, and advance in their Place; or elſe, that the ſaid *Antients* will give leave to the *Moderns* to come with Shovels and Mattocks, and level the ſaid Hill, as low as they ſhall think it convenient. To which, the *Antients* made Anſwer; How little they expected ſuch a Meſſage as this, from a Colony, whom they had admitted

out

out of their own Free Grace, to so near a Neighbourhood. That, as to their own Seat, they were *Aborigines* of it, and therefore, to talk with Them of a Removal or Surrender, was a Language they did not understand. That, if the Height of the Hill, on their side, shortned the Prospect of the *Moderns*, it was a Disadvantage they could not help, but desired them to consider, whether that Injury (if it be any) were not largely recompenced by the *Shade* and *Shelter* it afforded them. That, as to levelling or digging down, it was either Folly or Ignorance to propose it, if they did, or did not know, how that side of the Hill was an entire Rock, which would break their Tools and Hearts, without any Damage to it self. That they would therefore advise the *Moderns*, rather to raise their own side of the Hill, than dream of pulling down that of the *Antients*, to the former of which, they would not only give Licenſe, but also largely contribute. All this was rejected by the *Moderns*, with much Indignation, who still insisted upon one of the two Expedients; And so this Difference broke out into a long and obstinate War, maintained on the one Part, by Re-
                                                solution,

solution, and by the Courage of certain Leaders and Allies: but, on the other, by the greatness of their Number, upon all Defeats, affording continual Recruits. In this Quarrel, whole Rivulets of *Ink* have been exhausted, and the Virulence of both Parties enormously augmented. Now, it must here be understood, that *Ink* is the great missive Weapon, in all Battels of the *Learned*, which, convey'd thro' a sort of Engine, call'd a *Quill*, infinite Numbers of these are darted at the Enemy, by the Valiant on each side, with equal Skill and Violence, as if it were an Engagement of *Porcupines*. This malignant Liquor was compounded by the Engineer, who invented it, of two Ingredients, which are *Gall* and *Copperas*, by its Bitterness and Venom, to *Suit* in some Degree, as well as to *Foment* the Genius of the Combatants. And as the *Grecians*, after an Engagement, when they could not *agree* about the Victory, were wont to set up Trophies on both sides, the beaten Party being content to be at the same Expence, to keep it self in Countenance (A laudable and antient Custom, happily revived of late, in the Art of War) so the *Learned*, after a sharp and bloody
Dispute,

Difpute, do on both fides hang out their Trophies too, which ever comes by the worft. Thefe Trophies have largely infcribed on them the Merits of the Caufe; a full impartial Account of fuch a Battel, and how the Victory fell clearly to the Party that fet them up. They are known to the World under feveral Names; As, *Difputes, Arguments, Rejoynders, Brief Confiderations, Anfwers, Replys, Remarks, Reflections, Objections, Confutations.* For a very few Days they are fixt up in all Publick Places, either by themfelves or their * Reprefentatives, for Paffengers to gaze at: From whence the chiefeft and largeft are removed to certain Magazines, they call, *Libraries*, there to remain in a Quarter, purpofely affign'd them, and from thenceforth, begin to to be called, *Books of Controverfy.*

* *Their TitlePages.*

IN thefe Books, is wonderfully inftilled and preferved, the Spirit of each Warrior, while he is alive; and after his Death, his Soul tranfmigrates there, to inform them. This, at leaft, is the more common Opinion; But, I believe, it is with Libraries, as with other Cemetaries, where
fome

some Philosophers affirm, that a certain Spirit, which they call, *Brutum hominis*, hovers over the Monument, till the Body is corrupted, and turns to *Dust*, or to *Worms*; but then vanishes or dissolves: So, we may say, a restless Spirit haunts over every *Book*, till *Dust* or *Worms* have seized upon it; which to some, may happen in a few Days, but to others, later; And therefore, *Books* of Controversy, being of all others, haunted by the most disorderly Spirits, have always been confined in a separate Lodge from the rest; and for fear of mutual Violence against each other, it was thought Prudent by our Ancestors, to bind them to the Peace with strong Iron Chains. Of which Invention, the original Occasion was this: When the Works of *Scotus* first came out, they were carried to a certain great Library, and had Lodgings appointed them; But this Author was no sooner settled, than he went to visit his Master *Aristotle*, and there both concerted together to seize *Plato* by main Force, and turn him out from his antient Station among the *Divines*, where he had peaceably dwelt near Eight Hundred Years. The Attempt succeeded, and the two Usurpers have reigned ever

ever since in his stead: But to maintain Quiet for the future, it was decreed, that all *Polemicks* of the larger Size, should be held fast with a Chain.

BY this Expedient, the publick Peace of Libraries might certainly have been preserved, if a new Species of controversial Books had not arose of late Years, instinct with a most malignant Spirit, from the War above-mentioned, between the *Learned*, about the higher Summity of *Parnassus*.

WHEN these Books were first admitted into the publick Libraries, I remember to have said upon Occasion, to several Persons concerned, how I was sure, they would create Broyls whereever they came, unless a World of Care were taken; And therefore, I advised, that the Champions of each side should be coupled together, or otherwise mixt, that like the blending of contrary Poysons, their Malignity might be employ'd among themselves. And it seems, I was neither an ill Prophet, nor an ill Counsellor; for it was nothing else but the Neglect of this Caution, which gave Occasion

casion to the terrible Fight that happened on *Friday* last, between the *Antient* and *Modern Books* in the *King's Library*. Now, because the Talk of this Battel is so fresh in every body's Mouth, and the Expectation of the Town so great to be informed in the Particulars; I, being possessed of all Qualifications requisite in an *Historian*, and retained by neither Party; have resolved to comply with the urgent *Importunity of my Friends*, by writing down a full impartial Account thereof.

THE *Guardian* of the *Regal Library*, a Person of great Valor, but chiefly renowned for his *Humanity*, had been a fierce Champion for the *Moderns*, and in an Engagement upon *Parnassus*, had vowed, with his own Hands, to knock down two of the *Antient* Chiefs, who guarded a small Pass on the superior Rock; but endeavouring to climb up, was cruelly obstructed by his own unhappy Weight, and tendency towards his Center; a Quality, to which, those of the *Modern* Party, are extream subject; For, being light-headed, they have in Speculation, a wonderful Agility, and conceive nothing too high for them to mount; but in reducing

cing to Practice, discover a mighty Pressure about their Posteriors and their Heels. Having thus failed in his Design, the disappointed Champion bore a cruel Rancour to the *Antients*, which he resolved to gratify, by shewing all Marks of his Favor to the *Books* of their Adversaries, and lodging them in the fairest Apartments; when at the same time, whatever *Book* had the Boldness to own it self for an Advocate of the *Antients*, was buried alive in some obscure Corner, and threatned upon the least Displeasure, to be turned out of Doors. Besides, it so happened, that about this time, there was a strange Confusion of Place among all the *Books* in the Library; for which several Reasons were assigned. Some imputed it to a great Heap of *learned Dust*, which a perverse Wind blew off from a Shelf of *Moderns*, into the *Keeper*'s Eyes. Others affirmed, He had a Humor to pick the *Worms* out of the *Schoolmen*, and swallow them fresh and fasting; whereof some fell upon his *Spleen*, and some climbed up into his Head, to the great Perturbation of both. And lastly, others maintained, that by walking much in
the

the dark about the Library, he had quite loſt the Situation of it out of his Head; And therefore, in replacing his *Books,* he was apt to miſtake, and clap *des-Cartes* next to *Ariſtotle*; Poor *Plato* had got between *Hobs* and the *Seven Wiſe Maſters,* and *Virgil* was hemm'd in with *Dryden* on one ſide, and *Withers* on the other.

MEAN while, thoſe *Books* that were Advocates for the *Moderns,* choſe out one from among them, to make a Progreſs thro' the whole Library, examine the Number and Strength of their Party, and concert their Affairs. This Meſſenger performed all things very induſtriouſly, and brought back with him a Liſt of their Forces, in all Fifty Thouſand, conſiſting chiefly of *light Horſe, heavy-armed Foot,* and *Mercenaries*; Whereof the *Foot* were in general but ſorrily armed, and worſe clad; Their *Horſes* large, but extreamly out of Caſe and Heart; However, ſome few by trading among the *Antients,* had furniſht themſelves tolerably enough.

WHILE Things were in this Ferment; *Diſcord* grew extreamly high, hot Words paſſed

passed on both sides, and ill Blood was plentifully bred. Here a solitary *Antient*, squeez'd up among a whole Shelf of *Moderns*, offered fairly to dispute the Case, and to prove by manifest Reasons, that the Priority was due to them, from long Possession, and in regard of their Prudence, Antiquity, and above all, their great Merits towards the *Moderns*. But these denied the Premises, and seemed very much to wonder, how the *Antients* could pretend to insist upon their Antiquity, when it was so plain (if they went to that) that the *Moderns* were much the more * *Antient* of the two. As for any Obligations they owed to the *Antients*, they renounced them all. *'Tis true*, said they, *we are informed, some few of our Party have been so mean to borrow their Subsistence from You*; But *the rest, infinitely the greater Number (and especially, we* French *and* English *) were so far from stooping to so base an Example, that there never passed, till this very hour, six Words between us*. For, our Horses *are of our own breeding*, our Arms *of our own forging, and our* Cloaths *of our own cutting out and sowing*. Plato was by chance upon the next Shelf, and observ-

* *According to the Modern Paradox.*

ving thofe that fpoke to be in the ragged Plight, mentioned a while ago; their *Jades* lean and foundred, their *Weapons* of rotten Wood, their *Armor* rufty, and nothing but Raggs underneath; he laughed loud, and in his pleafant way, fwore, *By G—, he believed them.*

Now, the *Moderns* had not proceeded in their late Negotiation, with Secrecy enough to efcape the Notice of the Enemy. For, thofe Advocates, who had begun the Quarrel, by fetting firft on Foot the Difpute of Precedency, talkt fo loud of coming to a Battel, that *Temple* happened to over-hear them, and gave immediate Intelligence to the *Antients*; who thereupon drew up their fcattered Troops together, refolving to act upon the defenfive; Upon which, feveral of the *Moderns* fled over to their Party, and among the reft, *Temple* himfelf. This *Temple* having been educated and long converfed among the *Antients*, was, of all the *Moderns*, their greateft Favorite, and became their greateft Champion.

Things were at this Crifis, when a material Accident fell out. For, upon the higheft

The BATTEL.

highest Corner of a large Window, there dwelt a certain *Spider*, swollen up to the first Magnitude, by the Destruction of infinite Numbers of *Flies*, whose Spoils lay scattered before the Gates of his Palace, like human Bones before the Cave of some Giant. The Avenues to his Castle were guarded with Turn-pikes, and Palissadoes, all after the *Modern* way of Fortification. After you had passed several Courts, you came to the Center, wherein you might behold the *Constable* himself in his own Lodgings, which had Windows fronting to each Avenue, and Ports to sally out upon all Occasions of Prey or Defence. In this Mansion, he had for some Time dwelt in Peace and Plenty, without Danger to his *Person* by *Swallows* from above, or to his *Palace* by *Brooms* from below: When it was the Pleasure of Fortune to conduct thither a wandring *Bee*, to whose Curiosity a broken Pane in the Glass had discovered it self; and in he went; where expatiating a while, he at last happened to alight upon one of the outward Walls of the *Spider*'s Cittadel; which yielding to the unequal Weight, sunk down to the very Foundation. Thrice he endeavoured to force his Passage, and Thrice the Center shook.

shook. The *Spider* within, feeling the terrible Convulsion, supposed at first, that *Nature* was approaching to her final Dissolution; or else, that *Beelzebub* with all his Legions, was come to revenge the Death of many thousand of his Subjects, whom this Enemy had slain and devoured. However, he at length valiantly resolved to issue forth, and meet his Fate. Mean while, the *Bee* had acquitted himself of his Toils, and posted securely at some distance, was employed in cleansing his Wings, and disengaging them from the ragged Remnants of the Cobweb. By this Time the *Spider* was adventured out, when beholding the Chasms, and Ruins, and Dilapidations of his Fortress, he was very near at his Wit's end, he stormed and swore like a Mad-man, and swelled till he was ready to burst. At length, casting his Eye upon the *Bee*, and wisely gathering Causes from Events, (for they knew each other by Sight) *A Plague split you,* said he, *for a giddy Son of a Whore; Is it you, with a Vengeance, that have made this Litter here? Could you not look before you, and be d ——n d? Do you think I have nothing else to do (in the Devil's Name) but to Mend and Repair after your Arse? Good Words,*

Words, Friend, said the *Bee*; (having now pruned himſelf, and being diſpoſed to drole) *I'll give you my Hand and Word to come near your Kennel no more*; I was never in ſuch a confounded Pickle ſince I was born. *Sirrah,* replyed the *Spider, if it were not for breaking an old Cuſtom in our Family, never to ſtir abroad againſt an Enemy, I ſhould come and teach you better Manners. I pray, have Patience,* ſaid the *Bee, or you will ſpend your Subſtance, and for ought I ſee, you may ſtand in need of it all, towards the Repair of your Houſe. Rogue, Rogue,* replyed the *Spider, yet, methinks you ſhould have more Reſpect to a Perſon, whom all the World allows to be ſo much your Betters. By my Troth,* ſaid the *Bee, the Compariſon will amount to a very good Jeſt, and you will do me a Favor, to let me know the Reaſons, that all the World is pleaſed to uſe in ſo hopeful a Diſpute.* At this, the *Spider* having ſwelled himſelf into the Size and Poſture of a Diſputant, began his Argument in the true Spirit of Controverſy, with a Reſolution to be heartily ſcurrilous and angry, to urge *on* his own Reaſons, without the leaſt Regard to the Anſwers or Objections of his Oppoſite; and fully predetermined in his Mind againſt all Conviction

Not to disparage my self, said he, *by the Comparison with such a Rascal; What art thou, but a Vagabond without House or Home, without Stock or Inheritance? Born to no Possession of your own, but a Pair of Wings, and a Drone-Pipe. Your Livelihood is an universal Plunder upon Nature; a Freebooter over Fields and Gardens; and for the sake of Stealing, will rob a Nettle as readily as a Violet. Whereas I am a domestick Animal, furnisht with a native Stock within my self. This large Castle (to shew my Improvements in the Mathematicks) is all built with my own Hands, and the Materials extracted altogether out of my own Person.*

I am glad, answered the *Bee, to hear you grant at least, that I am come honestly by my Wings and my Voice, for then, it seems, I am obliged to Heaven alone for my Flights and my Musick; and Providence would never have bestowed me two such Gifts, without designing them for the noblest Ends. I visit, indeed, all the Flowers and Blossoms of the Field and the Garden, but whatever I collect from thence, enriches my self, without the least Injury to their Beauty, their Smell, or their Taste. Now, for you, and your Skill*

in

in *Architecture*, and other *Mathematicks*, I have little to fay: In that Building of yours, there might, for ought I know, have been Labor and Method enough, but by woful Experience for us both, 'tis too plain, the Materials are naught, and I hope, you will henceforth take Warning, and confider Duration and Matter, as well as Method and Art. You boaft, indeed, of being obliged to no other Creature, but of drawing, and fpinning out all from your felf; That is to fay, if we may judge of the Liquor in the Veffel by what iffues out, You poffefs a good plentiful Store of Dirt and Poifon in your Breaft; And, tho' I would by no means, leffen or difparage your genuine Stock of either, yet, I doubt, you are fomewhat obliged for an Encreafe of both, to a little forein Affiftance. Your inherent Portion of Dirt, does not fail of Acquifitions, by Sweepings exhaled from below: and one Infect furnifhes you with a fhare of Poifon to deftroy another. So that in fhort, the Queftion comes all to this; Whether is the nobler Being of the two, That which by a lazy Contemplation of four Inches round; by an over-weening Pride, which feeding and engendring on it felf, turns all into Excrement and Venom; producing nothing at laft, but Fly-bane and a Cobweb:

The BATTEL.

Cobweb: Or That, which, by an universal Range, with long search, much Study, true Judgment, and Distinction of Things, brings home Honey and Wax.

THIS Dispute was managed with such Eagerness, Clamor, and Warmth, that the two Parties of *Books* in Arms below, stood Silent a while, waiting in Suspense what would be the Issue; which was not long undetermined: For the *Bee* grown impatient at so much loss of Time, fled strait away to a Bed of Roses, without looking for a Reply; and left the *Spider* like an Orator, collected in himself, and just prepared to burst out.

IT happened upon this Emergency, that *Æsop* broke silence first. He had been of late most barbarously treated by a strange Effect of the *Regent's Humanity*, who had tore off his Title-page, sorely defaced one half of his Leaves, and chained him fast among a Shelf of *Moderns*. Where soon discovering how high the Quarrel was like to proceed, He tried all his Arts, and turned himself to a thousand Forms: At length in the borrowed Shape of an
Ass,

Ass, the *Regent* miſtook Him for a *Modern*; by which means, he had Time and Opportunity to eſcape to the *Antients,* juſt when the *Spider* and the *Bee* were entring into their Conteſt; to which He gave His Attention with a World of Pleaſure; and when it was ended, ſwore in the loudeſt Key, that in all his Life, he had never known two Caſes ſo parallel and adapt to each other, as That in the Window, and This upon the Shelves. *The Diſputants,* ſaid he, *have admirably managed the Diſpute between them, have taken in the full Strength of all that is to be ſaid on both ſides, and exhauſted the Subſtance of every Argument* pro and con. *It is but to adjuſt the Reaſonings of both to the preſent Quarrel, then to compare and apply the Labors and Fruits of each, as the* Bee *has learnedly deduced them; and we ſhall find the Concluſions fall plain and cloſe upon the* Moderns *and* Us. *For, pray Gentlemen, was ever any thing ſo* Modern *as the* Spider *in his Air, his Turns, and his Paradoxes? He argues in the Behalf of* You *his Brethren, and Himſelf, with many Boaſtings of his native Stock, and great Genius; that he Spins and Spits wholly from himſelf, and ſcorns to own any Obligation or Aſſiſtance from*

from without. Then he displays to you his great Skill in Architecture, and Improvement in the Mathematicks. To all this, the Bee, as an Advocate, retained by us the Antients, thinks fit to Answer; *That if one may judge of the great Genius or Inventions of the Moderns, by what they have produced, you will hardly have Countenance to bear you out in boasting of either. Erect your Schemes with as much Method and Skill as you please; yet, if the Materials be nothing but Dirt, spun out of your own Entrails (the Guts of Modern Brains) the Edifice will conclude at last in a* Cobweb: *The Duration of which, like that of other* Spiders Webs, *may be imputed to their being forgotten, or neglected, or hid in a Corner. For any Thing else of Genuine, that the* Moderns *may pretend to, I cannot recollect; unless it be a large Vein of Wrangling and Satyr, much of a Nature and Substance with the* Spider's Poison; *which, however, they pretend to spit wholly out of themselves, is improved by the same Arts, by feeding upon the* Infects *and* Vermin *of the Age. As for* Us, the Antients; *We are content with the* Bee, *to pretend to Nothing of our own, beyond our* Wings and our Voice: *that is to say, our* Flights *and our* Language; *For the rest, whatever we*

have

have got, has been by infinite Labor, and search, and ranging thro' every Corner of Nature: The Difference is, that *instead of* Dirt *and* Poison, *we have rather chose to fill our Hives with* Honey *and* Wax, *thus furnishing Mankind with the two Noblest of Things, which are* Sweetness *and* Light.

'T is wonderful to conceive The Tumult arisen among the Books, upon the Close of this long Descant of *Æsop*; Both Parties took the Hint, and heightened their Animosities so on a sudden, that they resolved it should come to a Battel. Immediately, the two main Bodies withdrew under their several Ensigns, to the further Parts of the Library, and there entred into Cabals, and consults upon the present Emergency. The *Moderns* were in very warm Debates upon the Choice of their *Leaders*, and nothing less than the Fear impending from their Enemies, could have kept them from Mutinies upon this Occasion. The Difference was greatest among the *Horse*, where every private *Trooper* pretended to the chief Command, from *Tasso* and *Milton*, to *Dryden* and *Withers*. The *Light-Horse* were Commanded by *Cowly*, and *Despreaux*. There, came

the

the *Bowmen* under their valiant Leaders, *Des-Cartes, Gassendi,* and *Hobbes,* whose Strength was such, that they could shoot their Arrows beyond the *Atmosphere,* never to fall down again, but turn like that of *Evander,* into *Meteors,* or like the *Canon-ball* into *Stars. Paracelsus* brought a *Squadron* of *Stink-Pot-Flingers* from the snowy Mountains of *Rhætia.* There, came a vast Body of *Dragoons,* of different Nations, under the leading of *Hervey,* their great *Aga :* Part armed with *Scythes,* the Weapons of Death ; Part with *Launces* and long *Knives,* all steept in *Poison*; Part shot *Bullets* of a most malignant Nature, and used *white Powder* which infallibly killed without *Report.* There, came several Bodies of *heavy-armed Foot,* all *Mercenaries,* under the Ensigns of *Guiccardine, Davila, Polydore Virgil, Buchanan, Mariana, Cambden,* and others. The *Engineers* were commanded by *Regiomantus* and *Wilkins.* The rest were a confused Multitude, led by *Scotus, Aquinas,* and *Bellarmine* ; of mighty Bulk and Stature, but without either Arms, Courage, or Discipline. In the last Place, came infinite Swarms of *Calones,* a disorderly Rout led by *L'strange*; Rogues and Raggamuffins, that follow the Camp for nothing

nothing but the Plunder; All without *Coats* to cover them.

THE Army of the *Antients* was much fewer in Number; *Homer* led the *Horse*, and *Pindar* the *Light-Horse*; *Euclid* was chief *Engineer*: *Plato* and *Aristotle* commanded the *Bow-men*, *Herodotus* and *Livy* the *Foot*, *Hippocrates* the *Dragoons*. The *Allies* led by *Vossius* and *Temple* brought up the Rear.

ALL things violently tending to a decisive Battel; *Fame*, who much frequented, and had a large Apartment formerly assigned her in the *Regal Library*, fled up strait to *Jupiter*, to whom she delivered a faithful Account of all that passed between the two Parties below. (For, among the Gods, she always tells Truth.) *Jove* in great Concern, convokes a Council in the *Milky-Way*. The Senate assembled, he declares the Occasion of convening them; a bloody Battel just impendent between two mighty Armies of *Antient* and *Modern* Creatures, call'd *Books*, wherein the Celestial Interest was but too deeply concerned. *Momus*, the Patron of the *Moderns*, made an excellent Speech in
the

The BATTEL.

their Favor, which was anſwered by *Pallas* the Protectreſs of the *Antients.* The Aſſembly was divided in their Affections; when *Jupiter* commanded the Book of Fate to be laid before Him. Immediately were brought by *Mercury,* three large Volumes in Folio, containing Memoirs of all Things paſt, preſent, and to come. The Claſps were of Silver, double gilt; the Covers, of Celeſtial Turky-leather, and the Paper, ſuch as here on Earth might almoſt paſs for Vellum. *Jupiter* having ſilently read the Decree, would communicate the Import to none, but preſently ſhut up the Book.

WITHOUT the Doors of this Aſſembly, there attended a vaſt Number of light, nimble Gods, menial Servants to *Jupiter:* Theſe are his miniſtring Inſtruments in all Affairs below. They travel in a Caravan, more or leſs together, and are faſtened to each other like a Link of Gally-ſlaves, by a light Chain, which paſſes from them to *Jupiter's* great Toe: And yet in receiving or delivering a Meſſage, they may never approach above the loweſt Step of his Throne, where he and they whiſper to each other thro' a long hollow Trunk. Theſe

The BATTEL.

These Deities are call'd by mortal Men, *Accidents,* or *Events;* but the Gods call them, *Second Causes. Jupiter* having delivered his Message to a certain Number of these Divinities, they flew immediately down to the Pinnacle of the Regal Library, and consulting a few Minutes, entered unseen, and disposed the Parties according to their Orders.

MEAN while, *Momus* fearing the worst, and calling to mind an antient Prophecy, which bore no very good Face to his Children the *Moderns;* bent his Flight to the Region of a malignant Deity, call'd *Criticism.* She dwelt on the Top of a snowy Mountain in *Nova Zembla;* there *Momus* found her extended in her Den, upon the Spoils of numberless Volumes half devoured. At her right Hand sat *Ignorance,* her Father and Husband, blind with Age; at her left, *Pride* her Mother, dressing her up in the Scraps of Paper herself had torn. There, was *Opinion* her Sister, light of Foot, hoodwinkt, and headstrong, yet giddy and perpetually turning. About her play'd her Children, *Noise* and *Impudence, Dullness* and *Vanity, Positiveness, Pedantry,* and *Ill-Manners.* The

Goddess

Goddess herself had Claws like a Cat; Her Head, and Ears, and Voice, resembled those of an *Ass*; Her Teeth fallen out before; Her Eyes turned inward, as if she lookt only upon herself: Her Diet was the overflowing of her own Gall: Her *Spleen* was so large, as to stand prominent like a Dug of the first Rate, nor wanted Excrescencies in form of Teats, at which a Crew of ugly Monsters were greedily sucking; and, what is wonderful to conceive, the Bulk of Spleen encreased faster than the Sucking could diminish it. *Goddess,* said *Momus, can you sit idly here, while our devout Worshippers, the* Moderns, *are this Minute entring into a cruel Battel, and, perhaps, now lying under the Swords of their Enemies; Who then hereafter, will ever sacrifice, or build Altars to our Divinities? Haste therefore to the* British *Isle, and, if possible, prevent their Destruction, while I make Factions among the Gods, and gain them over to our Party.*

Momus having thus delivered himself, staid not for an Answer, but left the Goddess to her own Resentments; Up she rose in a Rage, and as it is the Form upon such Occasions, began a Soliloquy.

'Tis

The BATTEL.

'*Tis I* (said she) *who give Wisdom to Infants and Idiots*; *By Me, Children grow wiser than their Parents*. *By Me, Beaus become Politicians*; *and* School-Boys, *Judges of Philosophy*. *By Me, Sophisters debate, and conclude upon the Depths of Knowledge*; *and Coffee-house Wits instinct by Me, can correct an Author's Style, and display his minutest Errors, without understanding a Syllable of his Matter or his Language. By Me, Stripplings spend their Judgment, as they do their Estate, before it comes into their Hands. 'Tis I, who have deposed Wit and Knowledge from their Empire over* Poetry, *and advanced my self in their stead. And shall a few* upstart Antients *dare to oppose me?* ⸺ *But, come, my aged Parents, and you, my Children dear, and Thou my beauteous Sister; let us ascend my Chariot, and haste to assist our devout* Moderns, *who are now sacrificing to us a* Hecatomb, *as I perceive by that grateful Smell, which from thence reaches my Nostrils*.

THE Goddess and her Train having Mounted the Chariot, which was drawn by *tame Geese*, flew over infinite Regions, shedding her Influence in due Places, till at length, she arrived at her beloved I-

Island of *Britain*; But in hovering over its *Metropolis*, what Blessings did she not let fall upon her Seminaries of *Gresham* and *Covent-Garden*? And now she reacht the fatal Plain of St. *James*'s Library, at what time the two Armies were upon the Point to engage; where entring with all her Caravan, unseen, and landing upon a Case of Shelves, now desart, but once inhabited by a Colony of *Virtuoso's*, she staid a while to observe the Posture of both Armies.

BUT here, the tender Cares of a Mother began to fill her Thoughts, and move in her Breast. For, at the Head of a Troop of *Modern Bow-men*, she cast her Eyes upon her Son *W--tt--n*; to whom the Fates had assigned a very short Thread. *W--tt--n.* a young Hero, whom an unknown Father of mortal Race, begot by stollen Embraces with this Goddess. He was the Darling of his Mother, above all her Children, and she resolved to go and comfort Him. But first, according to the good old Custom of Deities, she cast about to change her Shape; for fear the Divinity of her Countenance might dazzle his mortal Sight, and over-charge the rest

rest of his Senses. She therefore gathered up her Person into an *Octavo* Compass: her Body grew white, and arid, and split in Pieces with Dryness; the thick turned into Pastboard, and the thin into Paper, upon which, her Parents and Children, artfully strowed a Black Juice, or Decoction of Gall and Soot, in form of Letters; her Head, and Voice, and Spleen, kept their primitive Form, and that which before, was a Cover of Skin, did still continue so. In which Guise, she march'd on towards the *Moderns*, undistinguishable in Shape and Dress from the *Divine B--ntl--y, W--tt--n's* dearest Friend. *Brave W--tt--n,* said the Goddess, *Why do our Troops stand idle here, to spend their present Vigor, and Opportunity of the Day? Away, let us haste to the Generals, and advise to give the Onset immediately.* Having spoke thus, she took the ugliest of her Monsters, full glutted from her Spleen, and flung it invisibly into his Mouth; which flying strait up into his Head, squeez'd out his Eye-balls, gave him a distorted Look, and half overturned his Brain. Then she privately ordered two of her beloved Children, *Dullness* and *Ill-Manners,* closely to attend his Person in all Encounters.

Having thus accoutred him, she vanished in a Mist, and the *Hero* perceived it was the Goddess, his Mother.

THE destined Hour of Fate, being now arrived, the Fight began; whereof, before I dare adventure to make a particular Description, I must, after the Example of other Authors, petition for a hundred Tongues, and Mouths, and Hands, and Pens; which would all be too little to perform so immense a Work. Say, Goddess, that presidest over History; who it was that first advanced in the Field of Battel. *Paracelsus*, at the Head of his *Dragoons*, observing *Galen* in the adverse Wing, darted his Javelin with a mighty Force, which the brave *Antient* received upon his Shield, the Point breaking in the second fold. * * * * *

Hic pauca desunt. * * * * * * *
* * * * * * *

They bore the wounded *Aga*, on their Shields to his Chariot * * * * * *
* * * * * * *
Desunt nonnulla. * * * * * * *
* * * * * * * *
* * * * * * *

THEN

The BATTEL.

THEN, *Aristotle* observing *Bacon* advance with a furious Mien, drew his Bow to the Head, and let fly his Arrow, which miss'd the valiant *Modern*, and went hizzing over his Head; but *Des-Cartes* it hit: The Steel Point quickly found a *Defect* in his *Head-piece*; it pierced the Leather and the Pastboard, and went in at his right Eye. The Torture of the Pain, whirled the valiant *Bow-man* round, till Death, like a Star of superior Influence, drew him into his own *Vortex*. * * *
* * * * * * * * *
* * * * * * * * * *   *Ingens hiatus hic in MS.*
* * * * * * * * * *
* * * * * * * * * * *

when *Homer* appeared at the Head of the Cavalry, mounted on a furious Horse, with Difficulty managed by the Rider himself, but which no other Mortal durst approach; He rode among the Enemies Ranks, and bore down all before him. Say, Goddess, whom he slew first, and whom he slew last. First, *Gondibert* advanced against Him, clad in heavy Armor, and mounted on a staid sober Gelding, not so famed for his Speed as his Docility in kneeling, whenever his Rider would mount or alight. He had made a Vow to *Pallas*, that he would never leave the Field, till he had spoiled *Homer* of his Armor; Madman, who had never once *seen* the Wearer, nor understood his Strength. Him *Homer* overthrew, Horse and Man to the Ground, there to be trampled and choak'd in the Dirt. Then, with a long Spear, he slew *Denham*, a stout *Modern*, who from his Father's side, derived his Lineage from *Apollo*, but his Mother was of mortal Race. He fell, and bit the Earth. The Celestial Part *Apollo* took, and made it a Star, but the Terrestrial lay wallowing upon the Ground. Then *Homer* slew *W—sl—y* with a kick of his Horse's heel; He took *Perrault* by mighty Force out of his Saddle, then hurl'd him at *Fontenelle*, with the same Blow dashing out both their Brains.

* *Vid. Homer.*

On the left Wing of the Horse, *Virgil* appeared in shining Armor, compleatly fitted to his Body; He was mounted on a dapple grey Steed, the slowness of whose Pace, was an Effect of the highest Mettle and Vigor. He cast his Eye on the adverse Wing, with desire to find an Object worthy

worthy of his Valor: When, behold, upon a forrel Gelding of a monstrous Size, appeared a Foe, issuing from among the thickest of the Enemy's Squadrons; But his Speed was less than his Noise; for his Horse, old and lean, spent the Dregs of his Strength in a high Trot, which tho' it made slow Advances, yet caused a loud Clashing of his Armor, terrible to hear. The two Cavaliers had now approach'd within the Throw of a Lance, when the Stranger desired a Parley, and lifting up the Vizard of his Helmet, a Face hardly appeared from within, which after a Pause, was known for that of the renowned *Dryden*. The brave *Antient* suddenly started, as one possess'd with Surprize and Disappointment together: For, the Helmet was nine times too large for the Head, which appeared Situate far in the hinder Part, even like the Lady in a Lobster, or like a Mouse under a Canopy of State, or like a shrivled Beau from within the Pent-house of a modern Perewig: And the Voice was suited to the Visage, sounding weak and remote. *Dryden* in a long Harangue soothed up the good *Antient*, called him *Father*, and by a large deduction of Genealogies, made it plainly appear,

pear, that they were nearly related. Then, he humbly proposed an exchange of Armor, as a lasting Mark of Hospitality between them. *Virgil* consented, (For the Goddess *Diffidence*, came unseen, and cast a Mist before his Eyes) tho' his was of Gold, and cost a hundred Beeves, the others but of rusty Iron. However, this glittering Armor became the *Modern* yet worse than his Own. Then, they agreed to exchange Horses, but when it came to the Tryal, *Dryden* was afraid, and utterly unable to mount. * * * * * *

Vid. Homer.

After hiatus in MS.
* * * * * * * *
* * * * * * * *

* * * * * * *Lucan* appeared upon a fiery Horse, of admirable Shape, but head-strong, bearing the Rider where he list, over the Field; he made a mighty Slaughter among the Enemy's Horse; which Destruction to stop, *Bl--ckm--re*, a famous *Modern* (but one of the *Mercenaries*) strenuously opposed himself; and darted a Javelin, with a strong Hand, which falling short of its Mark, struck deep in the Earth. Then *Lucan* threw a Lance, but *Æsculapius* came unseen, and turn'd off the Point. *Brave* Modern, *said* Lucan,

Lucan, *I perceive some God protects you, for never did my Arm so deceive me before: But, what Mortal can contend with a God? Therefore, let us Fight no longer, but present Gifts to each other.* Lucan then bestowed the *Modern* a Pair of *Spurs*, and *Bl--ckm--re* gave *Lucan* a *Bridle*. *Pauca desunt.*

* * * * * * * * * * *

Creech; But, the Goddess *Dulness* took a Cloud, formed into the Shape of *Horace*, armed and mounted, and placed it in a flying Posture before Him. Glad was the Cavalier, to begin a Combat with a flying Foe, and pursued the Image, threatning loud; till at last, it led him to the peaceful Bower of his Father *Ogleby*, by whom he was disarmed, and assigned to his Repose.

THEN *Pindar* flew ——, and ——, and *Oldham*, and —— and *Afra* the *Amazon* light of foot; Never advancing in a direct Line, but wheeling with incredible Agility and Force, he made a terrible Slaughter among the Enemy's *Light-Horse*. Him, when *Cowley* observed, his generous Heart burnt within him, and he advanced against the fierce *Antient*, imitating
his

his Address, and Pace, and Career, as well as the Vigor of his Horse, and his own Skill would allow. When the two Cavaliers had approach'd within the Length of three Javelins; first *Cowley* threw a Lance, which miss'd *Pindar*, and passing into the Enemy's Ranks, fell ineffectual to the Ground. Then *Pindar* darted a Javelin, so large and weighty, that scarce a dozen *Cavaliers*, as *Cavaliers* are in our degenerate Days, could raise it from the Ground: yet he threw it with Ease, and it went by an unerring Hand, singing thro' the Air; Nor could the *Modern* have avoided present Death, if he had not luckily opposed the Shield that had been given Him by *Venus*. And now, both Hero's drew their Swords, but the *Modern* was so agast and disordered, that he knew not where he was; His Shield dropt from his Hands: thrice he fled, and thrice he could not escape; at last he turned, and lifting up his Hands, in the posture of a Suppliant, *God-like* Pindar, said he, *spare my Life, and possess my Horse with these Arms; beside the Ransom which my Friends will give, when they hear I am alive, and your Prisoner.* Dog, said Pindar, *Let your Ransom stay with your Friends;*

But

The BATTEL.

But your Carcafs shall be left for the Fowls *of the* Air, *and the* Beasts *of the* Field. With that, he raised his Sword, and with a mighty Stroak, cleft the wretched *Modern* in twain, the Sword pursuing the Blow; And one half lay panting on the Ground, to be trod in pieces by the Horses Feet, the other half was born by the frighted Steed thro' the Field. This *Venus* took, and wash'd it seven times in *Ambrosia*, then struck it thrice with a Sprig of *Amarant*; upon which, the Leather grew round and soft, the Leaves turned into Feathers, and being gilded before, continued gilded still; so it became a *Dove*, and She harness'd it to her Chariot.
* * * * * * *
* * * * * * * * *Hiatus valde deflendus in MS.*
* * * * * * * *
* * * * * * * * *

Day being far spent, and the numerous Forces of the *Moderns*, half inclining to a Retreat, there issued forth from a Squadron of their *heavy-armed Foot*, a Captain, whose Name was *B--ntl--y*; in Person, the most deformed of all the *Moderns*; Tall, but without Shape or Comeliness; *The Episode of* B-ntl-y *and* W-tt-n.

liness; Large, but without Strength or Proportion. His Armor was patch'd up of a thousand incoherent Pieces; and the Sound of it, as he march'd, was loud and dry, like that made by the Fall of a Sheet of Lead, which an *Etesian* Wind blows suddenly down from the Roof of some Steeple. His Helmet was of old rusty Iron, but the Vizard was Brass, which tainted by his Breath, corrupted into Copperas, nor wanted Gall, from the same Fountain; so, that whenever provoked by Anger or Labor, an atramentous Quality, of most malignant Nature, was seen to distil from his Lips. In his right Hand he grasp'd a Flail, and (that he might never be unprovided of an *offensive* Weapon) a Vessel full of *Ordure* in his left: Thus, compleatly arm'd, he advanced with a slow and heavy Pace, where the *Modern* Chiefs were holding a Consult upon the Sum of Things; who, as he came onwards, laugh'd to behold his crooked Leg, and hump Shoulder, which his Boot and Armor, vainly endeavouring to hide, were forced to comply with, and expose. The Generals made use of him for his Talent of Railing; which kept within Government, proved frequently of great

great Service to their Cause, but at other times did more Mischief than Good; For, at the least Touch of Offence, and often without any at all, he would, like a wounded Elephant, convert it against his Leaders. Such, at this Juncture, was the Disposition of *B--ntl--y*, grieved to see the Enemy prevail, and dissatisfied with every Body's Conduct, but his own. He humbly gave the *Modern* Generals to understand, that he conceived, with great Submission, they were all a Pack of *Rogues*, and *Fools*, and *Sons of Whores*, and *d—mn'd Cowards*, and *confounded Loggerheads*, and *illiterate Whelps*, and *nonsensical Scoundrels*; That if Himself had been constituted General, those *presumptuous Dogs*, the *Antients*, would long before this, have been beaten out of the Field. *You*, said he, *sit here idle, but, when I, or any other valiant* Modern, *kill an Enemy, you are sure to seize the Spoil. But, I will not march one Foot against the Foe, till you all Swear to me, that, whomever I take or kill, his Arms I shall quietly possess.* *B--ntl--y* having spoke thus, *Scaliger* bestowing him a sower Look; *Miscreant* Prater, said he, *Eloquent only in thine own Eyes, Thou rail:st*

Vid. Homer. de Thersite.

railest without *Wit, or Truth, or Discretion. The Malignity of thy Temper perverteth Nature; Thy* Learning *makes thee more* Barbarous, *thy Study of* Humanity, *more* Inhuman; *Thy* Converse *amongst* Poets, *more* groveling, miry, *and* dull. *All Arts of* civilizing *others, render thee* rude *and* untractable; Courts *have taught thee* ill Manners, *and* polite Conversation *has finish'd thee a* Pedant. *Besides, a greater Coward burtheneth not the Army. But never despond, I pass my Word, whatever Spoil thou takest, shall certainly be thy own; tho', I hope, that vile Carcass will first become a Prey to Kites and Worms.*

B--NTL--Y durst not reply; but half choaked with Spleen and Rage, withdrew, in full Resolution of performing some great Achievement. With him, for his Aid and Companion, he took his beloved *W--tt--n;* resolving by Policy or Surprize, to attempt some neglected Quarter of the *Antients* Army. They began their March over Carcasses of their slaughtered Friends; then to the Right of their own Forces: then wheeled Northward, till they came to *Aldrovandus's* Tomb, which they pass'd on the side of the declining Sun. And now

now they arrived with Fear, towards the Enemy's Out-guards; looking about, if haply, they might spy the Quarters of the Wounded, or some straggling Sleepers, unarm'd and remote from the rest. As when two *Mungrel Curs*, whom *native Greediness*, and *domestick Want*, provoke, and joyn in Partnership, though fearful, nightly to invade the Folds of some rich Grazier; They, with Tails depress'd, and lolling Tongues, creep soft and slow; mean while, the conscious *Moon*, now in her *Zenith*, on their guilty Heads, darts perpendicular Rays; Nor dare they bark, though much provok'd at her refulgent Visage, whether seen in Puddle by Reflection, or in Sphear direct; but one surveys the Region round, while t'other scouts the Plain, if haply, to discover at distance from the Flock, some *Carcass* half devoured, the Refuse of gorg'd Wolves, or ominous Ravens. So march'd this lovely, loving Pair of Friends, nor with less Fear and Circumspection; when, at distance, they might perceive two shining Suits of Armor, hanging upon an Oak, and the Owners not far off, in a profound Sleep. The two Friends drew Lots, and the pursuing of this Adventure, fell to *B--ntl--y*;

On

On he went, and in his Van *Confusion*
and *Amaze*; while *Horror* and *Affright*
brought up the Rear. As he came near;
Behold two Hero's of the *Antients* Army,
Phalaris and *Æsop*, lay fast asleep: *B--ntl--y*
would fain have dispatch'd them both,
and stealing close, aimed his Flail at
Phalaris's Breast. But then, the Goddess
Affright interposing, caught the *Modern* in
her icy Arms, and dragg'd him from the
Danger she foresaw; For both the dormant Hero's happened to turn at the
same Instant, tho' soundly Sleeping, and
busy in a Dream. For *Phalaris* was just
that Minute dreaming, how a most vile
Poetaster had lampoon'd him, and how
he had got him roaring in his *Bull*. And
Æsop dream'd, that as he and the *Antient* Chiefs were lying on the Ground, a
Wild Ass broke loose, ran about trampling and kicking, and dunging in their
Faces *B--ntl--y*, leaving the two Hero's asleep, seized on both their Armors,
and withdrew in quest of his Darling
W--tt--n.

H E, in the mean time, had wandred
long in search of some Enterprise, till at
length, he arrived at a small *Rivulet*, that
issued

issued from a Fountain hard by, call'd in the Language of mortal Men, *Helicon*. Here he stopt, and, parch'd with thirst, resolved to allay it in this limpid Stream. Thrice, with profane Hands, he essay'd to raise the Water to his Lips, and thrice it slipt all thro' his Fingers. Then he stoop'd prone on his Breast, but e'er his Mouth had kiss'd the liquid Crystal, *Apollo* came, and, in the Channel, held his *Shield* betwixt the *Modern* and the Fountain, so that he drew up nothing but *Mud*. For, altho' no Fountain on Earth can compare with the Clearness of *Helicon*, yet there lyes at Bottom, a thick sediment of *Slime* and *Mud*; For, so *Apollo* begg'd of *Jupiter*, as a Punishment to those who durst attempt to taste it with unhallowed Lips, and for a Lesson to all, not to *draw too deep*, or *far from the Spring*.

At the Fountain Head, *W---tt---n* discerned two Hero's; The one he could not distinguish, but the other was soon known for *Temple*, General of the *Allies* to the *Antients*. His Back was turned, and he was employ'd in Drinking large Draughts in his Helmet, from the Fountain, where he had withdrawn himself

himself to rest from the Toils of the War. *W--tt--n*, observing him, with quaking Knees, and trembling Hands, spoke thus to Himself: *Oh, that I could kill this Destroyer of our Army, what Renown should I purchase among the Chiefs! But to issue out against Him, Man for Man, Shield against Shield, and Launce against Launce; what* Modern *of us dare? For, he fights like a God, and* Pallas *or* Apollo *are ever at his Elbow. But, Oh,* Mother! *if what* Fame *reports, be true, that I am the Son of so great a Goddess, grant me to Hit* Temple *with this Launce, that the Stroak may send Him to Hell, and that I may return in Safety and Triumph, laden with his Spoils.* The first Part of his Prayer, the Gods granted, at the Intercession of His *Mother* and of *Momus*; but the rest, by a perverse Wind sent from *Fate*, was scattered in the Air. Then *W--tt--n* grasp'd his Launce, and brandishing it thrice over his head, darted it with all his Might, the *Goddess*, his *Mother*, at the same time, adding Strength to his Arm. Away the Launce went hizzing, and reach'd even to the Belt of the averted *Antient*, upon which, lightly grazing, it fell to the Ground. *Temple* neither felt the Weapon touch him,

Vid. Homer.

nor

nor heard it fall; And *W--tt--n*, might have escaped to his Army, with the Honor of having remitted his Launce against so great a Leader, unrevenged; But, *Apollo* enraged, that a Javelin, flung by the Assistance of so foul a *Goddess*, should pollute his Fountain, put on the shape of ———, and softly came to young *Boyl,* who then accompanied *Temple:* He pointed, first to the Launce, then to the distant *Modern* that flung it, and commanded the young Hero to take immediate Revenge. *Boyl,* clad in a suit of Armor which had been *given him by all the Gods,* immediately advanced against the trembling Foe, who now fled before him. As a young Lion, in the *Lybian Plains,* or *Araby Desart,* sent by his aged Sire to hunt for Prey, or Health, or Exercise; He scours along, wishing to meet some Tiger from the Mountains, or a furious Boar: If Chance, a *Wild Ass,* with Brayings importune, affronts his Ear, the generous Beast, though loathing to distain his Claws with Blood so vile, yet much provok'd at the offensive Noise; which *Echo,* foolish Nymph, like her *ill-judging Sex,* repeats much louder, and with more Delight than *Philomela*'s Song: He vindicates the Honor of

the

the Foreſt, and hunts the noiſy, long-ear'd Animal. So *W--tt--n* fled, ſo *Boyl* purſued. But *W--tt--n* heavy-arm'd, and ſlow of foot, began to ſlack his Courſe; when his Lover *B- ntl--y* appeared, returning laden with the Spoils of the two ſleeping *Antients*. *Boyl* obſerved him well, and ſoon diſcovering the Helmet and Shield of *Phalaris*, his Friend, both which he had lately with his own Hands, new poliſh'd and gilded; Rage ſparkled in His Eyes, and leaving his Purſuit after *W--tt--n*, he furiouſhly ruſh'd on againſt this new Approacher. Fain would he be revenged on both; but both now fled different Ways: And as a Woman in a little Houſe, that gets a painful Livelihood by Spinning; if chance her *Geeſe* be ſcattered o'er the Common, ſhe courſes round the Plain from ſide to ſide, compelling here and there, the Straglers to the Flock; They cackle loud, and flutter o'er the Champian. So *Boyl* purſued, ſo fled this Pair of Friends: finding at length, their Flight was vain, they bravely joyn'd, and drew themſelves in *Phalanx*. Firſt, *B--ntl--y* threw a Spear with all his Force, hoping to pierce the Enemy's Breaſt; But *Pallas* came unſeen,
and

Vid. Homer.

and in the Air took off the Point, and clap'd on one of *Lead*, which after a dead Bang againſt the Enemy's Shield, fell blunted to the Ground. Then *Boyl*, obſerving well his Time, took a Launce of wondrous Length and ſharpneſs; and as this Pair of Friends compacted ſtood cloſe Side to Side, he wheel'd him to the right, and with unuſual Force, darted the Weapon. *B--ntl--y* ſaw his Fate approach, and flanking down his Arms, cloſe to his Ribs, hoping to ſave his Body; in went the Point, paſſing through Arm and Side, nor ſtopt, or ſpent its Force, till it had alſo pierc'd the valiant *W--tt--n*, who going to ſuſtain his dying Friend, ſhared his Fate. As, when a skilful Cook has trufs'd a Brace of *Woodcocks*, He, with Iron Scewer, pierces the tender Sides of both, their Legs and Wings cloſe pinion'd to their Ribs; So was this pair of Friends transfix'd, till down they fell, joyn'd in their Lives, joyn'd in their Deaths; ſo cloſely joyn'd, that *Charon* will miſtake them both for one, and waft them over *Styx* for half his Fare. Farewel, beloved, loving Pair; Few Equals have you left behind: And happy and immortal ſhall you be, if all

all my Wit and Eloquence can make you.

And, now * * * * * *
* * * * * * * * * *
* * * * * * * * * *
* * * * *Desunt cætera.*

FINIS.

A DISCOURSE

Concerning the

Mechanical Operation

OF THE

SPIRIT.

IN A

LETTER

To a FRIEND.

A

FRAGMEMT.

LONDON:
Printed in the Year, MDCCIV.

THE BOOKSELLER's Advertisement.

THE following Discourse came into my Hands perfect and entire. But there being several Things in it, which the present Age would not very well bear, I kept it by me some Years resolving it should never see the Light. At length, by the Advice and Assistance of a judicious Friend, I retrench'd those Parts that might give most Offence, and have now ventured to publish the Remainder; Concerning the Author, I am wholly ignorant; neither can I conjecture, whether it be the same with That of the two foregoing Pieces, the Original having been sent me at a different Time, and in a different Hand. The Learned Reader will better determine; to whose Judgment I entirely submit it.

A DISCOURSE

Concerning the

Mechanical Operation

OF THE

SPIRIT, &c.

For T. H. *Esquire, at His Chambers in the Academy of the* Beaux Esprits *in* New-Holland.

SIR,

IT is now a good while, since I have had in my Head, something, not only very material, but absolutely necessary to my Health, that the World should be informed in. For, to tell you a Secret, I am able to *contain* it no longer. However, I have been perplexed for some time

time, to resolve what would be the most proper Form to send it abroad in. To which End, I have three Days been coursing thro' *Westminster-Hall*, and St. *Paul's Church-Yard*, and *Fleet-street*, to peruse *Titles*; and, I do not find any which holds so general a Vogue, as that of, *A Letter to a Friend*: Nothing is more common, than to meet with long Epistles, addressed to Persons and Places, where, at first thinking, one would be apt to imagine it, not altogether so Necessary or Convenient; Such as, *a Neighbour at next Door, a mortal Enemy, a perfect Stranger*, or *a Person of Quality in the Clouds*; and these upon Subjects, in appearance, the least proper for Conveyance by the Post; as, *long Schemes in Philosophy*; *dark and wonderful Mysteries of State*; *Laborious Dissertations in Criticism and Philosophy, Advice to Parliaments*, and the like.

Now, Sir, to proceed after the Method in present Wear. (For, let me say what I will to the contrary, I am afraid you will publish this *Letter*, as soon as ever it comes to your Hands;) I desire you will be my Witness to the World, how careless and sudden a Scribble it has been; That it was

was but Yesterday, when You and I began accidentally to fall into Discourse on this Matter: That I was not very well, when we parted; That the Post is in such haste, I have had no manner of Time to digest it into Order, or correct the Style; And if any other Modern Excuses, for Haste and Negligence, shall occur to you in Reading, I beg you to insert them, faithfully promising they shall be thankfully acknowledged.

PRAY, Sir, in Your next Letter to the *Iroquois Virtuosi*, do me the Favor to present my humble Service to that illustrious Body, and assure them, I shall send an Account of those *Phænomena*, as soon as we can determine them at *Gresham*.

I have not had a Line from the *Litterati* of *Tobinambou*, these three last Ordinaries.

AND now, Sir, having dispatch'd what I had to say of Forms, or of Business, let me intreat, you will suffer me to proceed upon my Subject; and to pardon me, if I make no further Use of the Epistolary Style, till I come to conclude.

SECT.

SECT. I.

'TIS recorded of *Mahomet*, that upon a Visit he was going to pay in *Paradise*, he had an Offer of several Vehicles to conduct him upwards; as fiery Chariots, wing'd Horses, and celestial Sedans; but he refused them all, and would be born to Heaven upon nothing but his *Ass*. Now, this Inclination of *Mahomet*, as singular as it seems, hath been since taken up by a great Number of devout *Christians*; and doubtless, with very good Reason. For, since That *Arabian* is known to have borrowed a Moiety of his Religious System from the *Christian* Faith; it is but just he should pay Reprisals to such as would Challenge them; wherein the good People of *England*, to do them all Right, have not been backward. For, tho' there is not any other Nation in the World, so plentifully provided with Carriages for that Journey, either as to Safety or Ease; yet there are abundance of us, who will not be satisfied with any other Machine, beside this of *Mahomet*.

For my own part, I muſt confeſs to bear a very ſingular Reſpect to this Animal, by whom I take human Nature to be moſt admirably held forth in all its Qualities as well as Operations: And therefore, whatever in my ſmall Reading, occurs, concerning this our Fellow Creature, I do never fail to ſet it down, by way of Common-place; and when I have occaſion to write upon Human Reaſon, Politicks, Eloquence, or Knowledge; I lay my *Memorandums* before me, and inſert them with a wonderful Facility of Application. However, among all the Qualifications, aſcribed to this diſtinguiſh'd Brute, by Antient or Modern Authors; I cannot remember this Talent, of bearing his Rider to Heaven, has been recorded for a Part of his Character, except in the two Examples mentioned already; Therefore, I conceive the Methods of this Art, to be a Point of uſeful Knowledge in very few Hands, and which the Learned World would gladly be better informed in. This is what I have undertaken to perform in the following Diſcourſe. For, towards the Operation already mentioned, many peculiar

liar Properties are required, both in the *Rider* and the *Aſs*; which I ſhall endeavour to ſet in as clear a Light as I can.

But, becauſe I am reſolved, by all means, to avoid giving Offence to any Party whatever; I will leave off diſcourſing ſo cloſely to the *Letter* as I have hitherto done, and go on for the future by way of Allegory, though in ſuch a manner, that the judicious Reader, may without much ſtraining, make his Applications as often as he ſhall think fit. Therefore, if you pleaſe, from hence forward, inſtead of the Term, *Aſs*, we ſhall make uſe of, *Gifted*, or, *enlightned Teacher*; And the Word, *Rider*, we will exchange for that of *Fanatick Auditory*, or any other Denomination of the like Import. Having ſettled this weighty Point; the great Subject of Enquiry before us, is to examine, by what Methods this *Teacher* arrives at his *Gifts* or *Spirit*, or *Light*; and by what Intercourſe between him and his Aſſembly, it is cultivated and ſupported.

In

IN all my Writings, I have had constant Regard to this great End, not to suit and apply them to particular Occasions and Circumstances of Time, of Place, or of Person; but to calculate them for universal Nature, and Mankind in general. And of such Catholick use, I esteem this present Disquisition: For I do not remember any other Temper of Body, or Quality of Mind, wherein all Nations and Ages of the World have so unanimously agreed, as That of a *Fanatick* Strain, or Tincture of *Enthusiasm*; which improved by certain Persons or Societies of Men, and by them practised upon the rest, has been able to produce Revolutions of the greatest Figure in History; as will soon appear to those who know any thing of *Arabia*, *Persia*, *India*, or *China*, of *Morocco* and *Peru*: Farther, it has possessed as great a Power in the Kingdom of Knowledge, where it is hard to assign one Art or Science, which has not annexed to it some *Fanatick* Branch: Such are the *Philosopher's Stone*; * *The Grand Elixir*; *The Planetary Worlds*; *The Squaring of the Circle*; *The Summum bonum*; Utopian Commonwealths;

* Some Writers hold them for the same, others, not.

wealths; with some others of less or subordinate Note: Which all serve for nothing else, but to employ or amuse this Grain of *Enthusiasm*, dealt into every Composition.

But, if this Plant has found a Root in the Fields of *Empire*, and of *Knowledge*, it has fixt deeper, and spread yet farther upon *Holy Ground*. Wherein, though it hath pass'd under the general Name of *Enthusiasm*, and perhaps, arisen from the same Original, yet hath it produced certain Branches of a very different Nature, however often mistaken for each other. The Word in its universal Acceptation, may be defined, *A lifting up of the Soul or its Faculties above Matter*. This Description will hold good in general; but, I am only to understand it, as applied to *Religion*; wherein there are three general Ways of ejaculating the Soul, or transporting it beyond the Sphere of Matter. The first, is the immediate Act of God, and is called, *Prophecy* or *Inspiration*. The second, is the immediate Act of the Devil, and is termed, *Possession*. The third, is the Product of natural Causes, the Effect of strong Imagination, Spleen, violent Anger, Fear, Grief,

Grief, Pain, and the like. These three have been abundantly treated on by Authors, and therefore shall not employ my Enquiry. But, the fourth Method of *Religious Enthusiasm*, or launching out the Soul, as it is purely an Effect of Artifice and *Mechanick Operation*, has been sparingly handled, or not at all, by any Writer; because, though it is an Art of great Antiquity, yet having been confined to few Persons, it long wanted these Advancements and Refinements, which it afterwards met with, since it has grown so Epidemick, and fallen into so many cultivating Hands.

It is therefore upon this *Mechanical Operation of the Spirit*, that I mean to treat, as it is at present performed by our *British Workmen*. I shall deliver to the Reader the Result of many judicious Observations upon the Matter; tracing, as near as I can, the whole Course and Method of this *Trade*, producing parallel instances, and relating certain Discoveries that have luckily fallen in my way.

I have said, that there is one Branch of *Religious Enthusiasm*, which is purely an

Effect

Effect of Nature; whereas, the Part I mean to handle, is wholly an Effect of Art; which however, is inclined to work upon certain Natures and Constitutions, more than others. Besides, there is many an Operation, which in its Original, was purely an Artifice, but through a long Succession of Ages hath grown to be natural. *Hippocrates*, tells us, that among our Ancestors, the *Scythians*, there was a Nation call'd, * *Long-heads*, which at first began by a Custom among Midwives and Nurses, of molding, and squeezing, and bracing up the Heads of Infants; by which means, Nature shut out at one Passage, was forc'd to seek another, and finding roome above, shot upwards, in the Form of a Sugar-Loaf; and being diverted that way, for some Generations, at last found it out of her self, needing no Assistance from the Nurse's Hand. This was the Original, of the *Scythian Long-Heads*, and thus did Custom, from being a second Nature proceed to be a First. To all which, there is something very analogous, among Us, of this Nation, who are the undoubted Posterity of that refined People. For, in the Age of our Fathers, there arose a Generation

* *Macrocephali*.

neration of Men in this Iſland, call'd *Round-heads,* whoſe Race is now ſpread over three Kingdoms, yet in its Beginning, was meerly an Operation of Art, produced by a pair of Cizars, a Squeeze of the Face, and a black Cap. Theſe Heads, thus formed into a perfect Sphere in all Aſſemblies, were moſt expoſed to the view of the Female Sort, which did influence their Conceptions ſo effectually, that Nature, at laſt, took the Hint, and did it of her ſelf; ſo that a *Round-head* has been ever ſince as familiar a Sight among Us, as a *Long-head* among the *Scythians.*

UPON theſe Examples, and others eaſy to produce, I deſire the curious Reader to diſtinguiſh, Firſt, between an Effect grown from *Art* into *Nature,* and one that is natural from its Beginning; Secondly, between an Effect wholly natural, and one which has only a natural Foundation, but where the Superſtructure is entirely Artificial. For, the firſt and the laſt of theſe, I underſtand to come within the Diſtricts of my Subject. And having obtained theſe Allowances, they will ſerve to remove any Objections that may be raiſed hereafter againſt what I ſhall advance.

THE Practitioners of this famous Art, proceed in general upon the following Fundamental; That, *the Corruption of the Senses is the Generation of the Spirit:* Because the *Senses* in Men are so many Avenues to the Fort of *Reason*, which in this Operation is wholly block'd up. All Endeavours must be therefore used, either to divert, bind up, stupify, fluster, and amuse the *Senses*, or else to justle them out of their Stations; and while they are either absent, or otherwise employ'd, or engaged in a Civil War against each other, the *Spirit* enters and performs its Part.

NOW, the usual Methods of managing the Senses upon such Conjunctures, are what I shall be very particular in delivering, as far as it is lawful for me to do: But having had the Honor to be initiated into the Mysteries of every Society, I desire to be excused from divulging any Rites, wherein the *Profane* must have no Part.

BUT here, before I can proceed further, a very dangerous Objection must, if possible, be removed: For, it is positively denied

nied by certain Criticks, that the *Spirit* can by any means be introduced into an Affembly of Modern Saints, the Difparity being fo great in many material Circumftances, between the Primitive Way of Infpiration, and that which is practifed in the prefent Age. This they pretend to prove from the fecond Chapter of the *Acts*, where comparing both, it appears; Firft, that *the Apoftles were gathered together with one accord in one place?* by which is meant, an univerfal Agreement in Opinion, and Form of Worfhip? a Harmony (fay they) fo far from being found between any two Conventicles among Us, that it is in vain to expect it between any two Heads in the fame. Secondly? the *Spirit* inftructed the Apoftles in the Gift of fpeaking feveral Languages; a Knowledge fo remote from our Dealers in this Art, that they neither underftand Propriety of Words, or Phrafes in their own. Laftly, (fay thefe Objectors) The Modern Artifts do utterly exclude all Approaches of the *Spirit*, and bar up its antient Way of entring, by covering themfelves fo clofe, and fo induftrioufly a top. For, they will needs have it as at Point clearly gained, that the *Cloven Tongues* never

never fat upon the Apoftles Heads, while their Hats were on.

Now, the Force of thefe Objections, feems to confift in the different Acceptation of the Word, *Spirit:* which if it be underftood for a fupernatural Affiftance, approaching from without, the Objectors have Reafon, and their Affertions may be allowed; But the *Spirit* we treat of here, proceeding entirely from within, the Argument of thefe Adverfaries is wholly eluded. And upon the fame Account, our Modern Artificers, find it an Expedient of abfolute Neceffity, to cover their Heads as clofe as they can, in order to prevent Perfpiration, than which nothing is obferved to be a greater Spender of Mechanick Light, as we may, perhaps, farther fhew in convenient Place.

To proceed therefore upon the *Phænomenon* of *Spiritual Mechanifm*. It is here to be noted, that in forming and working up the *Spirit*, the Affembly has a confiderable Share, as well as the Preacher; The Method of this *Arcanum*, is as follows. They violently ftrain their Eye-balls inward, half clofing the Lids; Then, as they fit,

fit, they are in a perpetual Motion of *See-saw*, making long Hums at proper Periods, and continuing the Sound at equal Height, chusing their Time in thoſe Intermiſſions, while the Preacher is at Ebb. Neither is this Practice, in any Part of it, ſo ſingular or improbable, as not to be traced in diſtant Regions, from Reading and Obſervation. For, firſt, the * *Jauguis*, or enlightned Saints of *India*, ſee all their Viſions, by Help of an acquired ſtraining and preſſure of the Eyes. Secondly, the Art of *See-ſaw* on a Beam, and ſwinging by Seſſion upon a Cord, in order to raiſe artificial Extaſies, hath been derived to Us, from our † *Scythian* Anceſtors, where it is practiſed at this Day, among the Women. Laſtly, the whole Proceeding, as I have here related it, is performed by the Natives of *Ireland*, with a conſiderable Improvement ; And it is granted, that this noble Nation, hath of all others, admitted fewer Corruptions, and degenerated leaſt from the Purity of the Old *Tartars*. Now, it is uſual for a Knot of *Iriſh*, Men and Women, to abſtract themſelves from Matter, bind up all their Senſes, grow vi-

* *Bernier, Mem. de Mogol.*

† *Guagnini Hiſt. Sarmat.*

ſionary

sionary and spiritual, by Influence of a short Pipe of Tobacco, handed round the Company; each preserving the Smoak in his Mouth, till it comes again to his Turn to take in fresh: At the same Time, there is a Consort of a continued gentle Hum, repeated and renewed by Instinct, as Occasion requires, and they move their Bodies up and down, to a Degree, that sometimes, their Heads and Points lye parallel to the Horizon. Mean while, you may observe their Eyes turn'd up in the Posture of one, who endeavours to keep himself awake; by which, and many other Symptoms among them, it manifestly appears, that the Reasoning Faculties are all suspended and superseded, that Imagination hath usurped the Seat, scattering a thousand Deliriums over the Brain. Returning from this Digression, I shall describe the Methods, by which the *Spirit* approaches. The Eyes being disposed according to Art, at first, you can see nothing, but after a short Pause, a small glimmering Light begins to appear, and dance before you. Then, by frequently moving your Body up and down, you perceive the Vapors to ascend very fast, till you are perfectly dosed and flustred like one
who

who drinks too much in in a Morning. Mean while, the Preacher is also at work; He begins a loud Hum, which pierces you quite thro'; This is immediately returned by the Audience, and you find your self prompted to imitate them, by a meer spontaneous Impulse, without knowing what you do. The *Interstitia* are duly filled up by the Preacher, to prevent too long a Pause, under which the *Spirit* would soon faint and grow languid.

THIS is all I am allowed to discover about the Progress of the *Spirit*, with relation to that Part, which is born by the *Assembly*; But in the Methods of the Preacher, to which I now proceed, I shall be more large and particular.

SECT. II.

YOU will read it very gravely remarked, in the Books of those illustrious and right eloquent Pen-men, the Modern Travellers; that the fundamental Difference in Point of Religion, between the wild *Indians* and Us, lyes in this; that

We

We worship *God*, and They worship the *Devil*. But, there are certain Criticks, who will by no means admit of this Distinction; rather believing, that all Nations whatsoever, adore the *true God*, because, they seem to intend their Devotions to some invisible Power, of greatest *Goodness* and *Ability* to help them, which perhaps, will take in the brightest Attributes ascribed to the Divinity. Others, again, inform us, that those Idolaters adore two *Principles*; the *Principle* of *Good*, and That of *Evil*; Which, indeed, I am apt to look upon as the most universal Notion, that Mankind, by the meer Light of Nature, ever entertained of Things Invisible. How this Idea hath been managed by the *Indians* and Us, and with what Advantage to the Understandings of either, may well deserve to be examined. To me, the difference appears little more than this, That They are put oftner upon their Knees by their *Fears*, and We by our *Desires*; That the former set Them a *Praying*, and Us a *Cursing*. What I applaud them for, is their Discretion, in limiting their Devotions and their Deities to their several Districts, nor every suffering the Liturgy of the *white* God, to cross or interfere with that

that of the *Black*. Not so with Us; who pretending by the Lines and Measures of our Reason, to extend the Dominion of one invisible Power, and contract that of the other, have discovered a gross Ignorance in the Natures of Good and Evil, and most horribly confounded the Frontiers of both. After Men have lifted up the Throne of their Divinity to the *Cælum Empyræum*, adorned him with all such Qualities and Accomplishments, as themselves seem most to value and possess: After they have sunk their *Principle* of *Evil* to the lowest Center, bound him with Chains, loaded him with Curses, furnished him with viler Dispositions than any *Rake-hell* of the Town, accoutred him with Tail, and Horns, and huge Claws, and *Sawcer Eyes*; I laugh aloud, to see these Reasoners, at the same Time, engaged in wise Dispute, about certain Walks and Purliews, whether they are in the Verge of God or the Devil, seriously debating, whether such and such Influences come into Mens Minds, from above or below, or whether certain Passions and Affections are guided by the Evil Spirit, or the Good.

Dum

Dum fas atque nefas exiguo fine libidinum Difcernunt avidi ———

Thus do Men eftablifh a Fellowfhip of *Chrift* with *Belial*, and fuch is the Analogy between *cloven Tongues*, and *cloven Feet*. Of the like Nature, is the Difquifition before us: It hath continued thefe hundred Years an even Debate, whether the Deportment, and the Cant of our *Englifh* Enthufiaftick Preachers, were *Poffeffion*, or *Infpiration*, and a World of Argument has been drained on either Side, perhaps, to little purpofe For, I think, it is in *Life* as in *Tragedy*. where, it is held, a Conviction of great Defect, both in Order and Invention, to interpofe the Affiftance of preternatural Power, without an abfolute and laft Neceffity. However, it is a Sketch of Human Vanity, for every Individual, to imagine the whole Univerfe is interefs'd in his meaneft Concern. If he hath got cleanly over a Kennel, fome Angel, unfeen, defcended on purpofe to help him by the Hand; if he hath knockt his Head againft a Poft, it was the Devil, for his Sins, let loofe from Hell, on purpofe to *buffet* him. Who, that fees a little paultry Mortal, droning

A FRAGMENT.

ning, and dreaming, and drivelling to a Multitude, can think it agreeable to common good Senſe, that either Heaven or Hell ſhould be put to the Trouble of Influence or Inſpection upon what he is about? Therefore, I am reſolved immediately, to weed this Error out of Mankind, by making it clear, that this Myſtery, of venting ſpiritual Gifts, is nothing but a *Trade*, acquired by as much Inſtruction, and maſtered by equal Practice and Application, as others are. This will beſt appear, by deſcribing and deducing the whole Proceſs of the Operation, as variouſly as it hath fallen under my Knowledge or Experience.

* * * * * * * * * * *
* * * * * * *
* * * * * * * *Here the whole Scheme*
* * * * * * * *of ſpiritual Mechaniſm*
* * * * * * * *was deduced and explain-*
* * * * * * * *ed, with an Appearance*
* * * * * * * *of great Reading and Ob-*
* * * * * * * *ſervation; but it was*
* * * * * * * *thought neither Safe nor*
* * * * * * * *Convenient to Print it.*
* * * * * * * * * * *

HERE it may not be amiſs, to add a few Words upon the laudable Practice of
wearing

wearing *quilted Caps*; which is not a Matter of meer Cuftom, Humor, or Fafhion, as fome would pretend, but an Inftitution of great Sagacity and Ufe; thefe, when moiftned with Sweat, ftop all Perfpiration, and by reverberating the Heat, prevent the Spirit from evaporating any way, but at the Mouth; even as a skilful Houfewife, that covers her Still with a wet Clout, for the fame Reafon, and finds the fame Effect. For, it is the Opinion of choice *Virtuofi*, that the Brain is only a Crowd of little Animals, but with Teeth and Claws extremely fharp, and therefore, cling together in the Contexture we behold, like the Picture of *Hobbes*'s *Leviathan*, or like Bees in perpendicular Swarm upon a Tree, or like a Carrion corrupted into Vermin, ftill preferving the Shape and Figure of the Mother Animal. That all Invention is formed by the Morfure of two or more of thefe Animals, upon certain capillary Nerves, which proceed from thence, whereof three Branches fpread into the Tongue, and two into the right Hand. They hold alfo, that thefe Animals are of a Conftitution extremely cold; that their Food is the Air we attract, their Excrement Phlegm; and that what we vulgarly

vulgarly call Rheums, and Colds, and Diſtillations, is nothing elſe but an Epidemical Looſeneſs, to which that little Commonwealth is very ſubject, from the Climate it lyes under. Farther, that nothing leſs than a violent Heat, can diſentangle theſe Creatures from their hamated Station of Life, or give them Vigor and Humor, to imprint the Marks of their little Teeth. That if the Morſure be Hexagonal, it produces Poetry; the Circular gives Eloquence; If the Bite hath been Conical, the Perſon, whoſe Nerve is ſo affected, ſhall be diſpoſed to write upon the Politicks; and ſo of the reſt.

I ſhall now Diſcourſe briefly, by what kind of Practices the Voice is beſt governed, towards the Compoſition and Improvement of the *Spirit*; for, without a competent Skill in tuning and toning each Word, and Syllable, and Letter, to their due Cadence, the whole Operation is incompleat, miſſes entirely of its Effect on the Hearers, and puts the Workman himſelf to continual Pains for new Supplies, without Succeſs. For, it is to be underſtood, that in the Language of the Spirit, *Cant* and *Droning* ſupply

ply the Place of *Senfe* and *Reafon*, in the Language of Men: Becaufe, in Spiritual Harangues, the Difpofition of the Words according to the Art of Grammar, hath not the leaft Ufe, but the Skill and Influence wholly lye in the Choice and Cadence of the Syllables; Even as a difcreet *Compofer*, who in fetting a Song, changes the Words and Order fo often, that he is forced to make it *Nonfenfe*, before he can make it *Mufick*. For this Reafon, it hath been held by fome, that the Art of Canting is ever in greateft Perfection, when managed by *Ignorance:* Which is thought to be enigmatically meant by *Plutarch*, when he tells us, that the beft Mufical Inftruments were made from the Bones of an *Afs*. And the profounder Criticks upon that Paffage, are of Opinion, the Word in its genuine Signification, means no other than a *Jaw-bone:* tho' fome rather think it to have been the *Os facrum*; but in fo nice a Cafe, I fhall not take upon me to decide: The Curious are at Liberty, to *pick* from it whatever they pleafe.

THE

"The firſt Ingredient, towards the Art of Canting, is a competent Share of *Inward Light:* that is to ſay, a large Memory, plentifully fraught with Theological Polyſyllables, and myſterious Texts from wholly Writ, applied and digeſted by thoſe Methods, and Mechanical Operations already related: The Bearers of this *Light,* reſembling *Lanthorns,* compact of Leaves from old *Geneva* Bibles? Which Invention, Sir *H------y E-----n,* during his Mayoralty, of happy Memory, highly approved and advanced; affirming, the Scripture to be now fulfiled, where it ſays, *Thy Word is a Lanthorn to my Feet, and a Light to my Paths.*

Now, the Art of *Canting* conſiſts in skilfully adapting the Voice, to whatever Words the Spirit Delivers, that each may ſtrike the Ears of the Audience, with its moſt ſignificant Cadence. The Force, or Energy of this Eloquence, is not to be found, as among antient Orators, in the Diſpoſition of Words to a Sentence, or the turning of long Periods? but agreeable to the Modern Refinements in Muſick, is taken up wholly in dwelling, and

dilating

dilating upon Syllables and Letters. Thus it is frequent for a single *Vowel* to draw Sighs from a Multitude; and for a whole Assembly of Saints to sob to the Musick of one solitary *Liquid*. But these are Trifles; when even Sounds inarticulate are observed to produce as forcible Effects. A Master Work-man shall *blow his Nose so powerfully*, as to pierce the Hearts of his People, who are disposed to receive the *Excrements* of his Brain with the same Reverence, as the *Issue* of it. Hawking, Spitting, and Belching, the Defects of other Mens Rhetorick, are the Flowers, and Figures, and Ornaments of his. For, the *Spirit* being the same in all, it is of no Import through what Vehicle it is convey'd.

It is a Point of too much Difficulty, to draw the Principles of this famous Art, within the Compass of certain adequate Rules. However, perhaps, I may one day, oblige the World with my Critical Essay upon the Art of *Canting, Philosophically, Physically, and Musically considered*.

BUT

BUT, among all Improvements of the *Spirit*, wherein the Voice hath born a Part, there is none to be compared with That of *conveying the Sound thro' the Nose*, which under the Denomination of *Snuffling*, hath paſſed with ſo great Applauſe in the World. The Originals of this Inſtitution are very dark; but having been initiated into the Myſtery of it, and Leave being given me to publiſh it to the World, I ſhall deliver as direct a Relation as I can.

THIS Art, like many other famous Inventions, owed its Birth, or at leaſt, Improvement and Perfection, to an Effect of Chance, but was eſtabliſhed upon ſolid Reaſons, and hath flouriſhed in this Iſland ever ſince, with great Luſtre. All agree, that it firſt appeared upon the Decay and Diſcouragement of *Bag-pipes*, which having long ſuffered under the Mortal Hatred of the *Brethren*, tottered for a Time, and at laſt fell with *Monarchy*. The Story is thus related.

As yet, *Snuffling* was not; when the following Adventure happened to a *Ban-*

bury Saint. Upon a certain Day, while he was far engaged among the Tabernacles of the *Wicked*, he felt the Outward Man put into odd Commotions, and strangely prick'd forward by the Inward: An Effect very usual among the Modern Inspired. For, some think, that the *Spirit* is apt to feed on the *Flesh*, like hungry Wines upon raw Beef. Others rather believe, there is a perpetual Game at *Leap-Frog* between both; and, sometimes, the *Flesh* is uppermost, and sometimes the *Spirit*; adding, that the former, while it is in the State of a *Rider*, wears huge *Rippon* Spurs, and when it comes to the Turn of being *Bearer*, is wonderfully head-strong, and hard-mouth'd. However it came about, the *Saint* felt his *Vessel* full *extended* in every Part (a very natural Effect of strong *Inspiration*;) and the Place and Time falling out so unluckily, that he could not have the Convenience of Evacuating upwards, by Repetition, Prayer, or Lecture; he was forced to open an inferior Vent. In short, he wrestled with the Flesh so long, that he at length subdued it, coming off with honourable Wounds, all *before*. The Surgeon had now cured the Parts, primarily affected;

A FRAGMENT.

affected; but the Disease driven from its Post, flew up into his Head; And, as a skilful General, valiantly attack'd in his Trenches, and beaten from the Field, by flying Marches withdraws to the Capital City, breaking down the Bridges to prevent Pursuit; So the Disease repell'd from its first Station, fled before the *Rod* of *Hermes*, to the upper Region, there fortifying it self; but, finding the Foe making Attacks at the *Nose*, broke down the *Bridge*, and retired to the *Head* Quarters. Now, the Naturalists observe, that there is in human Noses, an *Idiosyncrasy*, by Virtue of which, the more the Passage is obstructed, the more our Speech delights to go through, as the Musick of a Flagelate is made by the *Stops*. By this Method, the Twang of the Nose, becomes perfectly to resemble the *Snuffle* of a Bag-pipe, and is found to be equally attractive of *British* Ears; whereof the Saint had sudden Experience, by practising his new Faculty with wonderful Success in the Operation of the *Spirit:* For, in a short Time, no Doctrine pass'd for Sound and Orthodox, unless it were delivered thro' the Nose. Strait, every Pastor copy'd after this Original; and those,

those, who could not otherwise arrive to a Perfection, spirited by a noble Zeal, made use of the same Experiment to acquire it. So that, I think, it may be truly affirmed, the *Saints* owe their Empire to the *Snuffling* of one *Animal*, as *Darius* did his, to the *Neighing* of another; and both Stratagems were performed by the same Art; for we read, how the * *Persian Beast* acquired his Faculty, by *covering a Mare* the Day before.

<small>Herodot.</small>

I should now have done, if I were not convinced, that whatever I have yet advanced upon this Subject, is liable to great Exception For, allowing all I have said to be true, it may still be justly objected, that there is in the Commonwealth of *artificial Enthusiasm*, some real Foundation for Art to work upon in the Temper and Complexion of Individuals, which other Mortals seem to want. Observe but the Gesture, the Motion, and the Countenance, of some choice Professors, tho' in their most familiar Actions, you will find them of a different Race from the rest of human Creatures. Remark your commonest Pretender to a

Light

Light *within*, how dark, and dirty, and gloomy he is *without*; As Lanthorns, which the more Light they bear in their Bodies, caſt out ſo much the more Soot, and Smoak, and fuliginous Matter to adhere to the Sides. Liſten, but to their ordinary Talk, and look on the Mouth that delivers it; you will imagine you are hearing ſome antient Oracle, and your Underſtanding will be *equally* informed. Upon theſe, and the like Reaſons, certain Objectors pretend to put it beyond all Doubt, that there muſt be a ſort of preternatural *Spirit*, poſſeſſing the Heads of the Modern Saints; And ſome will have it to be the *Heat* of Zeal, working upon the *Dregs* of Ignorance, as other *Spirits* are produced from *Lees*, by the Force of Fire. Some again think, that when our earthly Tabernacles are diſordered and deſolate, ſhaken and out of Repair, the *Spirit* delights to dwell within them, as Houſes are ſaid to be haunted, when they are forſaken and gone to Decay.

To ſet this Matter in as fair a Light as poſſible; I ſhall here, very briefly, deduce the Hiſtory of *Fanaticiſm*, from the
moſt

most early Ages to the present. And if we are able to fix upon any one material or fundamental Point, wherein the chief Professors have universally agreed, I think we may reasonably lay hold on That, and assign it for the great seed or Principle of the *Spirit*.

THE most early Traces we meet with, of *Fanaticks*, in antient Story, are among the *Egyptians*, who instituted those Rites, known in *Greece* by the Names of *Orgya*, *Panegyres* and *Dionysia*, whether introduced there by *Orpheus* or *Melampus*, we shall not dispute at present, nor in all likelihood, at any time for the future. These Feasts were celebrated to the Honor of *Osyris*, whom the *Grecians* called *Dionysius*, and is the same with *Bacchus*: Which has betray'd some Superficial Readers to imagine, that the whole Business was nothing more than a Set of roaring, scouring Companions, over-charg'd with Wine; But this is a scandalous Mistake foisted on the World, by a sort of Modern Authors, who have too *literal* an Understanding, and, because Antiquity is to be traced *backwards*, do therefore, like *Jews*, begin their Books at the wrong

Diod. Sic. L. 1.
Plut. de Iside & Osiride.

wrong End, as if Learning were a sort of *Conjuring*. These are the Men, who pretend to understand a Book, by scouting thro' the *Index*, as if a traveller should go about to describe a *Palace*, when he had seen nothing but the *Privy*; or like certain Fortune-tellers in *Northern America*, who have a Way of reading a Man's Destiny, by peeping in his *Breech*. For, at the Time of instituting these Mysteries, * there was not one Vine in all *Egypt*, the Natives drinking nothing but *Ale*; which Liquor seems to have been far more antient than Wine, and has the Honor of owing its Invention and Progress, not only to the † *Egyptian Osyris*, but to the *Grecian Bacchus*, who in their famous Expedition, carried the Receipt of it along with them, and gave it to the Nations they visited or subdued. Besides, *Bacchus* himself, was very seldom, or never Drunk: For, it is recorded of him, that he was the first * Inventor of the *Mitre*, which he wore continually on his Head (as the whole Company of *Bacchanals* did) to prevent Vapors and the Head-ach, after hard Drinking. And for this Reason

* *Herod.* L. 2.

† *Diod. Sic.* L. 1. & 3.

* *Id.* L. 4.

(say

(say some *)* the *Scarlet Whore,* when she makes the Kings of the Earth drunk with her cup of Abomination, is always sober her self, tho' she never balks the Glass in her Turn, being, it seems, kept upon her Legs by the Virtue of her *Triple Mitre.* Now, these Feasts were instituted in imitation of the famous Expedition *Osyris* made thro' the World, and of the Company that attended him, where-

<small>See the Particulars in Diod. Sic. L. 1. & 3.</small> of the *Bacchanalian* Ceremonies were so many Types and Symbols. From which Account, it is manifest, that the Fanatick Rites of these *Bacchanals,* cannot be imputed to Intoxications by Wine, but must needs have had a deeper Foundation. What this was, we may gather large Hints from certain Circumstances in the Course of their Mysteries. For, in the first Place, there was in their Processions, an entire *Mixture and Confusion of Sexes;* they affected to ramble about Hills and Desarts: Their Garlands were of *Ivy* and *Vine,* Emblems of Cleaving and Clinging; or of *Fir,* the Parent of *Turpentine.* It is added, that they imitated *Satyrs,* were attended by *Goats,* and rode upon *Asses,* all Companions of great Skill and

Practice

Practice in Affairs of Gallantry. They bore for their Enſigns, certain curious Figures, perch'd upon long Poles, made into to the Shape and Size of the *Virga genitalis*, with its *Appurtenances*, which were ſo many Shadows and Emblems of the whole Myſtery, as well as Trophies ſet up by the Female Conquerors. Laſtly, in a certain Town of *Attica*, the whole Solemnity * ſtript of all its Types, was performed in *puris naturalibus*, the Votaries, not flying in Coveys, but ſorted into Couples. The ſame may be farther conjectured from the Death of *Orpheus*, one of the Inſtitutors of theſe Myſteries, who was torn in Pieces by Women, becauſe he refuſed to † *communicate his Orgyes* to them; which others explained, by telling us, he had *caſtrated* himſelf upon Grief, for the Loſs of his Wife.

* *Dionyſia Brauronia.*

† *Vid. Phœtium in excerptis è Conone.*

OMITTING many others of leſs Note, the next *Fanaticks* we meet with, of any Eminence, were the numerous Sects of *Hereticks* appearing in the five firſt Centuries of the *Chriſtian Æra*, from *Simon Magus* and his Followers, to thoſe of *Eutyches.*

Eutyches. I have collected their Syſtems from infinite Reading, and comparing them with thoſe of their Succeſſors in the ſeveral Ages ſince, I find there are certain Bounds ſet even to the Irregularities of Human Thought, and thoſe a great deal narrower than is commonly apprehended. For, as they all frequently interfere, even in their wildeſt Ravings; So there is one fundamental Point, wherein they are ſure to meet, as Lines in a Center, and that is the *Community of Women:* Great were their Sollicitudes in this Matter, and they never fail'd of certain Articles in their Schemes of Worſhip, on purpoſe to eſtabliſh it.

THE laſt *Fanaticks* of Note, were thoſe which ſtarted up in *Germany*, a little after the *Reformation* of *Luther*; Springing, as *Muſhrooms* do at the *End of a Harveſt*; Such were *John* of *Leyden, David George, Adam Neuſter,* and many others; whoſe Viſions and Revelations, always terminated in leading about half a dozen *Siſters, apiece,* and making That Practice a Fundamental Part of their Syſtem. For, Human Life is a continual Navigation, and if we expect our *Veſſels* to paſs

with

with Safety, thro' the Waves and Tempests of this fluctuating World, it is necessary to make a good Provision of the *Flesh*, as Sea-men lay in store of *Beef* for a long Voyage.

Now from this brief Survey of some Principal Sects, among the *Fanaticks*, in all Ages (having omitted the *Mahometans* and others, who might also help to confirm the Argument I am about) to which I might add several among our selves, such as the *Family of Love*, *Sweet Singers of Israel*, and the like: And from reflecting upon that fundamental Point in their Doctrines, about *Women*, wherein they have so unanimously agreed; I am apt to imagine, that the Seed or Principle, which has ever put Men upon *Visions* in Things *Invisible*, is of a Corporeal Nature: For the profounder Chymists inform us, that the Strongest *Spirits* may be extracted from *Human Flesh*. Besides, the Spinal Marrow, being nothing else but a Continuation of the Brain, must needs create a very free Communication, between the Superior Faculties and those below: And thus the *Thorn in the Flesh* serves for a *Spur* to the *Spirit*, I think, it is agreed among Physicians, that nothing affects the Head so much, as a tentiginous Humor, repelled and elated to the upper Region, found by daily practice, to run frequently up into Madness. A very eminent Member of the Faculty assured me, that when the *Quakers* first appeared, he seldom was without some Female Patients among them, for the *furor Uterinus*. Persons of a visionary Devotion, either Men or Women, are in their Complexion, of all others, the most amorous: For, Zeal is frequently kindled from the same Spark with other Fires, and from inflaming Brotherly Love, will proceed to raise That of a Gallant. If we inspect into the usual Process of modern Courtship, we shall find it to consist in a devout Turn of the Eyes, called *Ogling*; an artificial Form of Canting and and Whining by rote, every Interval, for want of other Matter, made up with a Shrug, or a Hum, a Sigh or a Groan; The Style compact of insignificant Words, Incoherences and Repetition. These, I take, to be the most accomplish'd Rules of Address to a Mistress; and where are these performed with more Dexterity, than by the *Saints?* Nay, to bring this Argument

ment yet closer, I have been informed by certain Sanguine Brethren of the first Class, that in the Height and *Orgasmus* of their Spiritual Exercise, it has been frequent with them * * * * * ; immediately after which, they found the *Spirit* to relax and flag of a sudden with the Nerves, and they were forced to hasten to a Conclusion. This may be further Strengthened, by observing, with Wonder, how unaccountably all Females are attracted by Visionary or Enthusiastick Preachers, tho' never so contemptible in their *outward Men*; which is usually supposed to be done upon Considerations, purely Spiritual, without any carnal Regards at all. But I have Reason to think, the *Sex* hath certain Characteristicks, by which they form a truer Judgment of Human Abilities and Performings, than we our selves can possibly do of each other. Let That be as it will, thus much is certain, that however Spiritual Intrigues begin, they generally conclude like all others; they may branch upwards toward Heaven, but the Root is in the Earth. Too intense a Contemplation is not the Business of Flesh and Blood; it must by the necessary Course of Things, in a little

Y   Time,

Time, let go its Hold, and fall into *Matter*. Lovers, for the fake of Celeſtial Converſe, are but another ſort of *Platonicks*, who pretend to ſee Stars and Heaven in Ladies Eyes, and to look or think no lower; but the ſame *Pit* is provided for both; and they ſeem a perfect Moral to the Story of that Philoſopher, who, while his Thoughts and Eyes were fixed upon the *Conſtellations*, found himſelf ſeduced by his *lower Parts* into a *Ditch*.

I had ſomewhat more to ſay upon this Part of the Subject; but the Poſt is juſt going, which forces me in great Haſte to conclude,

S I R,

Yours, &c.

Pray, burn this Letter as ſoon as it comes to your Hands.

F I N I S.